OLUBUNMI MABEL

The Last Time We Loved

First published by Olubunmi Mabel 2020

First edition

ISBN: 978-87-972624-0-5

Editing by Oladeji Jonathan D.

Contents

PRAISES FOR THE LAST TIME WE LOVED

"The opening of the book draws one in like a seductress good at what she does. Every delivery and act paints an actual image of the whole book in one's mind. It is more like seeing a movie inside a book. I read this book ignoring every other activity I needed to attend to.

That shows how engaging the book is, with a blend of emotions coursing through the mind —anger, love, forgiveness and of course, joy."—Yele Writes, *CEO Belle Chaow*

"Imagine a book with a plot that carries you the reader along, making you feel present in its plot, reminding you of one, two persons similar events happened to. That is the energy that this novel emits. The storyline is relatable, captivating, and intriguing. "Just one more page..." and you find yourself reading to the last page."—Christianah Ajiki, Content Developer, *OloriTana Solutions*

"A hard-to-put-down, kept-me-on-the-edge-of-my-seat kind of story.

An interestingly spiced narration that keeps you looking forward to the next page from the first page.

This is a novel you would want to read more than once, over and over again."—Abiodun Rhoda, *Obafemi Awolowo University*

"Olubunmi's ability to translate the basest and barest human emotions and imbue her characters with undiminished humanness is proof of an undeniable talent at work. She deserves to be read!"—Trust F. Òbe

"Emotional, intriguing, captivating, and relatable. Once I started reading, I couldn't put it down."—Enoch, Lead Pastor, *Champions' Chapel Copenhagen*

"This riveting drama trails a path of self-discovery, love and all the uncertainties that these imply for a single mother. Olubunmi writes such real faith-based drama that the reader easily can see themselves in it."—Damilola Jonathan Oladeji

ACKNOWLEDGMENTS

I'm so excited that you have this book in your hands, and I have some people to thank for it.

Adebola, thanks for your unwavering support and encouragement. You read the manuscript and loved it. You complement me so well, and I hope to tell our story one day. I'm sure many would call us 'crazy'.

Fimidara and Damifola, thanks for making me a mum. Your smiles are the highlight of my usually stressful day.

Biodun, your awesome contributions in this book cannot go unnoticed. I hope you see the potential that I see in you.

Omoyele, this book wouldn't have been this awesome without you. Thanks for your eagle eyes and for being my 'hype man'. Anyone who has you in their world is blessed.

Jonathan Oladeji, my editor, thank you for doing a great job and giving your helpful contributions.

Trust F Obe, thank you for working on this book first, and for always helping my reading habit.

Christianah Ajiki, thank you for working on this book when I couldn't and thank you for your helpful contributions.

To my readers who were on my neck and couldn't wait to read this novel, I appreciate you.

To God, for His unending grace and love that I don't deserve. I'm in awe of You!

To everyone who wants to make things right.

CHAPTER ONE

"Can you drive faster now, Susan?" Daniel said, tapping his feet and wiping off beads of sweat from his forehead in the fully air-conditioned car.

"For someone who just spent the last two hours in Lagos traffic, you sure sound impatient, bro," Susan replied as she turned the car into the street that led to their house.

"I don't know how people cope with living in this city."

"Says a twenty-eight-year-old man who spent the first twenty-five years of his life in Lagos."

They both laughed.

"You know, when you experience a good thing, you wonder how you managed without it."

Susan nodded in agreement. "Now you're sounding like those IJGB."

"What's IJGB?"

"I Just Got Back."

"Whatever. Are you sure my room is just the way I left it?" Daniel asked.

Susan scoffed. "You're asking this question the umpteenth time, and yes, it's the way you left it. Mum ensured that the maids clean it at least once a week. I have no business in your room. Your car was all I wanted, and I got it." She punched the steering wheel for effect.

Daniel looked around the car. "At least you did a good job maintaining it. That much makes me feel better."

"Why are you so particular about your room? You're not a politician, I'd have thought you had some cash stashed somewhere in your room."

Daniel laughed. "What I hope to find in there is more than cash."

"Huh. I wonder what is more important than money."

"You still haven't changed."

"God forbid that I change from being someone who loves the good things of life."

"Who are you dating this time? The President's son?"

Susan laughed as she brought the car to a halt before the house's gigantic black gate. She honked for the gateman.

Daniel unfastened his seatbelt. "I'll see you inside." He opened the car door and ran in through the small adjoining gate which the elderly gateman just opened.

He ran towards his mother's flat and briefly hugged his mum, who was standing outside with outstretched arms, before speeding into the house.

"Ah. Look at this boy! Is this how you greet your mother who has not seen you for two years?"

Susan laughed as she sauntered towards her mum.

"What is he looking for?" his mum asked.

"Something more important than money. He kept asking if we didn't touch anything in his room. I wonder what he's looking for," Susan replied.

Daniel appeared from the house, raising his hands in victory with a small notepad in his right hand.

"Yay! Hello, my people!" he screamed.

Susan and their mum exchanged glances.

* * *

Tolu squinted as she stepped out from the cold interior of her car into the scorching Friday afternoon sun. She locked her car and ambled towards her flat—looking forward to the pleasure of a cold shower.

"*O se,* Lamide," she said to her twelve-year-old neighbour's son who had helped her to open the gate, sparing her the pesky routine of alighting from her car, opening the gate, and closing it after parking her car. It had been a hectic morning shift at work.

Tolu loved her job as a nurse but a busy shift like today's shift could be quite upsetting. She opened the door and as usual, met her mother and daughter at home. They lived with her in a two-bedroom apartment she rented in Alagbaka Estate, one of the most sophisticated residential areas in Akure.

"Good afternoon, Gold." She kissed her mother on the cheek. 'Gold' was what she called her mother. Light-complexioned and five foot three, even at fifty-three, Gold looked so adorable. Tolu took after her, although she was taller. People attributed Gold's enviable figure to the fact that she had just one child; she had skipped the strains of multiple childbirths which would have taken a toll on her body.

"Hi, aunty," Omolola, her daughter greeted her without looking away from the TV.

Gold had always corrected the little girl, explaining to her that she was her grandmother and Tolu was her mother, but the explanation had yielded no result. Tolu had no issue with this and even felt her mother deserved for Lola to call her mum since she had been taking care of the girl since her birth. Tolu was convinced that Lola would as she grew older.

"Thank you, Lola," Tolu replied, lowering herself into the couch from across her mother. The sitting room was moderately furnished which made sure it was always spic-and-span. A lavender fragrance oozed from the air freshener. Gold had always been obsessively neat. Tolu had always thought her mother's neatness was annoying when she was younger; but now, she appreciated it. It would take an obsessively neat person to keep the house sparkling clean despite having a child in the house.

Tolu realized that her mother had not replied to her greeting and was staring at her strangely. "Is everything alright Gold?" she asked.

The older woman pursed her lips. Tolu stood up to sit beside her.

"Promise me you won't lose your temper, Tolu. Promise that you will be calm," Gold said.

"I promise," Tolu said, wondering what would make her mother issue such a plea before voicing her thoughts.

"Daniel called."

"Daniel, my cousin? Is he back home?"

Daniel who was Tolu's cousin, the son of Gold's younger sister, had moved out of his parents' house to live with Adetoun, a woman of thirty-five. He was twenty-five and had just gotten his Bachelor's in Business Administration from Obafemi Awolowo University. He claimed that he loved Adetoun and they wanted to get married. Adetoun is the daughter of a politician in Lagos and had a lot of money her father had passed to her after his demise. When Daniel brought Adetoun home to meet his parents, they told her she could only marry their son over their dead bodies. Daniel moved in with Adetoun in her duplex in Lagos and cut communication with his entire family. It had been over six months; everyone hoped that he would someday return home, to his right mind.

Gold shook her head. "It's not Daniel your cousin. It's Lola's father. He called me..."

"Who called you? You and I know Lola doesn't have a father," she blurted while struggling to be calm.

Lola glanced back at the two women for a second.

"You know that is not true. Listen, he called me this morning. He says he regrets his actions, and he's..."

"Gold, if I will keep my promise to you to remain calm, then I better be on my way to my room. I had a rough day. Anything that has to do with Daniel Okojie is the last thing I want to hear right now. Please excuse me." She picked her bag and headed to her room. "To hell with Daniel," she muttered and hissed.

Gold was not surprised at her daughter's reaction. She already guessed that it would be a hard nut to crack. She couldn't blame her. Daniel had left a bad taste in their mouths the last time his name had come up in a discussion.

* * *

Tolu took her time in the shower. The day had been eventful. She had earlier run into the staff toilet to cry after a patient's body was wheeled to the morgue. The patient had a twin boy and girl after being childless for ten years. Everything had happened in a rush. Tolu and her colleagues had observed that the woman was bleeding two hours after she was brought into the postnatal ward from the operating theatre. They had alerted the consultant on call who ordered that the patient should be wheeled back to the theatre. Tolu and her orderly wheeled the patient immediately out of the ward, but she started gasping for air before they could reach the theatre.

Tolu felt for the woman's husband who looked like he had been smashed in the skull when the doctor broke the news to him. He stared speechlessly until a nurse helped him into an office, consoling him all the while. He had had tears running down his face when the babies finally arrived.

"Ten years, ten good years; we have prayed, hoped, and waited for this day," he said as he held the babies.

Tolu cared about her patients and could not help but sympathise, sometimes to a fault, offering them financial assistance when necessary. Her colleagues would often dissuade her, saying the patients were not worth the stress, that they were mostly ingrates, and could even implicate her. They'd cited many examples to buttress their warnings, but Tolu would not be convinced.

Done with shower, Tolu helped herself to the fried rice and beef that Gold had prepared. She ate in the room, as she hoped to avoid running into her mum. She logged into her Facebook account to read what was trending but was intermittently distracted by thoughts of Daniel. She was scared too.

Daniel had better not think of taking Lola from her. As far as she was concerned, he had no child with her. She had aborted the one he was to have with her. Lola had no father, and she lacked nothing. She was a happy child and would do well without a father. Even if she needed a father, she deserved someone better, not Daniel. She owed her daughter that.

Tolu switched off her phone and allowed her mind to wander to the past, hoping that she would drift off to sleep.

CHAPTER TWO

Tolu met Daniel in her final year as a nursing student at the University of Ibadan. He was posted to her department as a youth corps member. She had gone to the departmental office for the yearly transcript collection.

"I'm sorry, your transcript is missing," he said after skimming through the files which were arranged in alphabetical order.

"What?"

"Got you," he laughed and pulled it out of the pack.

Tolu sighed in relief and smiled. "Thank you for the points you have taken off my blood pressure," she said.

Daniel laughed.

She decided there and then that she loved the sound of his laughter. It was playful and boyish yet somehow manly, and that drew her in. Well, that, and his looks. He stood at 5ft6 with the perfect body to match and a face that would make you agree with whatever he said. The kind of face that dared her to do more than exchange pleasantries whenever they ran into each other at the department after their first encounter.

Daniel wasn't the fittest or the most handsome man, but he appealed to Tolu and her senses in a way she could not grasp. At some point, she settled for the conclusion that it was his laughter that had her hooked. In the end, she thought it was his pleasant face. Daniel, on the other hand, felt at ease around her. He desired her company and found himself thinking about her at the end of each brief interaction.

On a Saturday, they had bumped into each other at a supermarket close to the UI Campus.

"Good to see you. Are you through with your shopping? I can drop you off at the hostel," Daniel hurriedly offered.

He came in a car. Tolu made a quick assessment of him. He wore a pair of jean shorts and a green T-shirt. Tolu ate him up with her eyes. It never seemed like she could get enough of him, no matter how much she looked.

"Almost - I have just a few items left to buy. I stay off-campus, close to the school."

"Alright, go ahead. I'll wait for you."

"Thank you."

She had not felt such an intense attraction to any man since her ex, Sylvester. It was not even so intense with Sylvester who worked in one of the banks in the school at the time. They dated through her third year before she broke up with him. She had discovered that he was cheating on her with another student in the Music Department. Sylvester was her first. He begged and begged when she announced the breakup. Though it was tough for her, she insisted.

Twenty minutes later, Daniel held open the door to his Toyota Prius to let her in.

"Thank you," she said and settled into the car, melting at his gentlemanly treatment. It had been a while since a man devoted that much attention to her. She missed it. Sylvester used to treat her that way, but he cheated on her. The car looked and smelled new. She wondered if he was from a wealthy home. Her curiosity was tickled, and she wanted to know more about him.

"Seat belt, please." His voice broke through her thoughts.

Tolu fastened her seat belt.

During the thirty minutes' drive to her house, Tolu had some of her curiosity satisfied. He was a graduate of Biomedical Engineering from the University of Lagos. From a family of four, his sister had just gained admission into the university to study Theatre Arts.

Tolu also told him bits about herself. She was an only child born to now retired civil servants. She came ten years into her parents' marriage. Her mother used to recount to her the many humiliations she endured from every angle.

"It is a horrible experience for any woman. I was made to challenge God during those years of waiting. I got married as a virgin, and so I believed that there was no reason I should have issues with being a mother. Had my husband not loved me to pieces, his family would have succeeded in breaking us apart," Gold would usually say while recounting her experiences.

"You must be spoilt," Daniel teased her, turning the car into the street that led to her house.

She laughed. "I was pampered, but not spoilt. Or should I say I was spoilt, but not rotten? My mother is a retired teacher and my father, a retired school principal. You know what that means."

"I'm not sure I do. Not all teachers are disciplinarians. I think personality plays a significant role."

"I agree," Tolu said," I believe you're the one who was and is overpampered. After all, you were an only child at some point. And the car..." she trailed off, hoping she hadn't overstepped her boundary.

He chuckled. "Well, you might be right. My dad promised me a car if I graduated with a first-class, and I did."

Tolu's eyes shone. A wave of admiration swept over her. He wasn't only handsome but also brilliant.

"Wow! I'm impressed."

"Thank you."

"So, the car was your motivation?"

"Not really. It wasn't my main motivation, but it was surely a part of it, I must confess."

They laughed.

"That's my house, the one painted brown," Tolu announced.

He pulled the car to a halt in front of the house. "Here we are."

"Thank you so much," Tolu said as she freed herself from the seat belt.

"It's my pleasure," he replied.

"Do you mind if we exchange phone numbers? I don't have friends here yet, and it gets boring sometimes."

"Sure, why not?" she replied and rummaged through her bag for her phone. There was no point playing hard to get. She liked him and she had nothing to lose. In fact, she felt lucky. Most of her classmates had a crush on him; they would jump at this kind of opportunity.

They became friends and started dating after five months. As much as they tried to hide it at the department, they couldn't. It was evident that something was going on between them. This earned Tolu some envy and admiration from her classmates.

They both had three months left to spend in school—for Daniel to finish the National Youth Service, and for Tolu to graduate. Daniel ensured she did well in her first semester exams. He gave her all the support and space she needed to study. They agreed to not having sex even though they weren't virgins. However, they did a lot of smooching, cuddling, and petting such that sex was almost the only thing off-limits. They agreed that was safer and Tolu would always rely on Daniel to bring them back whenever they were going too far. She found it hard to resist him.

One weekend, in the final semester of the school year, Tolu was in Daniel's house to spend the weekend. They were both lazing around on his bed, watching movies on TV. While they watched *Addicted,* they started making out. Tolu wanted to suggest that they stop the movie, but another part of her loved it. She had let Daniel lead as usual. She was confident of his willpower, that he would stop them before they went too far.

Daniel's hands roamed her body and freed her bra clasps. He paused for a bit as if looking for some sort of objection from Tolu. He continued when he got none.

"I'm sorry," he said moments later, their bodies wet with sweat.

"What are you sorry for?" She could still feel herself tingling from the sensations that ran through her body earlier.

"Okay, I'm not sorry," he said.

She giggled.

He tightened his embrace. Nothing compared to what she felt that night. If her entire life was a mountain climb, that night felt like the peak.

* * *

A month to her final exams, Tolu took ill. She self-diagnosed herself with malaria and had Daniel bring antimalarial drugs over to her house. She was relieved of the symptoms for two days.

"Why not go for a test? It could be some other ailment. You know better than to self-medicate," Daniel said to her. She agreed. He had been with her since the illness began. She decided not to tell her mum. They had both been recently struggling to heal from her father's passing. Tolu felt her father's demise was more than enough for her mum to deal with, so she kept mute about her ill-health. Tolu had lost her father to prostate cancer a day after she finished her last exam in the previous session.

The following day, Daniel drove her to a private clinic. She shunned the school's clinic because of its numerous protocols and procedures.

"We'll do a Pregnancy test alongside the Widal and Malaria Parasite tests," the doctor informed them.

"I don't think that would be necessary. I had my period last month." More so, she would have taken a urine pregnancy test herself if the thought of pregnancy ever crossed her mind.

Daniel nodded in agreement with her.

"It doesn't matter. You have nothing to lose after all," the middle-aged doctor insisted.

Two hours later, the test results and the scan revealed that Tolu was seven weeks pregnant. Though she wasn't thrilled about it, she did not think that having a baby would pose much of a problem. Daniel was capable of being a father. His family was comfortable; they would help him out. Her mother would be disappointed in her, but giving her a grandchild wasn't a bad idea, and she would become a graduate in a few weeks. She wasn't too young to have a baby at twenty-three. Daniel was twenty-six. Tolu soon noticed that Daniel had become restless and moody when the doctor announced the result. She thought she caught him swipe at a teardrop. He just wasn't himself. On their way out, he excused himself to have a word with the doctor. When they settled in the car, he asked her a question that made her heart thump.

"So, when are we coming back?"

"Coming back for what? I can't possibly have my antenatal care here -"

"Listen, I know we haven't had this conversation because we did not plan for it to happen, but I am not ready to be a father."

Tolu sat still in her seat, stunned. The weight of his words was too heavy to bear.

"Please," he pressed, "we can't have this baby now. See, there are some things I didn't tell you." He scratched his hairless head. "I'll be leaving for Canada in a few months for my Masters. I got a scholarship at the University of Southampton, but Dad insisted on Canada. Having a baby now could change things for me, and I have already turned down the scholarship from Southampton. You still have a lot ahead of you, and you're only twenty-three. I love you; you know that, but this isn't the best time."

Tolu stared at him in dumb silence.

"Did you hear me? Do you understand?" He placed an arm around her shoulders.

"Why now? Why are you just telling me about your school plans? So, you've been lying to me all along? God, I'm a fool!" Hot tears stung her eyes.

Daniel continued, "Oh no, Tolu. I've not been lying to you. I planned to tell you. I'm only telling you now because of this new development. Look, it extends beyond my career. I'm sorry I did not tell you that I am from a polygamous family. My father has three wives. I have seven other siblings apart from Susan, my sister. My mum is the third wife and might not be the last. Telling my mum that I am expecting a child could break her heart. I am her first son; all my older siblings went to the University of Alberta. I don't want to put her in that place, being her first son. Plus, she's hypertensive, I don't want to lose her."

But you can afford to lose me, Tolu thought. She had started to feel lightheaded. Tears clouded her vision.

"Drive me home," she said.

Daniel looked impatient. He wanted her to say something. A woman's silence is deadlier than her rants; he had two stepmothers and four female siblings, so he knew that for a fact.

"Talk to me, baby," he urged.

"I want to go home!"

Reluctantly, Daniel started the car. The drive to her house was quiet. Tolu kept sighing without breathing a word while Daniel cast frequented glances at her.

Thirty minutes later, they were in front of her house.

"I need to be alone for a while," Tolu said to him, a mix of anger and fatigue in her voice. She stopped him as he made to alight after her.

"Why, baby? We need to talk this through, please."

"Not today. I need some time alone." She alighted from the car and walked briskly through the gate without looking back.

Daniel knew better than to follow her. Tolu, although sweet, was strong-willed. He brought the car to life and drove off to his house. He thought the time apart from Tolu was much needed. He needed time to think, too. But no matter what he thought, he couldn't be cajoled into having a baby. He would come up with plans on how to convince Tolu to let go of the pregnancy. He loved her, but a lot was at stake.

* * *

Tolu flung her weight on the bed, her head aching terribly. Tears flowed freely down her face. How on earth did she get herself into this mess? She never imagined that she would get pregnant out of wedlock, at least not for a man who would put his career and his mother's impression of him over his love for her when it came to it. But if he ranked his mother over her, did this not mean that he'd always put family first? Maybe if she was patient and became his wife, nothing else would come first. What about polygamy? Why had he never mentioned that? What if it ran in the family? What if he would dump her just before he left?

She felt used. Her anger burned against him. If he loved her as he claimed, was this not the best time to prove it?

She blamed Daniel for not wearing a condom that night. She also blamed Sharon Leal for being a nymphomaniac in *Addicted*.

She hissed as she sobbed.

She knew she had no excuse for her foolishness. She could have used a contraceptive pill, even though it crossed her mind. But Daniel said they'd be fine, that it was only once. Even the shame of walking into a store and asking for it made her decide against it. Her period calendar app also said she was two days beyond her ovulation period, thus, the possibility of getting pregnant was slim. She should have been smart enough to clear every possibility. She was also confident in Daniel's love for her.

Tolu, enough of the regret and pity party. The deed has been done. You have to think of a way out of this. She counseled herself.

There was no way she was having an abortion. Not only did she fear for her life, she feared for her mother too. She was an only child, and it would be unfair to risk her life, even now that her father was no more. She knew everyone at the Obstetrics and Gynecology department at the University College Hospital. She couldn't bring herself to doing it there because they knew her too, and she'd never risk her life in the hands of any doctor she did not know.

She resolved that she would call Daniel the following day to discuss an alternative. If he insisted on an abortion, then that would be the end of their relationship. She would keep the pregnancy, tell her mother everything, and excavate everything about Daniel from her life. She would tell her baby that its father died before it was born. Yes, he was as good as dead.

Gold hadn't met Daniel but had spoken with him over the phone. Tolu told her about him when she went home for the first-semester break.

When Tolu told her mother that Daniel was from Abia state, Gold said jocularly, "*Sora fun awon omo Ibo o.*" (Beware of Igbo boys). Tolu had laughed.

She knew Gold was too enlightened for ethnic prejudice and discrimination to cloud her judgment of people. She believed her mum wouldn't remind her of her jocular warning. She would understand that Daniel's misbehaviour had nothing to do with his ethnicity. It was about him. It was his choice.

She wished that Daniel would change his mind about the abortion. She loved him. She wanted them to go through this together. Even if they wouldn't be getting married soon, she wanted him to be there for her, and be a pillar of support he used to be to her.

CHAPTER THREE

Tolu's eyes opened to the darkroom permeated by a streak of light from the partly closed door. She knew she was in her bed but didn't know what time it was. She reached for her phone and switched it on. It was 10 p.m. She had slept off while thinking about Daniel and his sudden reappearance in her life. Her body was covered with a blanket. She didn't remember sleeping with a cover. That was Gold's doing. She climbed out of bed and headed to the sitting room, feeling refreshed and weak at the same time. The TV was on, and Gold was lying down on the couch, wide awake.

"Why aren't you sleeping yet? Where's Lola?"

"She slept immediately after dinner."

Tolu took a seat from across Gold, hunger pangs tugging at her stomach. She knew her mum would talk about Daniel again, but she would face it this time. She didn't want anything to bother Gold. She would make her stance clear once and for all so that they wouldn't have to talk about it again.

"I'm hungry. What did you make for dinner?"

"*Amala ati efo riro.*"

Tolu's mouth watered. She knew she wasn't supposed to eat late, but she was hungry, and wouldn't miss the scrumptious dinner for the sexiest body in the world.

"I didn't want to wake you from your sleep," Gold said.

"I'm glad you didn't. I was so tired."

She excused herself and went into the kitchen. She returned five minutes later with her dinner on a tray.

"What will I do without you, Gold?" she said after the first bite. "This is delicious!"

Gold replied with a smile. *That should make discussing Daniel easier,* she thought as she sat up in her seat.

"Tolulope," she started.

Tolu knew the hour had arrived. Her mum would call her name in full whenever she wanted to discuss something serious. She smiled at her, urging her on.

"You know how much I love you. Your happiness is my primary concern. You're an adult, old enough to make your decision. The best I can do as a mother is give you my piece of advice," Gold continued.

Tolu hoped this piece of advice would not be too hard for her to swallow.

"Daniel did the abominable, I know. He deserves every bad thing you can ever wish him, but no matter what, he's still the father of your child."

Tolu hated that line. Which child? The child he never wanted? This line has been overused in defending men who come begging after denying pregnancies and neglecting their children. For her, it had lost its charm.

"I know he hurt you, and you are very mad at him, but he is alive, and he is Lola's father. Do you think Lola would be happy to know that she has a father after you have convinced her that she doesn't? She's still young; you can change that now. She might not forgive you if she finds out later. Moreover, if Daniel decides to take legal action against you to claim his daughter..."

Tolu's heart thumped. Fear threatened her appetite.

"He would do no such thing because I'll fight him tooth and nail."

"I'm pretty sure you don't want such drama in our peaceful lives. We don't have the money to engage in a legal battle; we also don't have the strength."

"I have the strength, Gold."

"You may be strong-willed like your father, but the emotional turmoil might break you. I don't want that for you. Look, I'm not saying you should marry him -"

"Over my dead body!" Tolu cut in, snapping her fingers over her head.

The thought of setting her eyes on Daniel disgusted her, let alone the idea of marrying him. She wouldn't want to touch him with a long pole, and she didn't want him around her daughter. In fact, did he talk about marrying her? Maybe he only wanted Lola. Gold was yet to tell her why he called; she had only been angry at the mention of his name.

"Why did he call you? What did he say? What exactly does he want? And how did he even get your phone number?" She only remembered him speaking to her mum on her phone.

"Tolu, you need to learn some patience. He got my number in an old diary he left in Nigeria. He returned from Canada three days ago and ransacked his room until he found the diary. He called me immediately. He said he couldn't reach you anywhere, even while he was over there."

Tolu chuckled. He could never reach her. She had broken her SIM card the day after her final paper and got a new line which she sent to some selected people. She also blocked him on Facebook. She wanted to wipe off every trace of Daniel from her life. He was as good as dead.

"So, what exactly does he want? Does he know about Lola?"

"He apologized for what he did after I gave him a piece of my mind. I don't know why I'm not as mad at him as I ought to be. Maybe he's not that bad after all."

Tolu shot her mother a pained look. A man who wanted to get rid of his child for his career pursuits and family?

"He just wants to see you. He asked if you kept the pregnancy as you intended. He wants to know how you're doing. I could feel the desperation in his voice, but I didn't tell him anything. I said I'd talk to you. You decide what you want him to know."

Tolu admired her mother for that. Despite the fact that Tolu was her only child, Gold never encroached on her freedom to make her decisions.

"Alright, thank you, Gold. I'll think about it."

"Please do. Whatever decision you make, I will support you." She rose to her feet. "Goodnight."

It was 10:45 p.m.

"Sweet dreams, Gold."

Tolu stretched on the couch to watch a movie. She would go to bed again two hours later because she was on morning duty the following day.

CHAPTER FOUR

Daniel turned in bed the umpteenth time. He had been awake since 3 a.m. and couldn't go back to sleep. His mind was too jumbled with a legion of thoughts to allow sleep. After speaking with Tolu's mother, the previous day, he had been expecting her call, or miraculously, Tolu's call. His heart skipped each time his phone rang. The woman's warm reception cum stern rebuke startled him. He had expected her to rain curses on him in fulfillment of the stereotype that Yoruba women spew curses like thunder. That further heightened his guilt and his hope of seeing Tolu.

He remembered vividly the day they broke up, rather, that she broke up with him. It was the day after they went to the hospital. He got to her house at 8 a.m. eager to know if she had agreed to get rid of the pregnancy.

"What is your decision?" She had asked him. She was seated on the bed with her back against the wall, while he sat on the only chair in the room from across her.

He cleared his throat and avoided her gaze. His eyes flickered around the room, looking at nothing in particular.

"Tolu, believe me when I say I love you, but I can't possibly raise a baby now. It's just not possible. That would mark the end of my dreams because my dad would ask me to marry you immediately. He is a polygamist, but he values children, and would never allow any of his children to have a baby out of wedlock. My mother would be heartbroken. She would lose her voice among her rivals. She needs to be proud of me. I'll become the laughingstock of the family, and my sister…"

Tolu cut in tearfully, "How can you be so selfish? Where did you place me in all your excuses?"

Daniel stood up and took a seat beside her.

"I'm just being sincere with you. It doesn't change the fact that I love you and would want to marry you. You're everything I want in a woman."

She shook her head. "You think you can bribe me with sweet words and the promise of marriage? You should know better."

"And you also should know that I'm not selfish. You know I love you, and I want the best for both of us."

She knew he loved her, but doubts clogged her heart. If he loved her as he claimed, he wouldn't suggest an abortion to her. What if she died in the process?

"No, you don't love me. You are selfish. You only care about yourself. You used me to pass time, which is so typical of you male *Corpers*. How could I have forgotten? I thought you were different. How foolish of me!"

A wave of anger shot through Daniel's body, but he managed to keep his emotions under control. She was hurting; she had every right to say anything to him. He deserved it.

"Your words break my heart. How could you say such a thing? Do you mean what we share is not real, that I'm just using you to pass my time here? That is an unfair thing for you to say. If that was my intention, there are many ladies at my disposal that I could use to achieve that. You know how they throw themselves at me in the department. I chose you because of what I felt for you."

Tolu knew that was true, but she didn't care.

"This is for the good of us. You are not ready for marriage, let alone a baby. Your mother would not be happy with us. I'm also not ready for marriage, let alone being a father. Think about it, Tolu." He reached for her hands. She allowed him to cup her hands in his. She wanted to feel his hands touch her for the last time.

"It's fine. I understand." She nodded.

Daniel's eyes shone. "Really? You understand? Thank you, baby. I love you! I promise -"

Tolu raised a finger. "No, don't make any promise. That would not be necessary."

"Why?"

She rose from the bed. "You should be on your way now. I'll take care of myself." She wiped her wet face with her palm.

Daniel's face fell. "Please, don't push me away. I want you in safe hands. I'll pay any amount to ensure that." He rose from the bed and stood to face her. Her bloodshot eyes bothered him. He felt guilty for the stress she was going through, but he had no choice.

"Daniel, you're a coward and a selfish being." Her body seethed with anger as her throat choked with tears. She sobbed for some seconds and continued, "How could you? Have you forgotten that I am an only child? Not only that, I recently lost my father, and I am the only one my mother has got. And you expect me to risk and maybe sacrifice my life on an abortion table to save your selfish dreams and to impress your family? How dare you!" Tears streamed down her face. Her head was spinning.

Daniel battled the tears in his eyes. Guilt tugged at his conscience, but he felt miserably helpless. Daniel was now on his knees, "Forgive me, Tolu. I'm at a crossroads here. Please, try to understand," he said sobbing. "You are a nursing student. Abortion is not a death sentence if we seek help from the right source. I really love you, but this is the only solution I can think up." Tears lined his dark handsome face.

Tolu had never seen him cry before, but she wasn't moved; it angered her.

"It's okay. You can leave now. I will be fine. Please leave."

Daniel rose from his kneeling position and moved closer to her, but she retreated.

"Please leave before I shout and the neighbours hear us."

He hesitated.

"Tolu, please let's do this together. Don't make rash decisions."

"Respect yourself and get out of here. My patience is thinning out."

He walked hesitantly to the door. "I'll call you."

Tolu walked briskly to the door, opened it to let him out, and slammed the door angrily behind him. She threw herself on the bed and wept her eyes out.

The memory of that day brought tears to Daniel's eyes. Tolu was right. He was a coward and a selfish being. How could he have suggested an abortion to her knowing how risky it was, coupled with the fact that she was an only child? He was indeed a spineless man who failed to take responsibility for his actions. How could he have been comfortable killing his child?

Daniel, you are a mess, he muttered to himself as he wiped his moist face with his blanket.

He hadn't told his mother and his sister, Susan, about it. He wanted to make up with Tolu before involving them. That was why he decided to stay with his friend, Wale, in Lekki, and not at his parents' house in Ikoyi, Lagos. He wasn't himself, and he didn't want them all over him as he wasn't ready to spill the beans. He swore he would do anything to be in Tolu's good books again.

He thought about her each passing day while he was in Canada. He still loved her, and he felt guilty for leaving her when she needed him most. That was so wicked of him. He would go to any length to make her smile at him again. It wouldn't be a piece of cake, but he was willing to do anything to achieve that. He only hoped she wasn't married. If she were, it would wreck him for life.

CHAPTER FIVE

"Seems like today promises to be a lot of fun," Tolu said on seeing the vacant beds in the postnatal ward. The ward, split into two wings, had the post-operative patients admitted on the right-wing, while new mothers who had *vaginal delivery* occupied the left-wing. Each wing contained ten beds, five on each side.

"Today will make up for yesterday. I learned you had a terrible shift yesterday," Josephine Okonkwo, one of the nurses on night duty replied. She sat on the chair with her legs resting on another chair at the nurses' station. Tall, with dark shiny skin, she was a thirty-eight-year-old mother of five and the most junior nurse in the ward, because she started working just six months ago.

Tolu had lost count of the number of times Josephine had recounted her story, but she never got bored each time Josephine told it as she was doing again. She finished from Akure Nursing School eighteen years ago, at age twenty, and was married off immediately to Obi, a successful businessman who dealt in car spare parts in Enugu. He didn't *allow* her to work. Instead, he had insisted that she become a full-time housewife. When she protested, he flared up.

"Why do you need to make money by washing other people's mess and smelly wounds, touching men's body and putting *pins* inside people's buttocks? Do you want to ridicule me? You want people to say I'm not capable of taking care of my wife? What do you need that I can't provide? Is it food, clothes, or money? Just stay at home and raise my children. That's all I want from you!"

Defeated by his views, Josephine tried to explain to him that people do not work only for material needs, but also to add value to humanity, which in turn guarantees one's fulfillment. She also explained that nursing isn't just about cleaning mess and wounds. Obi only attended primary school and later went to live with his uncle in Enugu. His uncle, an automotive spare parts dealer, gave him some money to start his own business after serving him for fifteen years. He had a good head for business, and he did well. All that mattered to him was money, so there was no point arguing with him.

Moreover, her father's warnings to her on the eve of her traditional wedding ceremony echoed in her ears. "*You must never argue with your husband. Don't ever raise your voice at him. He's your master. Obey everything he says and accept whatever he says as final. Do everything to please him because if you misbehave and he sends you packing, you will become homeless. You don't have a place in this house anymore after we have collected your bride price. You still have five siblings waiting to be married off.*"

Josephine accepted her fate, became a full-time housewife, and gave birth to five children—three boys and two girls, against her wish. She wanted just three children, but Obi loved sex more than his own life, and would even have sex with her when she was on her period.

Josephine would typically at this point mimic his ranting spree, "*Hia!* You want to enjoy my money alone, *okwaya*? Are you tired of giving birth to my children? What do you do but stay at home, cooking, cleaning, and raising my children? I do all the work. Woman, take your time, *inugo*? I want as many children as possible."

Obi died in a fatal car accident on his way to purchase some vehicle spare parts, and his family took over all his properties including his warehouses as if they had been waiting for him to die. Besides not leaving a will, he made his younger brother, Chidi, his next of kin.

Awake from her eighteen years slumber, Josephine realized how stupid she had been to have allowed Obi make her a woman with no life. She had no idea how he ran his business. All she did was cook, clean, and raise their children. She wasn't his next of kin, and her name was not on any of his properties' documents. She was indeed a *fool housewife.*

Life became tough. She received no support from her siblings. They accused her of not helping them financially when her rich husband was alive. Her children had to drop out of school when she couldn't afford their school fees. When feeding became a miracle to be hoped for, she decided to travel to Akure to retrieve her nursing certificate. She needed to work!

Josephine discovered to her embarrassment and luck that three of her classmates had become tutors in the school, and they informed her that Segun Akinola, one of the two guys in their class, was the current permanent secretary to the state commissioner for health. Segun and Josephine were lovers back in school. When Josephine's parents announced her betrothal, she told her mother about Segun. Not only did her mother object to their relationship because Segun was Yoruba, she also told her that love was an illusion. Her mom had told her how marriage was all about having a man who could take care of his wife and children.

Through the help of her classmates who were doing well, she was able to retrieve her certificate, renew her license, and get employed by the state government. After working for three months under close supervision, she got a two-bedroom apartment and moved her children down to Akure.

She had to start from scratch when her classmates had gone far ahead. Tolu could not help the sadness she felt for Josephine who had nothing to show for the previous eighteen years of her life, save her five children. Josephine never hesitated to share her story with whoever cared to listen. Moreover, talking about it helped her to keep frustration and depression away.

"I pray today makes up for yesterday indeed. Yesterday was crazy," Tolu replied, bringing her well-ironed white scrub out of her bag. "Where is Nurse Kofi-Attah?"

"She left already. She has a bride to make up," Josephine replied.

"Don't I just love her? She is so industrious. Entrepreneurship is one of the keys to financial independence. She inspires me."

"I should start thinking of what else to do aside from this job. If you single ladies are up and about, what should a widow with a battalion to feed, do?"

"Discover what you love doing and invest in it. Excuse me," Tolu said and headed to the changing room. Josephine could be quite loquacious, but Tolu understood that that was how she coped with her struggles.

Tolu took over monitoring the five stable patients from Josephine. The intercom buzzed as she sat down to go through their case files.

"Good morning, this is the theatre. You have a patient here who would be ready to be wheeled to the ward in fifteen minutes," the voice on the other end said.

Short of words, Tolu put down the receiver as she felt a mix of anger and disappointment. Would they ever learn to observe protocol? Why wasn't she informed before the surgery began? She would *punish* them by delaying for some minutes. The intercom buzzed three times before she eventually left with her orderly twenty-five minutes later.

"This act is unprofessional! Why would you come at this time when I called to tell you that this patient would be ready in fifteen minutes? Why would you leave a patient out here in the recovery lounge for longer than necessary? I called the ward three times without an answer. Is this intentional or what?"

Again, Tolu was short of words as she stared down the speaker who was standing beside the patient. He was an inch taller than her, bespectacled, with a theatre scarf and face mask on. She couldn't see his face, but she could feel his eyes heavily on her. He wasn't a familiar sight. *Who was he to address her in such a manner? A surgeon, a perioperative nurse, or a...?*

He cut into her thoughts. "This is just unacceptable!"

Tolu found her voice. "And you think calling the ward after the completion of a surgery is professional and acceptable, hmm?"

"What?"

"Yes. If you had any idea of what is professional and acceptable, you would have done the right thing, which is calling to inform the ward about the surgery so that we could prepare for the patient. You cannot just barge in on our procedures. I'm the only nurse on duty; you don't expect me to leave my ward to obey your impromptu instruction. Next time, if you want to get the right result, you do the right thing, young man." She had no idea how young he was but just had to chip in that part for effect.

He shook his head and dropped the patient's case file on the stretcher beside the patient. "You women are so ridiculous," he said and walked out on her.

Tolu stood there stunned as she watched his retreating figure. Women? That was it?

"Seriously? So, he's not going to hand over this patient? This is not funny at all," she said when he was already out of earshot. Beads of sweat gathered on her forehead.

"*Oga mi,* don't mind him. He will come to the ward to finish his work," the middle-aged orderly, who had been watching said. She removed the IV fluid from the drip stand and put it beside the patient.

Tolu assessed the patient and went through her case note. She was semi-conscious, and the operation site was well plastered. She was a thirty-five-year-old woman who chose to have her first baby in a church where she was attended to by an unregistered midwife. She was rushed to the hospital when she started bleeding after spending three days there. Not only did she lose the baby to fetal distress, but her womb also had to be removed because it had ruptured. Although Tolu felt sorry for her, she was irritated by her foolishness. She was literate, a teacher by profession. Conceiving for the first time at thirty-five was enough cause for concern, yet, she chose to give birth in a church!

Tolu fetched two of her relatives who were at the waiting arena. They, together with the orderly, wheeled her to the ward, while Tolu supervised them.

* * *

Thirty minutes later. Tolu heard someone talking to her.

"Please, can I have Adebayo Juliet's case note? I need to review it."

Tolu looked up from the case file to notice the owner of the now-familiar voice who was standing at the door of the nurses' station. He had removed his face mask and spectacles, so his features were now visible. He was dark, with well-groomed beards. Tolu could see the small-sized keloid on his jaw.

It was barely noticeable, courtesy of his beard. She wondered what happened to him there while she concluded that he was handsome at a second glance.

"I'm busy with the case note, as you can see," she replied.

"Alright, I'll wait.".

"Like you have a choice," Tolu muttered.

Tolu caught him smiling as he leaned on the table outside the office. He must have heard her.

"Here." Tolu handed the case file to him five minutes later.

"Thank you," he said and collected it from her.

Tolu walked into the ward to administer medications to patients. There were just six patients in the ward, including the woman who had just been wheeled in from the theatre. Ten minutes later, she was with the last patient, a thirty-two-year-old mother of five, who gave birth to a baby girl the previous night. She was Hausa.

"Mrs. Zakiyyah Danjuma, were you told to come next two weeks for family planning?"

The patient nodded.

"So, you'll be coming for IUD insertion, that is, Intrauterine Device. You need to stop giving birth to more children and take good care of yourself and your five children."

The woman nodded again.

Tolu knew she didn't understand a word, which she found so frustrating. It would be futile telling her more. The two nurses who could speak Hausa were off duty. Tolu hoped that Zakiyyah would have a reason to come back to the hospital so that she would get some orientation in her language. She served the patient with her medication and went back into the nurses' crib.

"Here's the case note. I'm done with it. Thank you," the guy said.

Tolu collected the case note from him and dropped it on the table without looking at him.

"I'm sorry about what happened at the theatre. I didn't mean to insult you or anything. I was just…" He waved a hand. "Never mind, I have no excuse. I am sorry."

Tolu could not help but look up at him. His sincere expression made her feel guilty for prejudging him. He wasn't arrogant after all.

"I am sorry too," she said.

"Adebisi Ayoade, the new anesthetist." He extended his hand for a handshake.

Tolu's eyes widened just before she took his hand.

"Adebisi sounds feminine, I know. I get this kind of look every time I tell people my name."

Tolu scoffed.

"I wish you a great time here," she replied.

"Thank you. I didn't plan to start my first weekend call on a quarrelsome note."

"It's fine. It is settled now."

"Good. It is dangerous for any doctor to be in the bad books of a nurse."

She replied with a faint smile, not wanting to indulge him. Though she was usually friendly with her co-workers, she didn't get too intimate with them, especially the men. She knew a few of them were attracted to her, but she tried, maybe too hard, not to give them an audience. She was yet to get over Daniel's betrayal. Did she miss being in love and having someone to share the love with? Yes, she did. But it was better than being fooled and used again. Once bitten, twice shy.

"You didn't tell me your name," he said.

"Tolu. Tolulope Makinde."

"I look forward to working with you."

"Same here." She didn't just say that.

Tolu could feel the embarrassment on her face, but he had left the ward.

CHAPTER SIX

"Dan, you no try. Haba! I can't believe you did all these without telling anyone, not even me. You didn't do well at all," Wale said after Daniel told him everything that transpired between Tolu and him.

Wale was Daniel's best friend; they shared a room in the two-bedroom flat they rented with six other guys back in the university. Daniel was the sole occupant of the room before Wale, who was looking for a room to stay, joined him. Wale studied computer science, light-complexioned and of average height, he was not particularly handsome but was well-groomed. He worked in a telecommunications company located in Lekki, Lagos. It was Saturday and they were in the kitchen. Daniel sat at the table, while Wale prepared lunch – beans porridge, and fried plantain.

"I could not tell anyone because I was so ashamed of myself. I would have told you; you know I don't keep things from you. But your line was never available."

"I know, right? I hated that village I was posted to for my service. I don't know how I survived there for a year. I felt like I was dying each day. I almost lost my mind. I mean, without access to the internet, I was cut off from the world."

"I couldn't even bring myself to tell you when we eventually got to talk."

"I have to be sincere with you Daniel; you were cruel. How could you leave Tolu in such a situation? I understand that you suggested abortion because of the things that were at stake. Of course, I know the kind of family you come from, but you should have considered her too. She is an only child. She loved and trusted you, and you left her alone with the consequences of what you both did. That's not good enough, man," Wale said. Picking a knife from the plate rack, he started to slice the plantains.

"She walked me out of her room, Wale. She stopped taking my calls. When I approached her in school, she threatened to disgrace me and report me to the school security. I stayed away from her so she could study for her final exams, but when I called her after then, her line was not reachable. She blocked me on Facebook and WhatsApp. When I summoned the courage to go to her house, I was told she had moved out. What else could I have done?"

"You could have done more. You still don't have any excuse. Why did you wait until now before you called her mother?" Wale poured the sliced plantain into the hot oil.

"It was three weeks to my return home that I remembered that I'd written her mother's number in a diary that I used back at her school while serving. I'd written down her mum's phone number in my diary that day hoping to call her later because I was charging my phone. I can't stop asking myself what would have happened if I had not written down the number. I feel so terrible."

"Relax; it's going to be alright, especially now that her mum is involved. You are lucky she's taking it cool with you. Some mothers would have cursed your generations to come. If she were my sister, I would have gotten you beat up, like Sonny in *The Godfather* does to his brother-in-law."

"Argh!"

Their laughter bounced off the kitchen walls as they walked.

"I'm not that bad. It was just the circumstances."

"Yeah, right! Just prepare for the worst. It might take a while for her to forgive you -"

"And to take me back," Daniel added.

Wale shot him a surprised glance as he turned off the gas cooker.

"You are asking for too much."

"Really? Are you saying she can't love me again or take me back? What if she has my child?"

"So what? What child are you even talking about? The one you wanted her to abort? It's like you don't know the gravity of what you did."

"You are making me feel worse, Wale. You are not giving me any hope at all."

"I am just being realistic. Don't raise your hopes. Get her to forgive you first, and then let things unfold." He set the table.

Daniel allowed the aroma of the food to permeate his nostrils. Wale had always been an excellent cook. Daniel always looked forward to his meals, right from their university days. He was the first of five children, so his mother made cooking mandatory for him. His kitchen was always neat and filled with the best culinary sets.

"No lady would believe you are a bachelor," Daniel used to tease him.

Wale joined Daniel at the table.

"Your woman is lucky," Daniel said, munching the well-fried plantain.

"I wish she knew that."

"We are still going to talk about your issue, but let's solve mine first as it's more complicated. I am the bad guy here. Don't you think I should call her mum again? I am anxious. At least, it will show that I am serious."

Wale shrugged." Go ahead."

Daniel picked his phone on the table to dial Gold's number.

* * *

Tolu arrived home at 3 p.m. Her stomach churned when she met Gold and Lola eating yam porridge garnished with vegetables and fish. She dropped her bag on the couch, rushed into the kitchen to serve her lunch, and joined them in the living room.

"I am so famished. I didn't want to buy food at the hospital cafeteria because I knew something delicious would be awaiting me at home," she said, placing her tray of food on the glass table. She removed her knee-length flared Ankara gown and was left with her underwear.

"To your room, young lady," Gold instructed.

Tolu laughed. "Let me enjoy my lunch, please. It's not like we are expecting a guest."

"You think so."

"Are we?"

"You never can tell."

"Are you expecting anyone?"

"Daniel called some minutes ago."

Tolu continued with her meal. The pleasure of the delicious meal swallowed her rage against Daniel.

"He's not coming here. You did not give him our address, did you?" she asked, partly confident that her mother would not do such a thing, but also afraid that she could, because of the way she had been going on about Daniel's issue.

"You know I wouldn't do that," Gold replied.

"I do, but you mothers sometimes can't be trusted."

Gold laughed.

"Let's continue this talk later," Gold said when she realized that Lola was listening in on their conversation.

* * *

Still in her underwear thirty minutes later, Tolu laid on the couch rubbing her stomach as the cold air from the air conditioner caressed her skin. Lola was on the verandah with her playmate, Myla, their next-door neighbour's daughter.

"So what is your decision? I don't take pleasure in hearing that regretful voice of his, "Gold said.

"You can bar his calls. It's not that difficult. Don't be fooled by his apologetic voice. That is men for you. They can pretend to be anything just to get whatever they want. Once they get it, they will show you their true colours."

Gold laughed. "Look at my daughter teaching me about men."

Tolu laughed.

"Why not? We are of different generations. I'm telling you about the men of my own generation. They are not as faithful as the men of your generation, like Dad. That's why you are soft on Daniel."

"Says who? Where did you get that from? Listen, a faithful man is a faithful man irrespective of the generation to which he belongs. Even your father was…" Gold trailed off.

"He was what?"

"Good. He was good," Gold replied in a low voice, avoiding her daughter's eyes.

Tolu suspected that her mother was trying to keep something away from her.

"Are you sure?"

"Tolu, the matter here is not whether Daniel is pretending or not, but your decision. If you think he is pretending, then tell him you don't want to have anything to do with him. He would know his fate and stop calling me," Gold replied, ignoring her question.

"I think that I will do just that. Give me his phone number."

* * *

Daniel's phone rang while he was doing the dishes.

"Guy, a private number is calling you," Wale announced. He was sitting at the kitchen table, working on his PC.

"Who could be hiding their number to call me? Not many people have this number."

"Better pick up. It might be her."

Daniel rinsed and dried his hands with a towel, but the phone had stopped ringing when he reached for it.

"Oh, snap!"

"Pray for a miracle."

Daniel sat. The phone rang almost immediately.

"Prayer answered."

"You better answer it before it goes off again."

Daniel answered it. He froze when he heard the voice of the caller. He jumped out of his seat and started pacing the kitchen while Wale looked up from his laptop to him. "Tolu," he said.

"Yes, cut to the chase. What do you want?"

"I know you are mad at me, and it is justified. But please, be easy on me. I know I don't deserve that you speak to me ever again."

"Good you know. I scheduled one minute for this call. You might want to make good use of it."

Daniel didn't miss the disgust in her voice. He ran his hand over his hair.

"I have so many things to say. I don't even know where to start."

"I guess we will talk when you do."

"Please, Tolu. I regret my action. I regret all that I put you through. Please forgive me."

"You have thirty seconds left."

"Why did you hide your number? Send it to me and I will call you."

Tolu hissed before the line went off.

Gold shook her head. "What have you achieved? Why did you call him when you knew you wouldn't give him a chance to talk?"

"That is nothing compared to what he put me through."

"Only a fool would argue that. But the past cannot be undone. The good thing is that he is ready to right his wrongs, but you are too bitter to let him."

"Mum, he cannot have his cake and eat it too. What does he take me for? Does he think he can just mess with my life, disappear, and come back at will? He must be a joker. People would laugh at my stupidity, so let him suffer for his misdeeds."

"People? Who are the people?"

"People! Gold, people! Even nature itself would protest."

Gold shrugged. "Be wise, Tolulope. Don't overdo things. You are not perfect either. After all, both of you were involved in this. Let him play his part too. Forgiveness isn't the same as accepting him back. Don't deny Lola of fatherly bond and affection."

"A father that rejected her!"

"Now, he's back. I'm off to catch a nap," Gold said, and headed for the bedroom.

* * *

Daniel blinked unbelievably at his phone. "You were right. It's not going to be easy," he said.

Wale shook his head. "I am trying to imagine what she would do when she eventually sees you. But I believe things would be better between the two of you before you get to meet. Just give her time to heal at her own pace. Don't rush her. Don't expect any magic too."

"I'm glad she called. She sounded so sweet and kind of...different," Daniel said slowly, feeling the taste of his words. "I want to talk to her. I want to hold her in my arms again and whisper to her how much I love her." He closed his eyes, imagining the reality of his fantasy. "I want to make things right with her. I don't care what it will cost me."

Wale stood up from his seat on noticing that his friend had started sobbing and had tears rolling down his face. He patted his shoulder.

"Hey, Dan. It's going to be alright. It's just a matter of time," he said. He didn't dissuade him from crying. He understood that crying helped to relieve tension, and being a man did not change that.

* * *

Tolu sighed.

Was she overreacting as Gold said? No, she wasn't. Her mother was too soft. Daniel cannot have his cake and eat it too. She would call him again and allow him to talk. But not today, she would call him whenever she felt like it.

At work, Tolu relived the days up until Daniel traveled. She also noticed that as much as she hated to admit it, she found the new anesthetist interesting. Since he was on weekend call, she would see him tomorrow as she was on the morning shift. A small smile stole her lips. She was surprised at herself. *It wasn't excitement; it was curiosity,* she argued.

She had been feeling lonely lately. She had no friends around. Though Gold and Lola were there for her, she desired a friend she could visit and share things with, maybe even share some of her nasty thoughts. Her school friends, Maryam and Chisom were far away in Abuja and Lagos respectively, and they only communicated over the phone. They even created a WhatsApp group chat, but Tolu also longed for physical contact. Maryam had gotten married immediately after NYSC and lived in Abuja with her husband and two-month-old daughter, while Chisom worked at the Lagos University Teaching Hospital (LUTH). Chisom never stopped asking Tolu to come work at LUTH too, but Tolu declined.

"Lagos is not for the fainthearted," she would say. She couldn't deal with Lagos life.

Born and bred in Lagos, Chisom could not imagine living elsewhere in Nigeria. Tolu tagged her ATL –' Addicted to Lagos'.

Tolu attributed her curiosity about Bisi to her loneliness. She once read somewhere that loneliness could accentuate the feeling of fondness.

CHAPTER SEVEN

The following day, Tolu had ten patients to care for. Adebayo Juliet, the patient she brought in from the theatre was sitting on a chair, sipping warm tea. Tolu pitied her. She was oblivious to the reality of her condition. Her relatives had lied to her that her baby was receiving treatment at the neonatal intensive care unit. They didn't dare to tell her that her baby did not make it, for fear of her breaking down or even dying from the shock of such news.

To Tolu, her baby didn't die; she killed him, through her negligence. The news of her baby's death paled in comparison to the fact that she would never be able to conceive. Tolu could bet it with her last penny that her husband would have children through another woman.

At 11 a.m. Tolu had served medications to patients and was reading a novel on her iPad. She wondered why the anesthetist was yet to make an appearance in the ward after his 7 a.m. review of Juliet. She had seen his review on Juliet's case note, and Tolu couldn't match his handwriting with his looks. He fulfilled the stereotype that most doctors have scrawny handwriting.

Maybe he wasn't as curious about her as she was about him. It wasn't like she cared, she only needed company. She wasn't into men anymore; she lost interest in them after her ordeal with Daniel, she thought.

A knock on the door shot her out of her reverie. Tolu looked up to see the subject of her musings standing before her. As if a missile of excitement pierced her heart, her face dissolved into a smile. He was wearing a set of green scrubs, his spectacles, and a smile.

"Someone looks happy today," Bisi said, crossing his legs and leaning against the wall.

Tolu had butterflies in her stomach. Was her excitement that obvious? She didn't want him to mistake her desire for company for an interest in him.

"Good morning, doc," she said, placing her iPad on the table.

"Morning. I can see our patient is doing just fine."

"Apparently."

He nodded his head. "It's just unfortunate what you women do to yourselves."

"You seem to have a problem with women," she replied. "You women can be so ridiculous," she mimicked him.

He laughed heartily, displaying his perfect dentition. "I thought we were over that?"

"Yes, we were. I just want to know the problem you have with the daughters of Eve."

"Oh. You got me all wrong. I mean, Juliet, for example," he lowered his voice, "who else should be running after trained medical personnel if not her—a thirty-five-year-old, pregnant for the first time— and about yesterday, well, something triggered that. I shouldn't have said that to you. It had nothing to do with you. I am sorry once again."

Tolu grinned. "What else can we do? No matter how much we health practitioners educate these women, some will still end up seeking medical care in the wrong places. Unfortunately, some literates are not exempted." She cast a glance in Juliet's direction. Bisi nodded in understanding. Tolu felt like they were intimate teenagers gossiping about a mutual enemy.

It is pathetic. I can't stop wondering how she would deal with the news of her baby's death, and the... you know...? He gave her a knowing look.

Tolu nodded. "Yeah."

He sighed. "May I sit?"

Tolu's face took on a glow on realizing that he intended to spend some more time with her. She pulled out a chair for him from across her. She caught a whiff of his perfume as he sat.

"Thank you. The hospital is quite calm today. We've not had any surgery since Juliet's case yesterday. Is this how it is on weekends?"

"I guess the hospital gods are trying to welcome you."

He laughed. "Really? So weekends are usually busy too?"

"This hospital is usually very busy."

"How long have you been working here?"

"A year," she said, "I was employed immediately after my NYSC".

"Lucky you."

"I know, right?"

"I returned from Australia three months ago after my specialty in anesthesia."

"That is cool. Why did you come back? I can't imagine anyone returning to this country after leaving."

He chuckled. "They say home is where the heart is. But really, I felt I should return home and give back to my country, besides the loved ones who wanted my butt back in Nigeria."

Tolu smiled and imagined what his family was like.

"As long as you enjoy what you do, then it is fine. That is the most important thing."

"I do. Do you?"

"I love nursing. I have always wanted to be a nurse."

"Good. I love people who know what they want and go for it. So tell me, where are you from and which school did you graduate from?"

Tolu was glad that the curiosity was mutual.

"I didn't offer you something to drink. My bad."

He removed his spectacles. "Never mind. I am fine. Your company is enough."

"You are just being polite." She reached for the medium-sized refrigerator in the cubicle and brought out a can of chilled malt drink.

"This is my favourite drink. Thank you," he said, opening the drink.

Tolu also brought out a can for herself.

"Excuse me. Let me check on my patients."

"Sure." He downed his drink to a half.

She walked around the ward. Six of the patients were sleeping, two were breastfeeding their babies, and the other two were discussing. *Hospital friendship*, Tolu thought as she walked back into the crib.

"I'm from Oka-Akoko, Ondo state, but I was born and brought up in Ile-Ife. My parents worked there, so that was where we were based. I've only been to my hometown once, when my paternal grandmother, whom I barely knew, died."

"In short, you are from Ile-Ife."

"Well, it shouldn't have been that way, there is no pride in not knowing one's roots, but it was like that due to family issues. My father's relatives are a bunch of trouble, so he kept us away from them, while he visited when necessary."

"Kept...Visited..."

"Yes, he is late."

She could see the sympathy in his eyes. "I'm sorry about that," he said.

"Thank you. It's been over two years now. I graduated from the University of Ibadan, the first and the best."

"Oh, please." He rolled his eyeballs.

Tolu laughed. "You can roll your eyeballs for all I care. It does not change the fact that we are the first and the best university in Nigeria."

"In Nigeria, not even in West Africa, I can live with that."

"Whatever."

They laughed. Tolu realized she hadn't laughed like that in a long time.

"I studied Medicine at the University of Benin, but I'm from Ekiti state, the fountain of knowledge, the state of the intellectuals..."

"It's my turn to roll my eyeballs," Tolu chipped in.

He laughed.

"Well," Bisi continued, "I was born and raised in Ado-Ekiti, so -" He was interrupted by the vibration of his phone in his breast pocket. He brought it out. "Excuse me, please. It's the doctor on call. Maybe there is emergency surgery."

Tolu gulped her drink while he answered the call.

"My guess was right. There's surgery."

"Oh," Tolu said, trying to stifle her disappointment. It had been a while since she had such a stimulating conversation, and she wasn't happy it ended so quickly.

"What's your shift like for the week?" He asked, picking his spectacles from the table.

"I'll be on morning shift till Wednesday, have two days off, and resume for night shift on Saturday."

"My weekend call ends tomorrow morning. I'll be resuming another call on Wednesday evening until Friday morning. That means we will see on Wednesday evening. It's a long time from now." The corner of his mouth curled up in a smile. "I'll give you a call; I hope you don't mind?"

He brought out his phone, which Tolu took from him to punch in her phone number. *She shouldn't be doing this. She was going against her principle of not getting intimate with a coworker.* Daniel had started this way with her. They had one interesting conversation, and then, he wanted more.

"You are an interesting person, I must say. We need to finish our conversation." He grinned and headed towards the exit.

Tolu smiled as she watched his retreating figure. She found him interesting too. He made her curious excitingly. She wouldn't mind getting close to him - as a friend. She could use his company, just as he could use hers too. He was new in town and would need a friend around. *Just like Daniel,* she thought.

* * *

Later in the evening, Tolu went to the cinema with Gold and Lola to see a movie. Gold was hesitant but agreed to go with them when Tolu insisted. When they got to the mall, Tolu did not feel like seeing the movie anymore. She just wanted to walk around and shop for provisions and pastries. After picking some items, she handed over the trolley with Lola in it to Gold. "Let me join the queue for bread and pastries."

She counted the people on the line and realized she was the tenth person. She could deal with that. The aroma from the bakery caressed her nostrils and made her mouth water. Her stomach rumbled. She only ate two pieces of cucumber and groundnut when she returned from work. While she was relishing the thought of eating the hot pastry with some frozen yogurt, she felt a tap on her shoulder. Her eyes screamed when she turned to see who it was.

"Doctor!"

He smiled. "Call me Bisi, please."

What is it with the men that showed up in my life and malls?

"You are the last person I expected to see this evening," she said, surprised.

He wore a pair of jeans and a green round neck T-shirt. Tolu admitted that he looked attractive. Suddenly, she was concerned about her appearance. She tried to remember what she looked like. She was wearing a black T-shirt on a pair of jean shorts and blue sneakers. Her weaves fell on her shoulders, unlike the ponytail she wore at work. With light makeup that accentuated her face, she remembered feeling pleased with her reflection in the mirror before she left the room. She was confident in her looks.

"Aren't you supposed to be on call?" she asked.

"Yes, and I am still on call. After the surgery that interrupted our conversation, all that filled my mind was a hot meat pie and chilled coke. So I came here to get some for myself and others. We deserve it."

She nodded. "I bet you do."

"You look great!" His eyes swept over her.

"Thank you."

"And why are you here? I guess you caught the pastry bug too."

"Just a Sunday evening outing with my family."

"You are married?"

"No."

Tolu thought she saw something like relief in his eyes. She wanted to ask him the same, but she didn't want to appear like she cared.

"And you?" She found herself asking.

"No."

She briskly looked away when she realized that her lips were parting in a smile. She was now the third person in line. When it was her turn, she ordered a loaf of bread and six pieces of chicken pie. She waved him goodbye, which he reciprocated. Before disappearing behind the racks at the exit, she stole a glance at him. Their eyes met. She looked away.

CHAPTER EIGHT

Daniel was jolted back to reality when his phone vibrated beside him on the bed. He hissed when he saw who the caller was. It was Uju, his mother's best friend's daughter. Both mothers had always wanted them to get together since their secondary school years. Uju's mother would always bring her along whenever she visited Daniel's mother.

Daniel had liked her. She was beautiful and fragile; she triggered his protective instincts. She swallowed everything he said, which made him feel respected as a teenager. But when they got to the university, he was repulsed by her inability to have a mind of her own. He wanted a lady with an independent mind who would question his opinions, not one who would nod to his every word. They both attended the University of Lagos, so she made it difficult for him to date another lady as everyone thought they were dating.

Theirs was a relationship of assumption as Daniel could not remember ever professing his love to her. Uju, being as dogmatic as ever, didn't care. Their relationship was mostly sexual, starting from kissing as teenagers to having sex as undergraduates. Daniel ensured that they never had unprotected sex; marrying her would be a nightmare. Both mothers were happy with their relationship, and Daniel often overheard them discussing their marriage. That was another reason he didn't tell his mother about Tolu. He didn't want her to encounter any opposition from his mother.

Daniel's joy knew no bounds when Uju was posted to Nasarawa for NYSC. The lack of network coverage in her place of primary assignment made communication difficult for them, and whenever they were able to talk, she would cry and express doubts about her survival. Daniel doubted if she would survive it too, being a pampered child. He was, however, happy that the place would toughen her a bit.

They didn't get to talk much and didn't even see each other till he traveled to Canada. Daniel had lost count of the number of times she had called him since he arrived in Nigeria. He did not want to switch off his phone because he was expecting a miracle - Tolu's call. He decided to answer Uju's call so that she would stop bugging him.

"Why haven't you been answering your calls?" she queried.

"Good afternoon to you too," he replied.

"I'm in no mood for pranks. It's ridiculous enough that I am the one chasing you with calls, yet you are ignoring my calls."

Daniel was taken aback. She didn't sound like the naive Uju he used to know.

"What do you want from me, Uju?"

There was a long pause. He must have shocked her with his question.

"Seriously? You should have asked me before we became sex partners for five years." Uju studied Psychology, a four-year course, but she had an extra year.

Daniel didn't want to be dragged down memory lane.

"That was what we were, nothing more, and that ended in school. There is no point bringing back the past. It's for over three years. You should have moved on by now. I'm very sure you have dated other guys and probably still dating them, so why are you on my case?"

She let out a cynical laugh. "It's none of your business how many guys I've dated. You were the one I gave my youth and my heart to. Your mum kept persuading me that you would come for me when you return from Canada. So good you are back."

Daniel felt his head spinning. He seethed with anger. Uju was still naïve after all. How on earth could she think he would marry her after three years of being incommunicado? More so, he didn't love her.

"Uju, you are a very beautiful lady. I liked you, and I enjoyed our friendship, but that's all there is to it. I cannot marry you. Leave our mothers out of this. You and I know better. This is between us. It's our lives, not theirs."

"After warming your bed for five years, this is all I get?"

"I warmed yours too. It takes two people to have sex, as long as I did not force you." He wouldn't fall for her emotional blackmail.

"Fuck off," she said in a shaky voice and ended the call.

Daniel heaved a sigh of relief. She could hurl whatever insults she desired at him as long as she was off his case. He didn't want her to be a clog in the wheel of the new life he was about to begin. He had gone with Wale to church, where Wale was a drummer. Daniel was touched by the sermon that Sunday and later yielded to the altar call. Though raised an Anglican, he was never really a church person. He didn't see a reason to be. Everything he needed was made available by his parents. He only went to church on Sundays because it was Sunday. As a child, going to church on Sunday was an opportunity to show off his new clothes and shoes. But back in Wale's church, he felt the need for a higher power. His life was muddled, and he needed some clarity and direction, so he decided to give Jesus a chance.

"Congratulations, man. One needs the Big Man up there," Wale had said to him in the car after service.

Daniel looked forward to a life directed by God because he had always lived life on his terms, which had been all good, but maybe he could have it better with God.

His phone rang again. It wasn't a known number. When he answered it, he froze at the caller's voice.

"Tolu?"

"Yes, it is me."

"Thank you."

"Save that for my mum. What do you have to say? This might be our last conversation."

Daniel didn't think so. If that was it, she would have hidden her phone number. But then, he took her partly seriously. Tolu could be unpredictable at times.

He sighed. "Thank you for calling. I know I don't deserve it one bit."

"You've said that earlier."

He smiled. "I have missed you, Tolu." He had been waiting for a chance to say that and he meant it also. He missed her company, stubbornness, smile, laughter, wit, and friendship. He felt bad that he hurt her that much. How could he have suggested an abortion? What was he thinking? He wanted them back together, and if that happened, he would never take the privilege for granted.

"I didn't call to hear how much you missed me." Memories of the past flooded her mind and sent chills down her spine. No, she couldn't miss him. She remembered their kisses. Shockingly, she found herself desiring to see what he now looked like. She gave herself a mental shake. The appropriate emotion she should feel was anger.

"Alright. Please give me the chance to right my wrongs. Will you?" he asked.

"It depends on what you are asking for."

He sighed and hesitated. "Can...can... I... see you?"

Tolu was torn between two conflicting desires. She wanted to see him. She also felt she should be too angry to want to see him. Not after what he did.

"I can't promise that," she replied. She needed to clarify her emotions before making a decision.

"Please," he begged.

"I will think about it."

Daniel's heart leapt for joy.

"Thank you. But can I call you?"

"No, you can't. I guess that is it. Bye."

"I cannot wait to see you again, Tolu."

"Don't push your luck with me."

The line went dead.

CHAPTER NINE

Tolu's attempt not to grin when Bisi walked into the ward at 11:45 p.m. proved futile as she grinned from ear to ear. Did she desire his company that much? It was Saturday, and she had resumed her night shift. She had been shocked to see Bisi on Wednesday morning when she went to the theatre. He was supposed to be on call from Wednesday evening. He told her he would be on weekend call again because the anesthetist who was supposed to be on weekend call called in sick. That meant they would see throughout the weekend. She had thirteen relatively calm patients.

"Good to see you again," he said, taking a seat.

She smiled.

"This is for you." He handed her a paper bag containing a medium-sized bowl of ice cream.

"Thank you." She collected it from him and opened it immediately. The weather was quite hot, and a bowl of ice cream was perfect for the moment. How thoughtful of him.

"Are you the only one on duty?" he asked.

"Yes, with my orderly."

"This is some work. There should be at least two of you."

"Yes, but the hospital is understaffed. What can we do?"

He shook his head. "It is not right. I know you are capable, but they shouldn't wear you out."

She replied with a smile, loving the way the ice cream melted into her mouth.

"Where do you live?" he asked.

"Alagbaka."

"I hear it's the most decent residential area here."

She shrugged. "Well, there are beautiful houses there."

"So, you live with your mum and your siblings?"

She smiled, but her smile disappeared when she remembered Lola. Should she tell him about her? Would he still be interested in her if he got to know she was a single mother? She knew how society discriminated against single mothers. Would he still hold her in high esteem? She could lie about anything, but not about her daughter. She wouldn't deny her daughter for any man in the world. Wasn't it better to tell him upfront so that she would know his intention early enough than to become emotionally involved and get hurt later?

"My mother and my daughter live with me," she said, her heart skipping many beats. She looked at him to see his reaction. If he was surprised, he didn't show it.

"Really? That is interesting," he replied, choosing his words carefully.

He waited to see if she would say more. There was a story behind it. Was she married, divorced, or widowed? Did she get pregnant in a relationship that didn't lead to marriage? When she didn't say more, he asked, "How old is she?"

"Two years old."

"I am sure she is as adorable as you. I'd love to meet her. I think I love kids."

Tolu laughed, feeling a bit relaxed. Bisi was glad to see her laugh. Although he was surprised at what he just heard, he wasn't disappointed. Instead, he got more curious about her.

"What about your siblings?"

"I don't have any."

"Really?" He didn't hide his surprise this time.

"Yes."

"Wow. You are an only child. What is it like? What was growing up like?

You enjoy the attention and love of both parents alone. You are a special being."

"Trust me; it's not fun. Even though I loved it as a child, I craved the company of siblings as I grew older, especially in my teenage years. But I had a good relationship with my parents, so they made the whole thing a little bearable. My mum is a very good friend."

"I envy you."

"Being an only child is not enviable. You get more concerned about your parents than about yourself. You exercise extra care in what you do, primarily for your parents' sake, because if anything bad happens to you, they will lose it."

"And that in turn, makes you unselfish, as opposed to the popular opinion that an only child is usually selfish."

She shrugged. "Well, it depends on how you are raised."

"I meant I envied your relationship with your parents, your mum especially."

"Why?"

He bit his lower lip. "My family..."

"Nurse!" A scream from the ward interrupted him, followed by the sound of someone dropping to the floor. Tolu and Bisi rose immediately and ran into the ward to see one of the patients sprawled on the floor. Tolu called her orderly, and the three of them carried the patient back to her bed. Her baby was sleeping calmly in her cot beside her mother's bed. The other patients who were sleeping were now fully awake, with some breastfeeding their babies. The orderly wheeled in the monitor to the patient's bedside while Bisi fixed it on her to measure her vital signs.

"She's probably weak," Bisi said, checking the woman's conjunctiva. "She's mildly pale."

"Why wouldn't she? I will report her husband to the hospital admin when I set my eyes on him," Tolu fumed.

"Why? What is the matter?" Bisi asked. The monitor beeped, notifying them of the patient's vital signs; the figures didn't look good.

"Mrs. Okon, get a bag of Dextrose Saline and a giving set," Tolu instructed the orderly, who rushed into the ward to get the items. The patient already had a cannula in her hand.

Twenty minutes later, Tolu and Bisi settled in the nurses' crib after stabilizing the patient and buying her some food at the hospital cafeteria for her to eat.

"Thanks for helping out," Tolu said. His presence calmed her immensely, and she enjoyed the way they worked together.

"I'm glad I could be of help. Why do you want to report her husband to the hospital admin?" Bisi asked again.

Tolu filled him in while she made a report in the patient's case file. "She is a thirty-eight-year-old mother of four girls, now five girls. Her husband was so furious and disappointed when he learned that his wife gave birth to another girl."

"Whose fault is that?"

"Ignorance. He had not touched the baby since she was born. I had to borrow some beverages from another patient when the man refused to buy some for her. I instructed him to get some food for her so that she could have some strength. It's been over two hours; he hasn't made an appearance. Why are men like this?"

"*Some* men," Bisi corrected.

"Whatever."

"Like you rightly said, the man is suffering from ignorance. He should be angry at himself, not the wife. A man determines the sex of a baby, not a woman. More so, women are achieving great feats in our world today. Greatness has nothing to do with gender."

"Tell me about it."

"I blame the woman more. Women need to step up their game. Whatever happened to family planning? Women should be aware of their reproductive rights. The man would gladly take another wife a few months after your demise."

"A few months is a long time. These women flee at the mention of 'fa…', then the nurse has to swallow the '…mily planning."

Bisi laughed, he liked her sense of humour. He sighed, yawned, and glanced at the wall clock. It read 1 a.m. Tolu looked at his sleepy eyes.

"I hate to announce my departure, but I've got to go before I crash here and become the one needing resuscitation," he said.

Tolu laughed. "Thank you for coming. I appreciate it."

"It's a pleasure. Take care and see you later." He patted her shoulder before leaving.

Tolu wished he could stay longer.

CHAPTER TEN

The week went as quickly as it came. It was Friday, and Tolu would be rounding off her night shift. She hadn't seen Bisi since they last spoke. He didn't call or send a text. She didn't have his phone number; she could have been tempted to call him. He wasn't at the hospital throughout the week because she didn't see his handwriting or name on the anesthetist's chart.

She couldn't deny that she missed him greatly. Different thoughts had been boggling her mind for the past three days. Had he lost interest in her? Was he ghosting her? Could it be because of what she told him about her being a single mother? She wouldn't be surprised if that was the case because society is not fair to single mothers. But somehow, she believed he wasn't like that. He seemed genuinely interested in her. Why then had he not contacted her for five days? What could be wrong with him? Was he sick or in trouble? Maybe she was overestimating their friendship.

Perhaps it was time she granted the wish of her daughter's father; since Bisi had gone AWOL and she wouldn't be going to work for the next six days. She put a call through to Daniel, who picked it almost immediately at 11 p.m.

"I live and work in Akure. Let me know when you are in town," she said.

Daniel's heart raced. "Can I come tomorrow?"

"Sunday is a better day."

"Thank you for this, Tolu."

"It's all for..." she halted. She wanted to say that it was all for Lola, but she had told him he had no child with her. He wanted him to believe that until she was ready to tell him the truth.

"It's all for who?" he asked.

"Never mind. Enjoy your weekend."

"You do the same."

As much as he was happy at the development, he wasn't happy that she was always eager to get off the phone with him. He understood he was suffering for the damage he caused. He went out of the room into the sitting room where Wale was watching a movie.

"I'll be traveling to Akure tomorrow. I am seeing Tolu," he announced, leaning on the couch.

Wale paused the movie. "Really?"

"Yes. She works and lives there. I've never been to Ondo state. Lagos and Ibadan are the only southwestern cities I have been to. Do you have an idea of how many hours it is from Lagos?"

"Well, count yourself lucky. I have a cousin who lives in Akure. He's a lecturer at FUTA. You know FUTA *now*?"

"Yes, I've heard about FUTA."

"He lectures there. He is thirty-three years old and single to stupor like you."

Daniel laughed. "It's not a crime to be single at thirty-three. I guess he's taking his time."

"Or he has too many options, so he has a problem making a choice."

"Having too many options leaves you confused."

"Exactly. I will call him so that you can put up with him for a while. He lives in a very decent three-bedroom apartment. I have been there a couple of times this year, and I did not want to leave. The town is so serene, unlike the hustle and bustle of Lagos. You can't tell how long this reconciliation process will take."

"Good. Good stuff."

"Now to answer your question, the journey is about four hours."

"Even if it's four times four hours, I don't mind. Please call your cousin right away. What's his name?"

"Tomiwa. He's a very cool dude. You have nothing to worry about."

"Isn't God awesome? Let me go in and start packing."

"But I will miss you."

"You have to deal with that, Wale. This is my life."

Wale nodded. "Yes, go and try the cutlass on your neck."

"Don't scare me."

They laughed.

"You will be fine, "Wale reassured him.

"I believe."

* * *

At 4 p.m. the following day, Tolu frowned when she picked up her phone and saw Daniel's name on the screen.

"Did I not tell you not to call me?" she queried immediately she answered it.

"Calm down, Tolu. You asked me to let you know whenever I was in town, and that is what I am doing."

"And I remember telling you to make it Sunday."

"I know. I'm just calling to let you know that I am in town so that we can make plans for tomorrow."

We? He sounded like it was a joint decision. No. She was in charge, and she would call the shots.

"Okay. I will call you tomorrow."

"Thank you," he said calmly and ended the call.

Tolu sensed his hurt. She knew she was too harsh on him. Guilt crept up in her heart, but she subdued it. She had every right to be harsh on him. It was nothing compared to what he did to her. He had better quit playing the victim because it wouldn't work.

"Be nice, Tolu", Gold's voice penetrated her thoughts. Tolu, Gold, and Lola were in the sitting room, watching a TV series, *Jenifa's Diary,* after a lunch of coconut rice and chicken stew.

"I am nice enough to have invited him to come over here."

"But you sounded too harsh on him. You didn't ask how his trip was; you didn't welcome him. You didn't even ask how he would fare in this town. Or are we hosting him?"

Tolu glowered at her mum.

Gold laughed. "Tolulope, you are the daughter of your father. You are just stubborn like him."

"I hope his other children aren't stubborn like him," Tolu whispered to herself.

"What did you say?" Gold asked.

"I remember dad. I keep wondering what he would have done if he was alive."

"He would have Daniel marry you or get him arrested."

"But he would have been so disappointed in me," Tolu said, biting her lower lip.

"That's a normal emotion to feel, but he wouldn't have stopped loving you and Lola."

Lola looked at them at the mention of her name.

"And I think that is the most important thing," Gold added.

Tolu nodded. Her mother was right. She knew that Gold was also disappointed in her, but that did not in any way affect her love for her.

* * *

Daniel dropped his phone on the table, drawn to tears. He had never felt so unwanted and rejected in his entire life. Tolu made him feel like a pain in the neck and a leech she could not wait to get rid of. She was mad at him, and he deserved it all. He wiped his misty face with his palms.

He had settled in Tomiwa, Wale's cousin's house. As Wale said, Tomiwa's apartment was cozy and his furnishing spoke a lot of his high taste. Daniel remembered Wale describing Tomiwa as single to stupor. Tomiwa was a typical ladies' man – tall, dark, and handsome with an amazing sense of humour. He had graduated with a first-class and won a UK scholarship for his graduate studies which was partly sponsored by his school. After obtaining his Master's Degree in Environmental Biology, he was retained as a lecturer in his department. He obtained his Ph.D. three years after that.

Daniel felt at home when he got into Tomiwa's apartment. Tomiwa had gone to pick him up from the car park when he got to Akure. He stopped by the restaurant to buy some food.

"Sorry, cooking is not my forte," Tomiwa said. "I don't want you to have an awful taste in your mouth on the first day of your visit."

Daniel laughed. "Thank you." That was thoughtful of him.

"But my kitchen is filled with foodstuffs and edibles. Apart from the fact that I don't have time to cook, I find cooking extremely boring. I don't enjoy it one bit. I have someone who does the cooking for me over the weekend. She cooks three different types of soup, makes *MoinMoin* and cooks beans sometimes, and stores them in the freezer. All I do is prepare the accompanying morsel meals, boil rice or yam. My cook is out of town this weekend."

"That is cool. Anything is possible at this age."

"You tell me. That's why it is completely unbelievable when couples quarrel over trivial things such as who cooks the food or does the laundry when you can hire people to do these things while you enjoy quality time with your family. After spending many years as a single, I will spend the rest of my years enjoying every time I get with my wife."

Daniel's laughter filled the car. "You are right but not everyone can afford extra help. So, household chores are a big cause of conflicts in many homes. I cook though, not because I love to, but because I have to."

"I know, right? Not every guy can be like Wale."

"He can cook to save the whole world."

They laughed. After twenty minutes' drive, they got to his house which was located very close to the university's second gate. Tomiwa led him to the guest room which contained a wardrobe, a large-sized well-laid bed, a reading table and chair, a trolley filled with toiletries, and a bedside lamp. The room, like the other parts of the house, was neat.

"Please, feel at home," Tomiwa said to him.

"I will. Thanks for your kind gesture. I appreciate it."

"It's a pleasure. Feel free to stay for as long as you want. I can't sleep in three rooms."

Daniel smiled and replied, "Thanks again," after which he called Tolu.

He felt hurt. Tolu didn't ask where he was, how he got to Akure, and where he would be staying. She even scolded him for calling to inform her of his arrival. His heart thumped at the anticipation of their meeting. What would she do when they meet? Slap him? Shout at him? Snub him? Whatever it would be, he couldn't wait to see her.

He headed for the bathroom to take a shower and later settled with Tomiwa in the sitting room for lunch.

* * *

Daniel shook his legs anxiously while waiting for Tolu at Nevado Gardens where she asked them to meet at 2 p.m. He arrived there at 1:30 pm. He didn't want to add to his offenses by arriving late. Tomiwa offered to drive him after lunch. They had attended church and returned at 11.30 a.m.

Nevado Gardens was an open space with tables and chairs arranged beneath small separate shades; Daniel sat at a table for two under one of the shades. There was also a playground for children, a restaurant and a bar, a DJ booth and a big swimming pool. The aroma of fish barbecue from the restaurant wafted into Daniel's nostrils and made his mouth water, but he couldn't bring himself to order for anything for fear that his stomach would reject such a brazen attempt. He was too nervous to eat. He ordered for water to keep his dry throat lubricated as he fixed his gaze on the entrance. He wouldn't want to miss the grand entry of the queen. He also didn't want her to catch him unawares.

He looked around. The venue was yet to be filled with people. There were less than ten people present. He knew that would change as time progressed as people hung out more in the evening.

"Good," he said to himself. If Tolu would shout at him and disgrace him, less than fifteen people would witness it. That was bearable enough and also fair, compared to his crime. He took a sip of his water.

At 2:30 p.m., a familiar figure walked through the entrance and glanced around. When her eyes fell on Daniel, she started walking towards him.

Daniel's heart raced. He was tempted to run away or even better, the ground could have been kind enough to split open and swallow him. Before he could say, *Jack Robinson,* Tolu was standing right before him. He stood up from his seat with the speed of lightning, and their eyes leveled. She wore a flowery jumpsuit and a pair of black heels. Her weave fell on her shoulders. She still maintained the same beautiful face he knew. Even though she looked chubbier, she looked every inch as attractive as before. Daniel swallowed hard. A fresh wave of guilt descended on him. He felt like pulling her into his arms, but he restrained himself, as that could earn him a premature slap.

"Hi, Tolu. Thanks for coming," he said when he finally found his voice. He pulled out a chair for her to sit.

"Thank you," she muttered as she took her seat. She also did a cursory assessment of him. He looked chubbier and now kept a neat beard which made him look more handsome and a little different. He wore a white shirt on black pants. Tolu was shocked that she wasn't as mad at him as she had thought she would be, though she wasn't happy with him either.

"You look amazing," he said.

Tolu dropped her purse on the table and shot daggers at him. Memories of their time together came rushing back. She remembered the first time they saw each other at the departmental office. She remembered their friendship, the sleepovers, their laughter, and their quarrels. Tears formed in her eyes, but she wiped her eyes before the tears could flow down her face.

Daniel went on his knees. "Please forgive me. I regret my act of wickedness. I have no justifiable reason to have treated you the way I did. Like you rightly said, I was a selfish coward. I am deeply sorry, and I'm ready to do anything, I mean anything, to earn your forgiveness, and probably..." he stopped. It wasn't the right time to suggest that they continue from where they stopped. That would be too forward and insensitive of him.

Tolu couldn't hold back the tears anymore. She kept dabbing her face with her towel. She remembered the pain she went through during childbirth and how she requested a cesarean section when she couldn't bear the pain anymore. She didn't care that her recovery would be more painful. There was no one with her but her mother. Tolu still wondered what kept her from raining curses on Daniel while she went through it all as typical of women who had men that made life miserable for them.

"Daniel…" she sobbed.

"I know I hurt you."

"Just shut up," she snapped.

"Sorry."

"You have no idea."

He nodded.

"You don't have the faintest idea."

He dabbed his eyes with his handkerchief and dropped it on the table.

"Can I ever forgive you?"

"Please, Tolu. I beg you in God's name."

She shook her head. "I suffered."

"I know," Daniel said.

"No, you don't. You fucking don't!"

"I'm so sorry."

"You should be." She dabbed her face carefully, hoping that her makeup had not been smudged by tears.

"Please, Tolu." Tears coursed down his face. "If I could go back and choose again, I'd have stayed and married you before leaving for Canada. But no, I badly wanted to make my mum proud that I forgot you were somebody's daughter too." He sobbed. "I'm not asking you to forgive me instantly; I know it would take some time. I'm just here to let you know how sorry I am and how willing I am to right my wrong. I'll gladly carry out any punishment meted out to me." He picked his handkerchief from the table to mop his wet face.

By now, they've attracted the attention of others who kept glancing at them. It seemed strange to see a man kneel and sob in front of a woman. Daniel didn't care, neither did Tolu. If only they knew their story…

Tolu sniffed. "Whatever. Just get up."

"Are you sure?" he asked.

"No." She hissed.

Daniel smiled. "Thank you." He stood up and sat still for a while wondering how best to pursue a conversation. "They sell fish barbecue here. I know you like it."

"Hmmm."

He smiled. "I remember every tiny detail about you."

"Indeed."

They both remained silent for a while, each in their world. Daniel wanted to ask about the pregnancy, but he was scared. He did not want to upset her.

Tolu was touched by his remorse, but she couldn't forgive him right away. He said he would gladly carry out whatever punishment she doled out to him. How could she punish him? He shouldn't just be forgiven and freed.

"How is your mum, Gold?" he asked, interrupting her thoughts.

Tolu managed a smile. "She's doing great."

"And how is your family?"

"Very well, thank you."

They both realized that they had a lot of catching up to do.

"How was your schooling in Canada?"

"I had a distinction in my Masters."

"It's not that hard," she sneered.

Daniel laughed. When he couldn't hold it any longer, he asked in a whisper after a while, "What happened to the pregnancy? Did you...?" He did not want to taste the word 'abortion' with his lips.

Tolu hesitated. Should she tell him about Lola now or keep him in suspense until later?

"I kept it," she answered.

Daniel's eyes widened. "You did?"

"Yes, but it's not yours."

His face fell. "I don't get you."

"I carried out your wish. I aborted your pregnancy, but I kept mine."

Daniel almost laughed, but he curbed himself. "Tolu please..."

Tolu raised a hand in protest. "How can something you never wanted, become yours? Let's not go there today, please." That would be his punishment – keep Lola from him.

Daniel sighed. He knew it wasn't going to be a piece of cake. He would let her disclose things to him at her own pace.

"Can we make an order now?" he asked.

"Fine." Her stomach rumbled.

He signaled to the waiter who walked briskly to them and took their order.

"So where do you work?" he asked.

"One of the government-owned hospitals."

"I am happy for you. I know you've always loved your career."

"Thank you."

"Where are you putting up?"

"My best friend's cousin's house. Remember Wale?"

She nodded. Daniel used to tell her about him.

"His cousin, Tomiwa, lectures at FUTA and also lives close to the school. He has a very nice apartment."

"Good."

"Where do you live?" he asked.

"Like you know anywhere here."

He laughed. "You know I'm a fast learner and I can always find my way."

"I hope you are not thinking of visiting?"

"Come on, Tolu. It's going to happen sometime. I need to see Gold and appreciate her."

"You can do that on the phone."

"Tolu, as strong-willed as ever."

The waiter brought their order – fish barbecue, fries and salad, and a bottle of wine.

"Looks like you come here often," Daniel said.

"Yes."

"Uhm."

"What?"

"On dates?"

"Are you jealous or what?"

"Yes, I am," he said, his heart palpitating. He feared she was in a relationship. Maybe he should let her know how much he still loved her before another man beat him to it.

Tolu chuckled. "I guess coming here was a mistake. I shouldn't have come." She picked her purse from the table. "Don't waste your jealous emotions on me. I am not your girlfriend."

Daniel dropped his fork and stood up. "No no no, please don't leave. I'm so sorry for upsetting you. I'm grateful that you came. Please stay."

Tolu dropped her purse on the table and settled back in her seat. Daniel lowered himself in his chair, his appetite giving way.

He hesitated for a few seconds, thinking of what to say not to further upset her.

"Do you still read novels like before? I remember how you littered your room with novels," he said.

She smiled. "I still read, maybe not as before. Work could be very hectic sometimes that all I want to do when I get home is crash in bed. Social media could be so distracting as well. I cannot deny that surfing Facebook and Instagram eats into my reading time. But I try to read when I'm off duty and I don't have to litter my house with books anymore. I do more of eBooks."

"Cool. I read eBooks too."

"And you, do you still snore like a pig?" she asked.

Daniel laughed and almost choked on his food.

"Come on, Tolu. It's not that bad."

"Really? Don't get me started."

"You snore too, you know?"

"Mine is mild, and even sweet to the ears. Yours is…oh my God. Remember I usually blocked my ears with my pillow so I could sleep."

"But it was not all the time; maybe whenever I was extremely tired. You slept and woke up on my chest many times, remember?"

"Well," she drawled.

"And do you still fart like an elephant?"

Tolu laughed this time, much to Daniel's pleasure.

"I suffered. Jesus! Tolu, you were ruthless."

She was still laughing.

Tolu was surprised to realize that her heart was softening towards him as they reminisced. When she checked her wristwatch, it was 6 p.m., so she announced her desire to leave. She undoubtedly enjoyed her time with him, but that didn't mean she would let him into her heart again. She wouldn't let that happen, not after what he did.

"How are you getting home?" he asked.

"I came in my car."

"Let me drive you home, please."

"So that you'll know where I live. No, thank you. I can drop you off at your place if you don't mind."

"Don't worry, I'll find my way home," he replied.

They stood up from their seats and headed towards the gate.

"I need to get some barbecue for Gold and…" she stopped.

"Gold and who?"

"Everyone at home." She rolled her eyeballs.

Later, Daniel walked her to her car, a white Toyota Camry. It looked new. He guessed she had probably just bought it. Or could it be a gift from whoever she was dating?

"Can I call you, please?" he asked when she settled into her car.

"It's your choice to call; it's mine to answer or ignore it."

"What's your shift like this week?"

"Call me whenever you want, and I will let you know if it's a good time or not."

Daniel resigned. "Okay. Drive carefully."

"Like I've been doing since I started driving, thank you." She started the ignition and zoomed off. Daniel watched as her car disappeared out of sight. He still loved her. He would do anything within his power to win her heart again.

* * *

When Tolu got home, Gold kept looking behind her.

"What?" Tolu asked.

"Where is he?"

"Who?"

"Daniel, of course. I thought you'd bring him along with you."

"What for?" Tolu asked, throwing herself on the couch.

"To see Lola."

"I didn't tell him about Lola."

"Why?"

"Just like that?"

"The earlier, the better."

"I don't think so."

"When do you intend to?"

"When I feel like it."

"What else did he say?"

"Gold, I need to shower. I bought you some fish." Tolu put the fish on the table and stood up.

"I know you're trying to shut me up, young lady," Gold said, pulling the foil containing the fish towards her.

Tolu laughed. "Where is Lola?"

"Second flat."

"Good."

CHAPTER ELEVEN

Tolu had concluded that Bisi was ghosting her because she was a single mother. Bisi called her on Tuesday morning while she was drying her body after a bath, and she started doubting her conclusion. Even though she was angry with him, she was so excited to hear from him.

"The past week was so crazy for me," he said.

Tolu felt guilty for jumping to hasty conclusions about him. She wondered what the problem was. Before she could ask, Bisi said, "If you are not too busy today, I would like to see you. Do you mind if I invite you over to my place or I come over to your place?"

Tolu hesitated. Her heart leapt with joy at the thought that she would be seeing him soon.

"Give me your house address," she said. It was better that way. She didn't trust his intentions enough to let him into her abode.

Bisi gave her his house address. It was quite close to the hospital.

"Give me a call when you get to Oluwatuyi. I will come to pick you there."

Tolu glanced at the wall clock. It was 10 a.m. "Alright. Expect me in two hours," she replied and dropped the phone on the bed.

She flipped the wardrobe open to choose an outfit for the outing. After five minutes of rummaging her wardrobe, she settled for jeans and a white T-shirt. She knew she could never go wrong with jeans. She put on a skimpy gown and headed to the living room for breakfast. Gold was waiting for her so that they could have breakfast together.

When Tolu settled down to eat, Gold asked, "What's the news?"

"What?" she asked, looking lost.

"You are all smiles."

"Nothing, I'm just.... " She shrugged and tried unsuccessfully to stifle her smile.

Gold smiled and served their breakfast.

"I've been thinking of the possibility of getting a teaching job in any of the private schools around here. I miss teaching. It's been over two years. Lola who used to keep me busy has started schooling. It is boring staying at home doing nothing, except reading and watching TV. I can combine teaching with looking after you two. I am still young..."

Tolu giggled, lifting a cup of coffee to her lips.

"Yes, fifty-three is a young age to stay home doing nothing. I retired early because I started work earlier in life. I still have so much inside of me that I can give out."

Tolu nodded. She understood her mother perfectly. She knew her mother to be a passionate and outstanding Home Economics teacher. She won the 'Teacher of the Year' award several times before she retired. Everyone knew Mrs. Makinde—fondly called Mummy Makinde in every school she taught. Tolu had often wondered how her mum coped with retirement. Teaching was what she loved doing.

"Let's get to work then. We can visit some of the schools around here and find out if there's a vacancy. Your years of experience will give you an edge."

"I think so too. That gives me hope."

"Let's be on the lookout."

Tolu stood up after eating a piece of toast and two cups of coffee. The thought of seeing Bisi in less than two hours gave her butterflies in her stomach.

"Aren't you hungry?" Gold asked, looking from her daughter to the remaining two slices of toast on her plate.

"I am okay." She picked her phone and went into her room. She decided to kill time by watching a movie on YouTube. One hour later, she was in the sitting room, biding Gold goodbye.

"I need to see a friend at Oluwatuyi."

"You now have a friend? That's good," Gold replied.

Tolu smiled. "See you soon." She picked her car key from the glass center table and reached for the doorknob.

"Be careful," Gold warned.

What? Tolu almost threw her head back to look at Gold. She laughed silently as she opened the door. While driving, she thought about Gold's solemn warning. Besides her mother's keenness, Tolu had given signs that she was visiting a male friend. Gold had caught her smiling sheepishly to herself, she couldn't finish her breakfast out of anxiety, and she had hurried to her room immediately after breakfast. Usually, she would have continued discussing with Gold after breakfast.

"Be careful," she repeated her mother's words to herself. That could only mean one thing – not to repeat the same act that birthed Omolola. She knew that Gold loved her and was only looking out for her, yet, she felt a bit embarrassed. She had always thought herself to be too smart to have unprotected sex that would lead to pregnancy. She could count the number of times she had had sex, yet, her carelessness during one of those times made it seem like she had always been having sex.

Even if Gold had not warned her, she had decided to stay chaste until she got married, no matter how wild her hormones and emotions ran. Apart from her religious and moral inclinations, she believed staying away from premarital sex would help her to think clearly and prevent unnecessary emotional complications.

Tolu drooled when she spotted Bisi at the junction. He wore jean shorts and a white T-shirt; so casual, yet good-looking. The shorts exposed his hairy legs, which Tolu found so attractive. She couldn't help but stare when he joined her in her car. Even though he looked handsome, the stress on his face was obvious.

"Thanks for coming. It's so good to see you again," he said.

"Same here."

Following his directions, Tolu drove to his house. He lived in a mini flat, consisting of a medium-sized sitting room, a large bedroom, a kitchen, and the toilet and bathroom, appropriate for a bachelor like him. Two artworks and two wooden portraits adorned the wall. Tolu made a mental note to view the portraits later. She guessed Bisi repainted the house. When she asked, he confirmed her guess.

"It's not a new house, so I had to repaint it. The walls were stained and dull; I couldn't manage it," he said.

Tolu nodded. She would have done the same thing too.

"You were absent from work throughout last week. I kept on wondering."

"I should have called you, I'm sorry. It was crazy. It's my mum."

"What happened to her?" She couldn't imagine anything happening to her mum.

"She's sick."

"Oh, sorry."

"She's been mentally ill for ten years, depression." He fixed his gaze on his outstretched feet.

Tolu felt pity for him.

"She was a banker but had to stop working when it all started. We used to be a family of five, mum and dad had three of us. I had two older siblings, male and female. The firstborn of the family died ten years ago in a fatal road accident on his way from Anambra state where he was posted for his NYSC. He had finished serving and was heading home."

"Oh my God! I'm so sorry about that," Tolu said.

"Our family has not been the same since that ugly incident. Mum couldn't handle it. Her life stopped. She stopped living. She lost interest in life, in her career that she loved so much, and even in us. She had to be admitted to a psychiatric hospital a month after the incident when she didn't get better. The loss of our brother was so painful to all of us, and watching mum become a shadow of herself made things worse. Dad had to be the stronger one for us. At one point, I was angry with my mum. I thought she was selfish. She should have been strong for my sister and me. Was my brother more important than the rest of us? Didn't we love him too?"

Tolu swiped at a teardrop. She couldn't imagine the pain the family went through. It was as good as losing two people at a time. When her father died, Gold, though heartbroken, did not lose her mind. She couldn't say which was more painful between losing a spouse and losing a child.

"When she was eventually discharged from the hospital two months later, she couldn't go back to work. Even though she was placed on anti-depressants, she was never herself. She had relapses which took her back to the hospital."

"I'm so sorry. It must have been so difficult for the family." She wanted to put her arms around him to comfort him and whisper in his ears that it would be fine, but she didn't want to be too forward. Another part of her urged her on. If he didn't consider her friend enough, he wouldn't be pouring his heart out to her this way. Still, she hesitated.

"Difficult is an understatement. Our family used to be full of fun and happiness. Dad was a professor at the University of Ado-Ekiti; mum worked in a bank. We were doing so well, and there was great love in the family until tragedy struck." He shook his head.

Tolu rose from her seat on impulse and sat on one of the white chairs beside Bisi. She placed a hand on his shoulder and squeezed it lightly.

"Somehow, I believe our family could have been fine if mum had not broken down. I know losing a child is one of the most disastrous things that can happen to any parent, but all the same, as long as there are still other children, a parent shouldn't think life is hopeless when one of the children dies. It wrecks a family. I mean, it's just unfair."

Tolu sensed the mix of love, sadness, and anger he felt for his mother.

"I was already in my first year at university when it happened. The news from home almost affected my academics, but my friends were there for me. My dad is a strong man. He also encouraged me. I love him so much, and I pity him the most. Watching your beloved wife become a stranger in the family is a hard blow. My sister and I didn't like going home during the holidays because it wasn't the same sweet home we loved to go to. We just had to go because of dad." He sighed.

Tolu remembered their clash at the theatre and felt guilty for reacting in that manner towards him. She had had no idea what he was going through.

"She had a relapse last week and attempted suicide. Dad had taken some drugs from the medicine cupboard and forgot to lock it; he said his phone rang in the sitting room and hurried to pick it. She swallowed some drugs from the cupboard and passed out. It was the house help who discovered her and alerted Dad. He usually keeps it from us when mum has a relapse, but this was beyond him. He was so shaken and scared that he had to call us and some relatives."

By now, tears flowed freely from Tolu's face. When Bisi, whose eyes were misty, heard Tolu's sob, he turned to her and wrapped his arms around her.

"I'm so sorry. I shouldn't have burdened you with my woes. I just needed someone to talk to," he said amidst sobs.

Tolu wiped her face with her hand and disengaged herself from him gently. "No, not at all. I'm just touched, you know. I'm glad you can share your burdens with me. What are friends for? Not only for work and ice-cream."

Bisi laughed. He liked Tolu. He felt so at home with her and found it easy to unburden his mind to her. He didn't feel that way with any of his exes, and not even with Adaora, his girlfriend.

"Thank you; I feel a lot better."

"How is she now?"

"She's been resuscitated. She is back to her pre-suicidal state." He laughed bitterly." I wish I could say she is fine; you know."

Tolu smiled. "I know."

"I didn't even offer you anything, but my woes. My bad. Forgive me." He clasped his hands on his chest and stood up. Enough of the sad mood already. I feel so much better now. What would you like to drink? Juice, wine, water... I have fresh pineapple juice."

"I guess I'll have that." Tolu now felt hunger pangs. She was with the object of her excitement; the butterflies in her stomach were now coming to a rest.

"I hope you don't mind *jollof* rice and chicken? I have it in the freezer already. I'll just microwave it."

"That's fine."

Bisi headed to the kitchen while Tolu, who was resisting the urge to accompany him to the kitchen, stood up to have a closer view of the two portraits perched on the wall. The smaller of the portraits was of him in a graduation gown, which Tolu guessed he must have taken on his convocation day. The larger was an old family portrait with the five of them. They looked happy. The children were beautiful and well-fed. Tolu thought they looked like *ajebo* children, meaning children of educated parents who were living comfortably.

Tolu's phone rang after she received her tray of food from Bisi. She dropped the tray on the table and rummaged her bag for her phone. Dang! It was from Daniel. Why could he be calling at this time? She muted the call and placed the phone on the couch. Her phone rang again. Bisi appeared from the kitchen with his tray of food.

"Bad time?" he asked.

"Maybe."

He sat beside her on the couch and placed his tray of food on his lap. A jug of fresh pineapple juice was on the table.

"It's my daughter's father."

"Oh. Does he live here in Akure?"

"No, but he is currently in town. I don't know when he'd be leaving anyway." She took a sip of pineapple juice.

"You haven't told me about him yet. What's up with you guys?"

Tolu smiled.

"No pressures. I understand if you don't want to talk about it," Bisi said, even though he wanted to know.

"I would like to talk about it, but not today. I don't want to put you in a bad mood again." Rather, she didn't want to spoil the moment. They had had enough bad tales for the day.

Bisi laughed. "No problems. Some other time."

They talked as they ate. Tolu gave updates on how the remaining days of her night shift went.

"What about the woman that fainted the other night?" he asked. "Did the husband eventually show up?"

"Oh yes, he did."

"Did you report him to the hospital admin as you threatened?"

"No. I realized his was a case of ignorance. Reporting him to the hospital admin won't accomplish anything. So, I sat him down and explained to him what he did not know."

"Good."

"I told him a man determines the sex of a baby, not a woman. He is the giver; his wife is only a receiver who produces whatever he releases into her. I gave him examples of women who are conquering grounds and achieving great feats in our world today. Greatness isn't attached to a penis. I even used myself as an example."

Bisi laughed.

"Yes. Nursing is a noble profession, and I'm proud to be a nurse."

"That is right."

"He was nodding vigorously to my words and became calmer afterward. I was so happy that my words sank in. He thanked me profusely and later apologized to his wife. He promised to take good care of his girls and ensure they get an education."

"Wow. That's amazing. Great job you did there. You just saved a family, in fact, a nation."

"I know, right? I felt so fulfilled. If I had not educated him, I'm sure he would marry a second wife with the hope of having a male child."

"Yes, a typical uneducated African man believes a woman decides the sex of a baby. Funnily enough, some of them aren't usually lucky as the second wife gives birth to more girls."

Tolu laughed. "Tell me about it. I see enough of that in my ward. I don't know what the obsession with male children is in Africa."

"Let's not go there," Bisi said.

They laughed.

The next time Tolu checked the time, it was 4 p.m. Even though everything within her protested, she announced that it was time for her to leave.

"I hate to see you leave. I haven't had such a great time in a long while," Bisi said.

He saw her off to her car and embraced her before she entered the car. Tolu sniffed his fragrance as the hug lingered. Suddenly, she wanted more; a kiss. Her body responded to her desire as a sweet, warm sensation swept through her body. She wouldn't kiss him. No, she wouldn't make the first move. She wished he would. If he did, she couldn't resist. She missed the touch of a man. She had lived the last two years in her anger against Daniel and didn't want to have anything to do with men, but the man whose arms she was locked in had awoken desires inside her.

Gold's warning echoed in her ears, and before she could muster enough courage to disengage from him, Bisi did. She felt a bit embarrassed. She hoped her body had not given her away too much.

"Drive carefully and please let me know when you get home," Bisi said.

"I will."

Tolu relived her time with Bisi as she drove. She was grateful that nothing exactly romantic happened in his apartment, although she could sense the chemistry between both of them. She was attracted to him. She believed he was attracted to her too. He hadn't said anything to her about his love life. She decided she was not going to allow any romantic attachment to him until she knew his relationship status and intentions towards her. She wouldn't want to be led on by him or become an emotional wreck again. Once bitten, twice shy.

Immediately she stepped into the house, her phone rang. It was from Daniel again. She answered it immediately. She had decided to return his call when she got home, but he beat her to it.

"Why are you policing me?" she queried. She waved at Gold and planted a kiss on Lola's cheek. Gold was feeding Lola with noodles. Tolu went into her room, not wanting to have the conversation before her family.

"How do you mean?" Daniel asked.

"Never mind. Good evening and how may I help you?"

"*Haba.* Come on, Tolu, be nice."

"I am nice enough to answer your call." She rolled her eyeballs and tossed her bag on the bed.

Daniel laughed. "Alright."

"What do you want?"

"I missed you, Tolu. Can we hang out?"

"You are asking for too much."

"Please, I beg you."

"When?"

"This evening."

"That's impossible. I just got in from an outing."

"A date?"

"Something like that."

There was a pause. Tolu was enjoying it all. She turned to the mirror to have a view of herself. Her makeup had worn off, but she looked good, still.

"Tell me it's a joke. Don't break my heart please."

Tolu snapped, "What the hell are you talking about? Are you my boyfriend? Oh, you think no guy would be interested in me because I got pregnant for some guy who left me to deal with it?"

"Oh no! Tolu, that's not true. I would never think like that towards you, never. You are every inch a treasure to any man, no matter what...."

"No matter what mess I am, right?" she cut in.

"I don't like where this discussion is heading."

"Why then are you concerned about my love life?"

"Because I still love you!"

Tolu lowered herself on the bed.

"You must be kidding."

"I'm not. I wouldn't have come here if I didn't care about you."

"It doesn't matter. You might have come to relieve yourself of guilt, to clear your battered conscience."

Tolu heard him sigh.

"Now I feel like I'm the vilest criminal on earth who has committed the most unforgivable offence."

"Yes, that's what you are to me."

"Really? Is my crime that unforgivable or you are just unforgiving?"

"You can insult me for all I care. You already did the worst when you turned your back on me when I needed you the most. When you left me alone to deal with the consequence of what we both did."

"I said I was sorry!" he shouted.

"Sorry doesn't fix everything!" Tolu shouted back. The door creaked. She looked back to see Gold poking her head through the door.

"Is everything alright?" she asked, keeping her voice low.

Tolu took the phone away from her ear. "I'll see you in a bit," she whispered.

Gold nodded and closed the door.

"I know sorry doesn't fix everything. That is why I'm here to make amends."

"By telling me you still love me?"

"No, but that's just the truth."

"So how exactly do you want to make amends?"

"I don't know, Tolu. That's why I'm here. Anything; just tell me how you want me to."

"The only way I can think of is by you having nothing to do with me. Leave me alone."

"You know that is not possible. I can't do that. Say something else."

"I thought you said anything."

"Yes, that is to show my willingness."

Tolu couldn't help but laugh. "You are just impossible."

"I know. Please forgive me. Remember what we used to share."

"Wow. Now you want to resort to emotional blackmail. Dude, it's not going to work."

"You know that's not what I'm doing. I'm just... argh. Could you please stop reminding me of my mistakes? I'm still trying to forgive myself for them; you reminding me makes it more difficult for me. Let's move on, forget the past, and focus on the future."

"You're not the one to tell me that. I'll do that at my own pace."

"I'm not pushing you. I'm just... Okay, I'm sorry for upsetting you. What about a date tomorrow then?"

"A date? Call it something else."

"A meeting, an appointment, an outing, a trial. Whichever makes you happy."

"A trial."

"I am game, my lord."

"See you tomorrow then, criminal."

"You cannot call me a criminal yet until after the trial."

"Really? There's no need for a trial then since you're a confirmed hardened criminal."

"No, please. Be merciful, your honour."

"Get off my phone, criminal."

"Yes, my lord. See you tomorrow at 2 p.m."

"I decide the time."

"Oh. Sure."

"Bye."

"I love you, Tolu."

"You never stop pushing your luck."

Tolu heard him laugh before she ended the call.

CHAPTER TWELVE

The following day, Tolu drove around the neighbourhood with Gold in search of secondary schools that needed a Home Economics teacher. After a fruitless inquiry at three schools, Gold suggested that they return home. They would continue their search the following day.

"Why don't we just search on the internet instead of going from school to school? People go digital these days," Tolu said, driving out of the car park of the third school.

"I've thought about that too, but I doubt if schools in this community would have adopted such levels of technological advancement," Gold replied.

"Maybe not all, but some, especially the rich schools."

Gold nodded.

"And newspaper publications too," Tolu added.

"Oh yes. Schools make use of that a lot. Why didn't we think of these options?"

They chuckled.

"If only I had enough money, I would have loved to own a school. Maybe start with a primary school, and then extend it to a secondary school later if possible."

"Really? This is the first time I hear you say this."

"I know. That's my dream. Having a dream without the resources to bring it into fulfillment is as good as having no dream."

"I disagree, mum. If you believe in your dream and share it with the right people, you will attract the resources you need to achieve it."

"Maybe you are right."

"I am."

"I mean, we could have been saving towards it."

"No, you have your own life to live and your dreams to achieve."

"But I know you gave up your dreams for me to be what I am today."

"That is expected of every parent when torn between pursuing their dreams and securing the future of their children."

"Then it's not wrong if the children decide to reciprocate the same act."

"It's wrong if it becomes a cycle. The children don't have to give up their dreams for their parents. That's why the parents made the sacrifice in the first place. The parents can enjoy the fruits of their children's dreams, and if possible, help fund their parent's dreams."

Tolu sighed. She wished she could make Gold's dream come true. She deserved it.

"Did dad know about this before he died?"

"Well, yes, he did. In fact, he wanted the same too."

"And?" She believed that her parents could have owned a school if they wanted to. Even though civil servants were not well remunerated in the country, she believed they could have still tried.

"A lot of things happened in our marriage that you didn't know about," Gold said. She didn't plan on saying that. She didn't want to break the promise she made to her late husband.

"Things like what?" Tolu drove into the street that led to her house.

"Wait. When is Daniel traveling back to Lagos?" Gold asked.

Tolu had always suspected that her mum was keeping some things away from her, but now, she confirmed it. She felt bad and slightly pissed. How could she keep stuff from her only child? Did Gold not trust her enough? Did she love her husband that much or was she trying to protect him? Did Gold believe Tolu shouldn't be let into the deep secrets of their marriage? The mention of Daniel's name reminded her that she would be seeing him soon.

"I don't know," she replied.

"And you didn't ask him?"

Tolu shrugged.

"Since you have refused to tell me how things are between you two, I guess there's only a little I can say."

"I guess so too," Tolu replied, obviously angry with her mum. If she kept things about their family away from her, then she shouldn't know everything about her personal life too. She pulled up in front of the house. Since she would be going out to see Daniel, she didn't bother parking the car inside the house.

Gold noticed Tolu's change of mood. She knew why. She was an intelligent woman, and she knew her daughter so well. When they got inside, she asked, "Tolulope, what is the matter?"

Tolu was irked. She loved her mum to a fault, they rarely quarreled, but she could sense a quarrel brewing between them if Gold lingered on not telling her the truth about her dad or the both of them.

"Don't pretend like you don't know what the matter is, Gold!"

Gold folded her arms, feigning innocence.

When Tolu saw that her mum was not ready to talk, she picked the car keys which she earlier dropped on the table, and headed towards the door. "*Mo n bo*," she said. *I'll be back.*

Gold flopped on the couch. She would have to break the promise she made to her late husband. Her daughter was pissed at her, and she knew how stubborn Tolu could be. Things would not be fine between them until she told her the things she didn't know about their marriage, and that was the last thing she wanted. She didn't like seeing her daughter upset.

Tolu opened the car and threw herself in it, trying to control the rhythm of her breath. She left the house to avoid saying things that she would later regret. It was 1 p.m. and the sun was scorching. She needed to feel better before she returned to the house. As she fondled her phone, the thought of seeing Bisi appealed to her, but she kicked against it. She didn't want to appear emotionally needy to him. Plus, he would be preparing for work because he told her he would be on call today. *And Daniel?*

"*Yeye* guy," she said, her lips curving into a smile as she dialed his number.

"Chief Judge," he said when he answered it.

"Will you stop that nonsense?"

He laughed. "Aren't you? You decide the fate of my love life right now."

"Men and lies. Why do you sound like you've not dated other ladies since we broke up? Who even knows if you're dating many others presently? I can't be fooled by you guys anymore."

"Point of correction, you broke up with me."

"Whatever."

"And about dating other ladies since we broke up? Let's not go there."

"A-ha! Now I want to go there. Never mind. It's not like I care anyway. I just want to point out your deceit to you."

"I'll tell you about it when we see it. But most importantly, I'm as single as the word single. I'm not in any relationship, so you're safe."

Tolu hissed. "You are so annoying."

"I just can't help being silly with you."

"I don't even know why we are having this discussion."

"Because there is a part of you that still cares about me, maybe."

Tolu thought about it. Could it be?

"I'm careful not to say, love, you know. I don't want to push my luck."

"Good for you."

"When and where are we seeing?" he asked.

"You are still at FUTA, right?"

"Yes, I am. Are you coming over? Do you want me to host you?"

"You? Host me? I don't hate myself that much."

"That hurts, you know?"

"Not as much as what you did."

Daniel sighed. "When will you forgive me, Tolu?"

"Maybe I have, but I don't just trust you."

"Why? You think I will rape you or what?"

"Any man who did what you did is capable of doing worse. Why should I enable you?"

"Tolu, you're tormenting me."

"Just as you tormented me with your wickedness."

"Okay! Where are we meeting?"

"I'll come over to FUTA south gate. There is an eatery around the south gate junction. We can talk there."

"Okay, I know the place."

"I'm on my way now. Don't keep me waiting."

"I wouldn't dare. I can't wait to see you."

"Tsk tsk."

She ended the call.

* * *

Daniel stood up from the chair immediately he got off the phone with Tolu. He shut down his PC where he had been working on his CV. Since he wasn't sure how long he would be in Akure, he might as well get himself busy while he worked towards winning Tolu's heart again. He wasn't leaving until he achieved that. Tolu was a hard nut to crack, but he was willing to go all the way to earn her love.

He believed he could get a contract job. He would visit some hospitals in town to assess their medical equipment and see if they needed his service. He was sure they would. The condition of the health care system in the country was unpleasant, but convincing hospital heads and the concerned government officials was the main challenge. People could be resistant to change, especially if it would cost them money. He would try his best anyway and could even use his father's help if need be. His father had some friends who were into politics in Lagos and Abia states. Somehow, there would be someone who has a connection with the people in power in Ondo state. And yes, he would speak to Tolu about it.

He flung the wardrobe open. Tomiwa had done a good job of making him feel at home. Daniel always missed him whenever he went to work in the morning and looked forward to having him back at home. He was good company.

He picked a sky-blue long sleeve shirt and a pair of Jeans. He assessed his looks in the mirror as he brushed his hair. He knew he was good-looking. One major reason coupled with his intelligence that made him one of the most sought-after guys in school, both in Nigeria and Canada. He didn't indulge himself with the ladies that threw themselves at him at UNILAG because he wanted to make a first-class and get the car gift his father promised him. More so, there was Uju, who assumed they were in a relationship and was always acting like his girlfriend when he never professed his love to her. Daniel didn't care if she dated other men because he didn't love her. This irked Uju who expected him to exhibit some level of jealousy when necessary.

In his two year stay in Canada, he dated a couple of ladies. He couldn't call what he had with them relationships. They were more like friends with benefits. They kept him company and had sex. He didn't commit himself to any of them. His heart was still with Tolu. He didn't find anyone like her. What they shared remained fresh in his memory every day. Tolu was the only lady he had ever really loved.

He used some perfume on his body and took one last look at himself in the mirror before dashing out of the room. Tolu must not get there before him or else he would be in for it.

* * *

Daniel got up from his seat when he saw Tolu's car heading to the eatery's car park. He silently prayed that he received favour in her sight and that their date, rather 'trial,' would go well. He walked briskly to her car and poked his head in the car immediately she turned off the engine.

"Are you coming down?" he asked.

Tolu picked her purse and looked at him. "I don't remember stating my car as our meeting place," she replied.

Daniel laughed. "There we go. The ever-sarcastic Tolu."

"I wear my badge with pride. Excuse me."

Daniel stepped back as she opened the car door. His eyes swept over her when she got down from the car.

"You are pretty, Tolu," he said.

She rolled her eyes. She was wearing a knee-length fitted white gown and a pair of flat red sandals. "Thank you. But don't think that would reduce the weight of your punishment," she replied. He wasn't looking bad either, but she wouldn't tell him that.

Daniel laughed. "I wish you would just tell me my punishment, so I could start serving it immediately, no matter how hard."

"I already told you, but you refused."

"No, you didn't."

"Really? I told you to leave me alone. That's it."

"Come on, Tolu. You know I wouldn't do that."

"Really? But you did that once, and that's why we are here." She folded her arms and leaned on the car.

Daniel sighed. He was getting tired of Tolu's nagging.

"That was then. I'm here to fix my mistake. That was the past; this is the present, Tolu. How unforgiving can you be? Haven't you ever made a mistake in your life? Haven't you hurt anyone before? Why is it so difficult for you to forgive me seeing that I'm willing to do anything to be in your good books again?" He couldn't hide his anger this time. She was driving him crazy.

Tolu saw the hurt in his eyes, but he deserved every bit of the treatment she was dishing out to him.

"Really? Emotional blackmail again? Like I told you, it's not going to work on me, so quit playing the victim," she said, fighting the guilt that was tugging at her heart. She wondered if he was right about her being unforgiving. No, he wasn't right. He deserved to be treated anyhow she liked. How could he ask her to abort their pregnancy, travel to Canada, and expect her to give him a grand welcome just because he came back begging? What if she had died from abortion or childbirth complications? Would he seek forgiveness from her rotten bones? Yes, she destroyed her SIM card and blocked him on every social media platform, but he could have reached her if he wanted to.

"Suit yourself, Tolu," he replied. His anger was getting the better of him.

"I honoured your invitation, and what I get is an insult?"

"I didn't insult you; I'm just getting frustrated." He rubbed his forehead as if that would relieve him of the ache he was feeling.

"Alright. Go and deal with your frustration and let me go deal with mine!" She turned towards the car and opened the car door.

Daniel took hold of her hand and shut the door. "Okay, I'm sorry. Don't leave. I'm sorry for upsetting you. I know I deserve all the harsh treatment, but I'm human too. Be fair. Come on."

Tolu smiled to herself before turning to face him. "Okay," she said, trying to stifle a smile.

"Let's just sit inside the eatery and talk. I am famished."

Daniel fought the urge to hold Tolu's hand while they walked. He didn't want another outburst from her.

"What would you like to eat?" he asked her immediately as they settled at a table for two.

"Beans and *dodo*."

"I'll have the same too."

Tolu made a face.

"What? A criminal cannot eat what the judge eats?"

"Whatever, Daniel."

"Hey! You just called my name. That's a good sign."

"It doesn't mean anything."

"It does. You have not called my name since we reconciled. I love it when you do."

"Reconciled?"

"Well, since we met."

"I'm hungry, please." She felt her stomach rumble.

"Just a minute." He left to place their order.

Tolu's eyes followed him. Could she call him a good man? Would a good man do what he did to the woman he claimed to love? Even though he was showing remorse and willingness to make her happy with him, could he still earn the good man tag? She found it strange and embarrassing that she was still attracted to him. Maybe she still liked him even? Wasn't she supposed to stay angry with him after the unforgivable thing he did?

Daniel returned with a waiter, both carrying a tray of food and a bottle of water each.

"Thank you," he said to the waiter as he placed the food on the table. Tolu murmured the same.

Tolu's stomach rumbled aloud to Daniel's hearing.

"That's my stomach saying, 'thank you,' she said, pulling a tray of food to herself. Her mouth watered at the sight of the bean porridge, a big cut of croaker fish, and fried plantain.

"Tell your stomach that Daniel will do anything for it."

"I shouldn't even be eating this. I should have gone with you to make my order and brought my food myself." She started eating. The bean porridge tasted good.

"I'll take that as a joke that it is. You should learn to trust me. I cannot hurt you. You are safe with me."

"Yeah, right?"

"Please, excuse me," he said.

She watched with amusement as Daniel prayed briefly. When he opened his eyes and saw her looking at him, he said, "A criminal cannot pray again - at least for mercy?"

She covered her mouth and laughed. "Daniel prayed before eating. Wow!"

"It's not just because I'm about to eat. I'm breaking my fast."

Tolu's eyes widened.

"Yes, I was fasting."

"Really?"

He lifted a piece of the *dodo* to his mouth. "Yes. I am now a serious Christian *o*; trying to know God more."

Tolu kept staring at him.

He continued with a serious expression. "I realized I needed God. I had been a churchgoer all my life and never really taken God seriously."

Tolu hmmed. "I hope this isn't all to impress me."

"No! I did it for myself. It happened in Wale's church after listening to a sermon that opened my eyes to the poverty of my soul and spirit. I gave my life to J.C afresh."

"Who is J.C?" she asked, looking lost.

"Jesus Christ, of course."

"Oh." She smiled and muttered, "J.C."

"Funny?" he asked.

"No, interesting."

"Yeah. If I wanted to impress you, I know what to do. Not..."

"Really? What are you trying to insinuate? That I'm not spiritual?" she feigned annoyance.

"You know that is not what I mean. You and I know that you are not really into church or religious stuff."

"You are being euphemistic, Daniel."

He laughed.

"Anyways, I shamefully accept the truth that I have only been a churchgoer and not been serious with God. If I had been, if we both had been, we probably wouldn't have found ourselves in this mess."

"Forgetting those things which are behind, and reaching forth unto those things which are before..."

"You don't tell me that. I'll do that at my own pace."

"Not my words, Tolu. Those are the words of the Bible. Paul's to be precise."

Tolu laughed. "I know; it rings a bell. I see you have been reading the Bible."

He nodded lightly.

CHAPTER THIRTEEN

Bisi smiled as he approached the postnatal ward, but his smile disappeared when he entered the nurses' office and was welcomed by a different face. That was when it hit him that Tolu was off duty. She had been in his thoughts throughout yesterday, and he wished above everything else to see her today, even though he knew that she was off duty.

After recovering from his disappointment, he greeted the young nurse in a sky-blue scrub while managing a smile. "Good afternoon."

She looked up from the case note she was writing in. "Good afternoon."

Bisi sized her up. She was dark-complexioned with a beautiful oval face and had short twist braids on.

"I'm the anesthetist on call. I just came to check on the post-op patients." *But most importantly to see if I would stumble on Tolu.*

"Oh okay," she said and rose to her feet. Bisi realized that she was tall and had curves that couldn't go unnoticed.

"I'm Adebisi Ayoade. You can call me Bisi."

She smiled. Bisi knew it was because of his name. His Australian friends called him 'busy'.

"Lucia Kofi-Attah," she replied.

"Kofi-Attah. Ghanaian?"

She nodded.

"Interesting." He beamed. It seemed the ward boasted of interesting people.

"There are four of them," she said, sorting out the case files.

"I'm interested in the woman with the ruptured uterus." The surgeon and the anesthetist that handed over to him had told him about the patient. They called her the 'wonder woman' who survived after having a severe uterine rupture and had the attention of the surgical team for five hours. She almost emptied the hospital's blood bank as she was transfused with ten pints of blood during the surgery. She was fortunate to have had the most common blood group, O positive; else, she wouldn't have survived it.

"Okay." She handed over the case file to him. "The first bed by the right."

"Thank you," Bisi said and walked to the woman's bed. She was lying in bed with her head propped up with two pillows. Blood and intravenous fluid dripped simultaneously into each hand.

"Mrs. Bosede Alabi," Bisi called to confirm she was the patient.

"Siirrr," she answered, her speech dragged. She was thirty-two years old, fair and plump, looking unkempt.

"How are you feeling today," he asked, checking her eyes. Expectedly, she was mildly pale.

The patient nodded.

Bisi took her vital signs. Her pulse was quite rapid, her body temperature slightly elevated, her blood pressure and respiration borderline. He documented his assessment and care plan in her case note and returned to the nurses' station.

"Thank you. Let her continue to be under close monitoring," he said to Lucia, who responded with a nod. Bisi thought of her as snobbish. Don't ladies who know they are pretty and curvy tend to be? However, he understood that she had quite a lot on her plate as she was the only one on duty. He missed Tolu. Realizing it wasn't a good time for making an acquaintance, he left the ward.

* * *

"Thank you," Tolu and Daniel said simultaneously to the waiter who packed their dirty dishes and cleaned up the table.

"What is your hospital like? Do you have the latest medical equipment to work with?"

Tolu chuckled. "*For where?* We have a vital sign monitor that serves the ward though."

Daniel shook his head. "It's a pity. I'm thinking of meeting with the medical directors of some hospitals here and if necessary, go to the Ministry of Health. The health sector needs to be taken seriously. You wonder why our politicians travel outside the country when they have a headache."

Tolu laughed.

"Yes, it's because they don't trust our health care system. But the masses have no choice. So many deaths in the hospitals are preventable."

Tolu nodded. "Coupled with the fact that the hospitals are understaffed. Imagine having just one nurse on duty in the whole ward. If you are lucky, you have two."

"That's serious." He sighed.

"You can try your luck. We never can tell. It would -" her phone vibrated, cutting her short.

Daniel looked at the name on the phone screen. Bisi.

"Excuse me," she said and answered the call with her face full of smiles.

Daniel knew Bisi to be a girl's name, but the smile on Tolu's face confused him. That wasn't a girl-to-girl kind of smile.

"Hey. I envy you right now. Hope you're enjoying your duty off?" Bisi said.

"I don't have a choice. How is your call going?"

"The hospital is quite calm, only that you are off today, and I miss you, and that is why I called."

"I miss you too," she blurted and cast a glance at Daniel's crestfallen face.

"You wouldn't believe I went to your ward today with the hope that I would stumble on you, even though I knew you were not on duty."

"Really?"

"Yes. I met a young Ghanaian nurse…"

"Lucia?"

"Correct."

Tolu felt a tinge of jealousy. Lucia was a beauty queen with killer curves, and she could be quite flirtatious. Besides these, she was stylish. A certain married consultant couldn't hide his crush on her as he would always frequent the ward whenever she was on duty.

"So, you guys had fun since the hospital was calm," Tolu caught herself asking.

"Not at all. We didn't talk much. She was the only one on duty and had a lot to do. The judge in me nearly passed the snub verdict on her."

Tolu felt relieved. "She's a pleasant person. You only met her at the wrong time."

Daniel shared glances between his phone and Tolu.

"I think so too because there is a woman in your ward who is under close monitoring, another case of severe uterine rupture."

"Oh my God! Not again!"

Daniel looked at her, his face creasing into a frown.

"She's a thirty-two-year-old mother of a four-year-old boy. When she came to the clinic two days ago, she was told she would need a caesarean section because the baby was not only big but also breech. She refused and said she had prayed that she would never undergo an operation. She left the hospital and went to a church. She was rushed back to the hospital yesterday in a semi-conscious state, bleeding like no man's business."

"Jeez."

"It was crazy yesterday, I was told. She almost emptied the blood bank."

"Really?"

"Yes. She's conscious now. I went to see her."

Tolu sighed.

"I have given you the hospital gist. Now, when do we see again? I've missed you."

Tolu looked at Daniel; their eyes met.

"How about tomorrow? I could visit your place before I resume at the hospital if you don't mind. You are also welcome to my place. Or we could go out if you wish," Bisi said.

"Tomorrow is fine, but place and time will be communicated later." She would need to think over their meeting venue. She wasn't sure if she'd want him to know where she lived yet. Even though she liked him and was attracted to him, she didn't know him and his intentions well enough. Also, going to his house was quite risky. With the chemistry between them, she didn't trust herself enough to resist him if he made a move on her. Did that mean she would need to go visiting with some condoms stashed in her bag just in case? Or would he have some condoms in his house? Oh no! She should not be thinking about having sex with someone she barely knew.

Bisi cut into her thoughts, "Alright. I'll be expecting your call or message. Enjoy yourself."

"Thanks for the call." She dropped the phone on the table. "I'm so sorry for holding you up. I had to take the call," she said to Daniel, her lips parting in a smile.

He sighed. "A criminal has no choice. Are you in a relationship, Tolu?" he asked, skeptical of her answer. It was good he knew so that he would know his fate and think of his next line of action.

Tolu sighed. If she told him she wasn't in a relationship, Daniel would be encouraged in his pursuit to have her back in his life. But if she told him she had a boyfriend, he would let her be, and that would ruin any chance of that happening. Plus, she and Bisi were likely to end up together, so technically, she was in a relationship.

"Yes," she replied.

Daniel's face fell. "Was he the one who called?"

She nodded.

"Okay," he replied in a low voice. He might as well ask about the pregnancy and have his heartbroken all at once. "What about the baby? Did you keep it?"

"I already told you that I removed your pregnancy just as you wanted."

He nodded slowly. None of them said anything for the next three minutes. Daniel couldn't wait to be home, but he didn't want to be the one to end the date.

Tolu checked the time on her phone. It was 4:30 p.m. "I guess we are done here," she said.

"Yeah. Thanks for coming."

He saw her off to her car.

"Let me drop you off at home," she offered.

"No, I'll be fine. It's just a few minutes' walk to the house."

"Drive carefully," he managed to say.

Tolu got into the car and drove out of the park while Daniel watched till her car was out of sight. He started walking home, feeling as if the weight of the world was on his shoulders.

* * *

Daniel met Tomiwa in the house, eating *Booli* with palm oil. He usually bought the roasted plantain every day on his way from work to eat it with palm oil at home. Daniel had grown to love the food just like his host and always looked forward to eating it with him.

"I kept yours in the microwave," Tomiwa said after exchanging pleasantries with Daniel. He was clad in a pair of boxers that revealed his hairy thighs and legs.

"Thanks, Tom." He sank into a sofa. "I'll be travelling back to Lagos tomorrow," he announced.

Tomiwa stopped eating. "Why? Have you gotten your girl back?"

Daniel sat up and quickly hid the tears in his eyes. "Another guy has her. She has a boyfriend."

Tomiwa stood up from his seat and lowered himself beside Daniel, patting his back. Hot tears coursed through his face. He let himself cry to be relieved of his pent-up emotions. Tomiwa continued to pat him as he cried and sobbed. When his sobbing subsided, he said, "You are not travelling to Lagos tomorrow."

"Why? What's left for me? She said she has forgiven me, but she cannot trust me again. She also said she aborted the pregnancy. She is already in a relationship. She reminds me of my wrongs every time we talk. What then should I wait for? What hope is there for me?"

"Just calm down, there is hope for you. If you love her and you are serious about wanting her back in your life, trust me, you can have her," Tomiwa said.

Daniel looked at him. "What do you have for me?"

"I'm not a relationship counsellor, but I can share my experience with you. I hope it helps." He stood up and returned to his seat.

Daniel adjusted in his seat and mopped his wet face with a handkerchief.

"I'm about to open an old wound, but if it will be of help to you, why not? How much do bandages cost?"

Daniel laughed, unable to resist Tomiwa's humour.

"You must have been wondering why I'm not married despite my apparent readiness."

Daniel nodded and smiled when he remembered that Wale had called him "single to a stupor".

"Wale keeps saying I'm single to stupor."

Daniel laughed out at the coincidence of Tomiwa's words with his thoughts.

"He thinks it's because I'm picky. Well, I do not deny that, but there is more to it. I've always been a bookworm and never really been involved in love matters. Don't get me wrong; I love women, I mean, I admire them, so I have no doubts about my sexuality." He laughed and continued, "I have many of them as friends, and some want more than friendship, especially as an undergraduate. But I wasn't ready to love. I dreaded heartbreaks like death. When I love, I love too deeply. I didn't want anything to get in the way of achieving my goal, which was graduating with a first-class. My initial goal was to become the best graduating student."

"Wow. You are a highflyer," Daniel chipped in. He only aimed at making a First-Class and not becoming the best graduating student.

Tomiwa smiled. "It comes with a lot of prices. I don't believe in school love. I don't see why I should start a relationship when marriage is the last thing on my mind. So, during my service year in Lagos, I relaxed a little. I had some time on my hands to invest in love affairs. Luckily, I met Laide, also a corps member. We were posted to the same school to teach. We hit it off on the first day we reported at the school. She was a beautiful lady, but what attracted me to her was her personality. She was full of life, cheerful, and witty. There was never a dull moment with her."

Daniel began to feel hot. He removed his socks, shirt, and trousers, leaving on him his underwear.

"We became friends, fell in love with each other three months into our service year, and started dating. She was my first, and I loved her deeply. She brought light into my life and made my service year memorable. We were practically inseparable."

Daniel smiled.

"No, we did not have sex. She was a virgin just like me, and we promised to remain that way till we got married. We were not saints anyway. Of course, we shared some kisses, and you know..." Tomiwa smiled.

Daniel nodded in understanding as he remembered the intimate times he and Tolu shared.

"We wept during the last week of our service year because apart from the fact that we lived far apart; I was based in Abeokuta while she lived in Port Harcourt; I was to travel to the UK for my postgraduate studies. I assured her that with effective communication, we would be fine, and a year would be gone before we knew it. I learned later that it wasn't as easy as we had thought. During the first two weeks, we communicated well, but my obsession for success took over as I buried my head in my books. To be fair, I was encumbered with lots of tasks - lectures to attend, assignments to submit, lab practical, research, and project, and my personal reading. It got so bad that we only talked once a week. Even though she called almost every day, I couldn't pick her calls because I was either in the library or laboratory. I usually promised myself to call whenever I got to my room, but the brown bat has got nothing on me."

Daniel laughed.

Tomiwa continued, "She complained and complained. We fought each time we got to talk. I called her selfish, a nag, and an attention seeker." He shook his head in regret. "I think she got tired and stopped bothering me. She no longer cared if we talked or chatted. I felt relieved because I was able to concentrate on my tasks, so we stopped communicating altogether two months before my return. I still loved her very much and couldn't wait to see her. I believed it was the same thing with her, despite our being incommunicado. I thought she gave me time to concentrate because my schedule became tighter and I was close to returning to the country anyway. When I landed at the airport in

Nigeria, she was the first person I called. She answered my call and warned me never to dial her number again. I thought she was still angry with me, so I let her be and called the following day. To my greatest shock, a male voice answered the call and warned me to steer clear of his fiancée. I kept on calling until I started receiving threats. That was when it dawned on me that I had lost Laide. I was shattered. It's been seven years now. I keep comparing the ladies I meet with her."

Daniel sighed. He couldn't tell who had it worse between him and Tomiwa. "I am so sorry for your loss, Tom," he said.

"I guess it served me right. I was selfish and overly ambitious. Even though my schedule was always tight, I could still have communicated reasonably with her, knowing how tough a long-distance relationship could be, especially for a lady. If I could spare time to eat, sleep, and use the toilet, I could have kept in touch with her, even amid these necessary activities. It wasn't as if she was jobless too. She had a restaurant she was starting. Love is all about sacrifice sometimes."

"I know, right? But you should open your heart to love again. It's been long."

"I'm trying, but there are just too many ladies. Too many of them, beautiful and smart; just the way I like them, they leave me numb."

Daniel remembered that Wale had said a similar thing.

"I have my eyes on a lady though. She's a master's student in the department."

"That's good to hear. Why not go after her before some sharp dude does?"

He rubbed his forehead. "I will, maybe after her final exams. I just hope she wouldn't mind that a lecturer is asking her out."

"You are a fine young man; any lady would be happy to be your woman. Moreover, she's a postgraduate student, not an undergraduate."

He smiled." Now, let's talk about you."

"Yes," Daniel said, feeling so relieved and hopeful.

"If you love this lady, what's her name?"

"Tolu."

"Yes, if you love Tolu, then you've gotta fight for her. What is the assurance that her boyfriend genuinely loves her? The fact that she is in a relationship doesn't mean you should back off from her. All you need to do is show that you are a better option than the person she's dating."

"I hope I won't be a distraction or a threat to her relationship?"

"You won't. You are only fighting for your woman. If she sees your genuineness, she might reconsider. What is even the assurance that she has a boyfriend? What if she told you that just to keep you away?"

"The guy called her in my presence, and she was all smiles."

Tomiwa shrugged. "Well, it does not change the way you feel about her. The fact that she has forgiven you is a good sign that she might reconsider you."

"I don't know, Tom. I don't know what to think anymore."

"Do you know the guy?"

"No. But I think they both work in the same hospital."

Tomiwa thought for a minute. "I think you need to get a job on contract there as you intended. You need to be closer to your babe. You need to increase your visibility. Proximity increases attraction. We tend to fall in love with people we see often."

"You are so right. I must see the CMD of that hospital tomorrow."

"I will drop you off there. I don't mind waiting to bring you back too. I don't have any lectures until noon"

Daniel jumped up from his seat and slapped Tomiwa a high five.

"Let me go and warm my *Booli*," he said.

"Please warm this with it." Tomiwa passed the remaining of his roasted plantain that had become cold to Daniel.

* * *

Tolu took a deep breath as she turned off the engine. Many thoughts and questions boggled her mind. She knew that Daniel was hurt by the phone call she received and the answers she gave to his questions. But what could she do? She believed Daniel still loved her and cared about her, but how could she love and trust him again after what he did? A part of her wanted to, but what would people say? And what did Bisi want from her? The chemistry between them was palpable. She didn't even know his relationship status. What if he was in a relationship or engaged and was just leading her on? Maybe she was rushing things and expecting too much, after all, she just became friends with him? She would take her time and guard her heart. She hoped that Gold would be ready to tell her what she needed to know when she entered the house because there was no way she would pretend that all was well between them.

She alighted from the car and entered the house to meet Gold snoring on the couch, and Lola sleeping soundly on the floor with her arm clutched to her doll. Tolu headed to her room to undress after which she had a cold shower and later slept.

CHAPTER FOURTEEN

Tomiwa drove Daniel to the hospital as he had promised. They located the CMD's office following the directions of the security officer. The secretary, a middle-aged woman whose skin screamed of exhaustion from bleaching products, had her sunburnt face masked under heavy makeup. Daniel expected an awful reception, typical of an average secretary in a public organization, but to his surprise, she gave them a warm reception.

"He has a meeting with the Commissioner of Health today," she said, wearing a smile.

Daniel had disappointment written on his face.

"He will be around tomorrow," she added immediately, seeing Daniel's sad expression.

Tomiwa patted Daniel's back while the woman asked, "Do you have an appointment with him?"

"No."

"No problem. Come tomorrow at this same time. What is your name?"

"Daniel Okojie," he told her, and she scribbled on a piece of paper.

"He will be here tomorrow," she said.

Daniel thanked her and left with Tomiwa.

* * *

At 9:30 a.m., Gold had not returned home after taking Lola to school at 7:40 a.m. The school was only ten minutes' walk and four minutes' drive from home, but Gold preferred to walk as a form of exercise. Tolu knew her mother was avoiding her. When she woke up at 8 p.m. the previous night to have dinner, she found Gold and Lola already sleeping in their room. It was quite unusual because Lola's sleeping time was 8 p.m. while Gold usually slept at 10 p.m.

Tolu dialed Gold's number which she answered after the third ring. When Tolu asked her where she was, she replied that she was taking a walk and would soon be home. Tolu shrugged. Gold could walk around the whole town if she liked, but she wouldn't leave for Bisi's place until her mother returned to spew whatever she was hiding, even if it meant cancelling her visit to Bisi's house.

"I'll be going out very soon. I just called to know where you are," Tolu told her.

"I have my key. I'll be home very soon."

After the call, Tolu went back inside her room to get dressed.

* * *

At 10:30 a.m., Gold arrived at the house. She gasped at the sight of her daughter who sat with her legs crossed in the sitting room.

"Is it that serious, mum? Why are you avoiding me?" Tolu queried.

Gold sat on a couch opposite Tolu, looking down. She took a deep breath and spoke, "I don't know how to say this to you. Apart from the fact that I vowed to your father not to tell you, I don't want you to get hurt."

"I won't," Tolu promised. She had imagined the worst.

Gold hesitated before dropping the bombshell, "Your father had another family back in his hometown."

Tolu nodded slowly. She wasn't surprised. Somehow, she had always suspected it. Why would her father keep her and Gold away from his people? Were they that bad? He visited his hometown alone. Also, her parents didn't have a house of their own and Tolu knew that Gold shouldered most of the family's expenses, leaving her to wonder what her father, who was a senior-level officer for fifteen years before his retirement, spent his money on.

"I knew it," she said.

Gold, who had been looking down at her hands raised her head, her face filled with surprise. "How did you know?"

Tolu shared her suspicions with her mother. Then she asked, "How many are they? The kids and maybe the women too."

"Stop being sarcastic." Gold eyed her.

"Well, I'm not."

"There's only one woman. She has three children for him, two girls and a boy, ages twenty, seventeen, and fourteen."

Tolu nodded.

"He had them after I had you and couldn't have more kids."

Even though Tolu had her suspicions confirmed, she felt so bad; not because her father had other kids apart from her, but the fact that he kept them away from her and made her believe she was his only child. His other family, which was larger, took up most of his income.

Gold continued, "Don't take it the wrong way. Your father was a good man, and he loved us deeply. Remember how he loved and adored you. We stayed ten years before we had you. He fought with his relatives who asked him to take another wife, his mother especially."

"So, what happened? Why did he eventually succumb to their wish when he already had me?" Tolu asked, her anger burning against her late father.

"I found out about his other family a year after they had a second child. He told me his mother said she wouldn't be happy with him if she died without him having more kids because he was her only child. He said she threatened to place a curse on him."

Tolu sneered. "Witchcraft."

"His mother got him a twenty-year-old secondary school-leaver. She told him the lady was a virgin and so would be fertile. Indeed, she was."

"What is the assurance that the children are his?"

Gold shrugged. "Of course, they are his. He would have known if they were not."

"How? Did he carry out a DNA test on them? He left a young woman in the village and visited her occasionally, and you think she wouldn't have a man in the village to meet her sexual needs. That's his business anyway. How did you find out?" Tolu asked.

"Through his phone – I wasn't snooping. Your father and I trusted each other so much. We respected each other's privacy and never snooped on each other."

Tolu scoffed.

"On that fateful day, he was having his bath, and his phone kept ringing incessantly. The caller's name was saved as Mr. Ade. I knew him to be your father's friend, so I answered the call with the thought that he might be calling for a very urgent matter. I was shocked when I heard the voice of an angry lady, speaking in your father's dialect, which I mildly understood. She was saying something about a sick child needing a blood transfusion. I hung up and checked his message folder. I had read only the last message your father sent to the number by the time he stepped into the room."

"What was the content of the message?"

"He warned the person never to call him again because they had agreed that he would be doing the calling. All 'Mr. Ade' had to do was send an empty message and he would call back."

Tolu sighed.

"Have you met the woman and her children?"

"No. I'd rather not. Knowing that they exist is traumatic enough for me. I don't know if I can handle meeting them. I don't want images of them to mess up my mind or the memory I have of your father. Your father respected my wish and ensured that our paths never crossed. He even warned them not to attend his funeral so that we would never meet."

"Wasn't that nice of him?" Tolu chipped in.

Gold gave her a reprimanding look.

"Stop painting the man as a saint. He did what he did because he wanted to, not because his mum manipulated him. Was he a baby? He went ahead to have another child even after you knew about his other family. What explanation will you give for that? 'He was trying to have a male child' you'd say. The man thwarted your dream of owning a school. He spent his money on his other family while you ran our family with yours. Yet you carried on as if all was well and even fell for his deceit to keep it from me. Dad used you, Gold!" A tear escaped from the corner of her right eye.

"I loved him. I loved him so much. I couldn't just -" Gold choked on her words as tears poured down her face.

"Love? Why do women make ridiculous decisions in the name of love? No, I think you were deceived. God! How did you live with such a level of deception?"

"What could I have done? Divorce him and start from where? Moreover, he loved and respected me."

"He used you," Tolu insisted.

"You don't know my husband more than I do, Tolulope. You don't know what we shared," Gold snapped.

"Oh well. He was your husband, not mine but you should have informed me. Didn't you think I would have loved to have siblings? Did you think I enjoyed being an only child?" She paused, and after releasing a deep breath, she said rather calmly, "Just like you, I'm not interested in meeting the other family." She stood up. "I'll see you later."

For the first time in a long time, Gold wept in remembrance of her late husband. He was only a man webbed in unpleasant life circumstances and as a good wife, she had to be there for him. She loved him wholeheartedly and she believed the feeling was mutual. He didn't use her. Or did he?

* * *

When Tolu hit the road, she sent a text to Bisi, informing him that she was on her way to his house. He replied immediately, expressing his excitement at her coming.

Although Tolu had prepared her mind for the worst, she couldn't help feeling sad and betrayed. She was even angrier that Gold was living in denial of the fact that her husband used her. If her father respected Gold as she claimed, he wouldn't have done that. Her father was selfish, Tolu concluded. Would he have forgiven Gold if she did the same to him? Tolu was angry at her mum's passivity. She should have also tried her luck with another man to see if the problem was with her. Then, Gold would prove her husband's 'love' and 'respect' for her. Adultery was taboo for the woman, but for the man, it was acceptable. Amazing! Tolu thought.

"What a patriarchal society we live in!" she said angrily as she put the car to a halt in front of Bisi's house.

"Hey!" Bisi said excitedly and held out his arms for an embrace. Tolu melted into his open arms as she let tears flow freely. He led her to sit on the couch and placed her head on his right shoulder. He rubbed her back gently while she cried her heart out.

When her cry reduced to sobs, Bisi asked, "Do you want to talk about it?"

I" just found out that my father had another family in our hometown. She had three kids for him, two girls and a boy."

"Oh!" He raised his eyebrows.

"What is wrong with having one child? I am still alive, after all."

He smiled.

"I don't have anything against his having more kids from another woman but keeping it away from me and having talked my mum into doing the same is heartbreaking."

"I guess they didn't want to hurt you."

"And now?"

He shrugged.

"I am angrier at my mum's naivety—she did not realize that he played her. He spent most of his salary on his other family while my mum ran our family with hers. She keeps saying he loved and respected her so much. Like seriously? A man who loves you would never hurt your feelings, right?"

"Sometimes it's complicated, Tolu. Life is not black and white. We are humans after all, and we mess up at times," he replied.

She sighed. Did it mean Daniel could love her as he claimed? Maybe things just got complicated between them too.

"Should I get you something to drink?"

"Yes, please. Thank you." She lifted her head from his shoulder, mopped her wet face with her palms, and watched as he made his way to the kitchen. She closed her eyes and relived the past ten minutes. She loved the way he received her. He was calm and seemed in charge of the situation. She found him so easy to talk to, just like he found her too and had told her about his family. *Could this be a sign?* She wondered.

"Here," Bisi's voice interrupted her thoughts.

She opened her eyes and collected the glass of chilled orange juice that he offered.

"Thank you," she muttered and took a sip. Bisi also took a sip from his glass. He wore a pair of khaki shorts and a T-shirt. Tolu's eyes ran through his hairy thighs and swallowed hard. If she ever doubted her ability to resist him should he make a move on her, now she doubted even more.

"How is your mum?"

"I don't know. I left her immediately after she told me everything."

He smiled. "This is the time she needs you the most. Please, don't be mad at her. Marriage is a mystery. Sometimes, a man and a woman share something so spectacular, that they make some jaw-dropping decisions that leave people wondering."

"I wish she had made a jaw-dropping decision too. Like, sleep with another man to see if she would have more kids."

Bisi burst into laughter. "Abomination!"

"And for the man, it's what?" she asked.

"You know a man can have more than one wife. Some religions and even our culture support it. But a woman cannot have more than one husband. In fact, she must not be caught having an affair."

"Wait, this is getting interesting." She set her half-empty glass on the table.

Bisi laughed and downed his drink.

"To start with, most religions and cultures, especially the African culture, are patriarchal, so I don't do any. But I think the Christian religion is quite fair. The Bible commands a man to love his wife unconditionally just as Christ loved the church and gave Himself for her. That is love and selflessness at its peak, but men still struggle with this injunction because they are naturally selfish."

"I think human beings generally are selfish."

"But men are more selfish than women," Tolu argued.

"You seem to have a thing against men."

She threw her head backward. "Do I? I don't think so. I'm just being realistic."

"Being realistic is subjective. What we call reality most times is a product of our experiences, preferences, desires, and views, which are often biased."

"We-e-ll," she dragged, rolling her eyes. "I'm forced to agree with you."

"Selfishness is more nature-inclined than it is gender-inclined."

"Hmm." Tolu nodded and sipped her drink.

"A child who grows up in a loving environment would find it easy to give love to others. Children who are taught to love and share with others are not likely to be selfish. I believe that we are products of our environment."

"You are correct. I never thought of it that deeply before now," she said. "It is so relieving sharing my burden with you." She exhaled loudly.

"I am happy you feel better," he said, looking into her eyes.

"Thank you," she replied, returning his look shyly. At that moment, she longed for a kiss. She caught him swallowing hard too. She could read hesitation in his eyes. He did not want to make the first move. Maybe he didn't want her to think he was taking advantage of the vulnerable situation she was in. Moreover, they were not dating yet, so there was no ground for such romance.

Tolu's heart raced as she toyed with the idea of making a move. What if he turned her down or considered her as easy? Although a lot was being done to correct the stereotype that sexually brazen women were loose, society still considered sexual passiveness as a feminine virtue.

"Can I kiss you?"

Bisi's words snapped her out of her thoughts. She tried to stifle a grin, but her lips betrayed her. Her face turned towards his and their lips locked.

* * *

While Tomiwa and Daniel sat at the reception waiting for Daniel to be called in, a middle-aged chubby nurse stumped in, expressing her frustration over the lack of equipment needed to perform some procedures. They could tell she was a matron from her uniform.

"If not for my love for this profession and our people, I would have quit and sought greener pastures in the UK many years ago. The working environment here is not encouraging. How can a surgical ward not have a functioning autoclave? The consequence is infection and breakdown of surgical wounds," she lamented to the secretary.

"I thought you sterilize your instruments at the central sterile supply department?" the secretary asked while Tomiwa and Daniel listened in.

"Is that supposed to be? Imagine the long distance between the ward and the CSSD. We use the CSSD because we have no other option. The ideal thing is for each ward to have its sterilizing machine. The two trolleys we have are bad. We carry them instead of wheeling them because if we dare wheel them, sleeping patients will first experience a nightmare before jumping out of their beds."

The secretary laughed loudly. "Matron! The noise *abi*?"

"Yes, the noise. I am not exaggerating. We have written several letters of complaints, yet nothing has been done about it. That is why I'm here in-person to see the Chief. My nurses are exhausted. We are tired. We can't continue like this. If nothing is done this time, we may have to close the ward until everything is fixed."

"Ah! Don't do that o, matron. I'm sure the Chief would do something about it now that you are here."

"I hope so," she replied.

Tomiwa and Daniel exchanged glances. Before either could say a word, a man came out of the CMD's office.

"Matron, you can go in now," the secretary said while she gestured to Daniel to be patient. "You can see she's upset. Moreover, she needs to return to the ward quickly."

Daniel nodded in understanding.

Twenty minutes later, the matron came out, and Daniel went in to see the

CMD. After Daniel stated the purpose of his visit and his qualification, the CMD, Dr. Mahmoud, replied, "I appreciate your zeal to work, young man, but the government is not recruiting at the moment."

"I know, sir. But this isn't about the government recruiting me, it's about us improving the health care delivery of this hospital through the provision of the latest hospital equipment."

"That is not my job, it is the government's, and I'm sure that it's not in the state's budget for now so I can't present it to the commissioner for health at this time."

"What if private individuals and organizations show interest in helping out?"

The Chief's eyes lit up and formed a frown almost immediately.

"We have written letters to many of these people. They only make promises but do not fulfill their promises."

"Maybe you haven't met those who are true humanitarians."

"Do you know any?"

He knew he could get his father and some of his father's friends to be of help. "I do know some people who would embrace and support this project."

The CMD narrowed his eyes at Daniel. "Young man, what is your motive? I thought you were some desperate graduate seeking a job, but you do not sound like one."

I'm desperate for Tolu's love. Daniel smiled at his thought. "I am passionate about the hospital workplace environment. I have less than three months to spend in this state, so I want to keep myself busy and give back to the community in my little way."

"So, what will be your take-home?"

Winning Tolu back into my life "Anything you are willing to give, but most importantly, my fulfillment."

The CMD sighed. "You can leave ten copies of your CV and two copies of your proposal letter. I have a meeting at the Ministry of Health on Monday morning. See me at 2:30 p.m. on Monday. I'll take you around the hospital so that you can see the situation of things for yourself."

"Thank you, sir." Daniel tried to contain his joy.

"I should thank you. I'm also not pleased with the situation of things here, so if you're offering us some help, I should appreciate you."

Three minutes later, Daniel walked out of the office.

"Besides my desire to get Tolu back, I'm passionate about the hospital workplace environment. Our hospitals are something else. I can't imagine working in any," Daniel said to Tomiwa, who shot him a glance.

"Are you saying you can't work in Nigeria?"

He laughed. "I don't have to work in a hospital. There are biomedical companies I can work in. I hope our healthcare system improves soon."

"That might take forever. Some states have it better though. No thanks to our greedy leaders who prefer to stash billions of naira meant for the country's development in their homes."

"It's so sad. Nigeria is a blessed country, but corruption is our undoing."

"In the meantime, you could work in companies instead of hospitals."

"I think I prefer it over there. Their dedication to research and development cannot be compared to what we have here. I don't want to be part of the brain-drain though."

Tomiwa laughed. "Tell me about it. That is why most of our excellent students and lecturers travel abroad to study and work because there are no resources to fund research and ideas. It's sad."

Daniel nodded in agreement.

CHAPTER FIFTEEN

Tolu, are you ready to make a fool of yourself again? Remember your 'no work romance policy'? You wouldn't want to be caught dating a coworker. You don't want to be the next topic of hospital gossip.

These thoughts clouded her head as she was engulfed with emotions and passionately kissing Bisi. He reminded her of what she'd been missing in the past two years. He had awakened her desires, and now she wondered how she had been coping. When he moved his hand from her neck down to her right breast, she jerked and broke the kiss.

"I'm so sorry. I didn't mean to make you uncomfortable," Bisi pleaded.

She nodded lightly. Her body was on fire. Her eyes went to the bulge under his trousers.

"Let me get us something to eat," he said and got up.

"Do you have a girlfriend?"

Tolu's question stopped him in his tracks. When he turned, Tolu could tell from his expression that his accompanying words wouldn't make her happy.

"Not exactly," he replied.

"How do you mean? It's either you are in a relationship or not." She was fast losing her patience.

"She's in Australia but -"

"Never mind," Tolu cut in. She picked her phone and headed towards the door.

"Where are you going?" Bisi asked, looking confused.

"Why not ask your distant girlfriend? You guys are all the same."

"Come on, Tolu. I can explain it. It's not what you think," he said, but she was already out of the house. He heard her start her car and drive off.

Tolu sobbed as she headed home. Her day was ruined. She thought she could find some succor in Bisi after what Gold had told her, but she was wrong. He was only using her to kill time until his girlfriend returned, just as Daniel used her to pass the time for his NYSC.

"Why do I keep attracting losers?" she screamed and hit the steering wheel.

Was that only what she was good for - men's pastime?

But was it reasonable to be angry with Bisi? He sought her consent before they kissed. They weren't dating and he never professed his love to her. They were just friends. Why then was she angry and jealous? Was she in love with him?

"My head is so messed up right now," she muttered amidst sobs.

She desperately needed a shoulder to cry on. Gold wasn't the right person to talk to at the moment neither were her two girlfriends, Chisom and Maryam. It's been a while since the trio of them chatted on their WhatsApp group page. Daniel was another person she found it easy to talk to, but he was obviously out of the question. Maybe it was time she talked with God, she thought.

* * *

Tolu rambled into the nurses' station on Monday at quarter to two in the afternoon and met two nurses, Josephine Okonkwo and Tomilola Davidson, who was ahead of her by one rank. They were gossiping as usual. Tomilola was dark and plump with an acne-battered face which she didn't bother to treat. She didn't use makeup or wore any jewelry. She believed that they were instruments of Jezebel to lure men into lust, and both the seducer and the lured would end up in hellfire.

After an exchange of pleasantries, Tomilola said to Tolu, "Don't you young nurses advise one another?"

Tolu's face creased into a frown.

"I learned Lucia is a mistress, dating married men and putting them under her thighs."

Half-mindedly, she replied, "You talk as if men are babies."

Josephine replied, "You don't understand idioms. She meant that your friend holds men captive. Who knows maybe she's using juju."

Tolu shot her a look. She wanted to reply to Josephine that she had a lot on her plate already with five children to cater to rather than to be gossiping with Tomilola, who was popularly called the hospital's CNN. Even Tomilola herself had enough going on in her life that could serve the hospital enough gossip for six months. Rumour had it that she usually delivered all her salary to her husband, who would, in turn, squander it on his numerous side chicks. She argued that it was a symbol of submission. People could count the number of clothes she had. She had only a pair of black shoes which she wore every other day.

"She is not using juju. Her body is juju enough," Tomilola chipped in.

"I agree with you. Her curves and her face that never lacks makeup" replied Josephine.

Tomilola hissed. "How are you even sure that she didn't have plastic surgery to have the body? Can it be natural?"

"It could be natural. African women are well-endowed. I used to be so beautiful before Obi and his children sucked the beauty out of me. I'm not saying Lucia couldn't have done cosmetic surgery to enhance her looks. These young ladies can do anything to keep men in their grasps."

"Excuse me, I need to change into my scrub," Tolu announced and headed to the changing room, hoping that the two women would have rounded off their gossip before she returned. Unfortunately, when she returned to the ward five minutes later, they were yet to change the topic. Since she had seven minutes left before she took over the ward, she sat on one of the chairs, rested her back, and shut her eyes, just to show her lack of interest in their gossip.

"I learned she has just opened a sophisticated salon and makeup studio in town. I'm sure that is some women's husbands' money speaking. The lady doesn't have a conscience. How can she even have peace knowing that she's breaking people's marriages? These girls don't know how unhappy they make other women."

Yeah, right? Tolu understood that Tomilola was speaking from experience as rumour also had it that she once caught her husband in the act on their matrimonial bed, and instead of showing remorse, he was mad at her for interrupting him. He instructed her to prepare food for him and his mistress afterward, which she did. Another version of the story stated that her husband, Davidson, neither loved nor intended to marry her. He only married her because she got pregnant while they were dating, and Tomilola's family threatened to cast a spell on him to run mad if he didn't marry their daughter.

Tomilola, on the other hand, had always felt privileged to 'have' him. He was a good-looking man, and she was nowhere close to being his type. He had dated her because she was responsible for his bills since she had a job, and he didn't. Six years into the marriage, she remained the breadwinner.

Josephine shook her head. "Women go through a lot in marriage. Although my Obi was a traditional man to the core and did not allow me to work, he was faithful to me. Even if he had other women, I didn't know about them."

"Good man! He respected you. All men cheat, only the good ones keep it away from their wives," Tomilola said.

Tolu stifled a sigh. Tomilola's experience with her unfaithful husband had left her with the impression that all men cheat. Tolu felt a tap on her thigh and opened her eyes to see Tomilola's eyes peering into hers.

"Why don't you advise your friend, Lucia?"

Tolu struggled to contain her annoyance. "Lucia is an adult, and so, old enough to make decisions for herself. I'm not privy to her personal life, it would be rude of me to poke my nose into her personal affairs." Her voice was now getting intense. "Besides, how true are these things you are saying about her? Rumours are just what they are—hearsays, which could have been started by someone who doesn't like her." She said with a tone of finality, more like she was done with the conversation.

Tomilola wouldn't give up. "Everyone cannot be all wrong or dislike her. They must have some proof. *Abi* how does she afford those outfits she wears? How much does she earn?"

"And she doesn't look like she was raised by wealthy parents," Josephine added.

Tolu shook her head at their shallowness. "So, a child from a wealthy family is supposed to fold her arms and not work for her money or pursue her passion? Jealousy and lack of correct information about people are usually at the root of hearsays. People should learn to mind their businesses. It's her business whatever she does with her life." She hoped she passed her message across.

Tomi protested, "It's not her business *o*! You don't know how it feels to have your husband cheat on you with another woman, painfully a younger woman, young enough to be your younger sister or even your daughter."

"Don't worry, she will understand when she gets married," Josephine said.

Tolu snapped her fingers over her head. "I reject such an experience. Marriage is a lifetime affair, but if it starts threatening my life and sanity, I'd rather take a walk."

Tomilola smiled ruefully. "If wishes were horses - it's not as easy as you think, Nurse Makinde."

Tolu had become really uncomfortable. She glanced at her wristwatch. "It's ten minutes past two," she said, standing up and heading out of the cubicle into the ward to prevent the discussion from lingering.

Tomilola still had more to say. She was overwhelmed and talking about her problems indirectly was the way she let off some steam instead of confronting the source of her problem—her husband, Davidson.

Thirty minutes later, Tolu was glad to be alone in the nurses' station. Her workplace principles, avoiding romantic affairs and gossip, had been nearly violated in a quick roll. As she went through the case files of the ten patients she had taken over, she let out sighs intermittently as though they would wipe the events off her memory. After one hour of going through the case files, she closed the last file.

Thoughts of Bisi flickered into her mind, and she fought hard to suppress them each time. She had been ignoring his calls and messages since the day she left his house angrily. He called her one hour after she left his place; he called several times and also sent text messages the following day. When she didn't answer his calls or reply to any of his texts, he stopped calling.

Tolu shook her head. She was not ready to listen to his *lies*. Bisi had stabbed her just when she decided to open her heart to love. Daniel didn't seem forthcoming anymore either. He had gone silent on her since the last time she saw him. Once again, she doubted his love for her.

"Who is here?" a familiar voice shot her out of her reverie.

She raised her head, transfixed as three pairs of eyes focused on her.

"Good afternoon, nurse. This is Mr. Daniel Okojie, a biomedical engineer. He will identify the equipment that each department needs. Hopefully, we will get some. He shall also see to the installation of all the equipment and facilitate the training of the entire staff on how to use them," the CMD said.

"Hi," Daniel said, extending his hand towards her. He was smiling. Daniel was dressed in a pair of black pants and a blue shirt with the sleeves rolled up.

Tolu hesitated before taking his hand. Many questions swam through her mind. What in the world was Daniel doing here? How did he convince the CMD to employ him?

"You are welcome, Dan... Mr. Daniel," she said briskly with a forced smile.

"I don't have to introduce Dr. Ayoade. We are on a hospital tour, and this ward happens to be our next point of call," the CMD briefed.

Tolu nodded, avoiding Bisi's eyes, which had been fixed on her since they entered the ward. Their eyes had locked while the CMD was introducing Daniel.

"Please, take us around your ward and tell us what you have."

Tolu led the tour around the ward with feigned confidence.

"The beds lack features suitable for post-operative patients. We have only one monitor for vital signs in the ward, which has even been malfunctioning lately," she rattled off. Daniel made some notes on his iPad.

"Is that all, nurse?" the CMD asked.

"Yes, that is all, from me anyway. The CNO will tell you if there is more."

"Alright. Thank you, nurse -"

"Makinde," Tolu supplied.

"Yes, Nurse Makinde. Do have a great shift." He led the way out of the ward.

Tolu returned to the nurses' station and settled slowly in her chair, drifting into a barrage of thoughts. She didn't think Daniel was still in town since she stopped hearing from him. She knew Daniel came to Akure because of her, however, after seeing him a few moments ago, she wondered if he had decided to settle in the town. What was he really up to?

She arranged the case files neatly. She would be serving medications in a few minutes.

"Hey!"

Tolu looked at the door to see Bisi standing there. He had entered the ward through the back door.

"Hi," she replied distantly.

He walked in. "May I sit?"

She shrugged.

He sat opposite her. "Where do I start? You are so mad at me."

She scoffed. "I have no right to be mad at you. I'm not your girlfriend. I'm afraid I don't have much time here. I have patients waiting to be attended to, as you can see." She gestured towards the stack of case files.

Bisi sighed. "First, I apologize for any clumsiness my actions might have caused. I can't deny that I'm attracted to you, and I like you a lot. We've only met a few weeks, and you've brought nothing but happiness into my life."

Tolu fought the temptation to grin. She was pleased with what he was saying.

"It's just kind of complicated. I'm sorry I kissed you. I should have exercised some self-control."

"There is nothing to be sorry about. You didn't kiss me. We kissed." *And I loved it.*

"Alright." He rubbed his palms. "So, you have forgiven me?"

He was trying to be sly, and Tolu wasn't going to play along. "Bisi, I won't have us pretend like we don't know what is going on here. You have a girlfriend, there is no need for getting amorous with me. We may feel something for each other, but I'll never be the second fiddle." She stressed the '*never*' and continued, "I am not a plan B."

Bisi let out a short breath. "My girlfriend, Adaora, is in Australia. I have called it quits with her many times, but she just wouldn't let go. There is no way I'm marrying the spoilt brat. She's the only daughter of a wealthy single mum. Initially, I was fascinated by her academic prowess and beauty. She's a computer scientist and a straight-A student. The six months of our relationship were characterized by constant sex and frequent fights over her extravagant lifestyle. There were no intellectual discussions, and whenever I attempted to share my burdens with her, she made promises to take me on a shopping spree to forget my worries. I got tired of her and the relationship."

Tolu swallowed her laughter.

"I can't marry that kind of woman. I'm sure she has got herself another guy in Australia to satisfy her high libido. Although she intends to come back to Nigeria after completing her program, I have been taking steps to sever ties with her."

Tolu took a deep breath.

"When I met you, and we got talking, my decision to break up with her was reinforced. You are deep and reflective. We connect on a deeper level. I don't find it difficult to share my burdens with you."

Tolu rolled her eyeballs.

"I'm not flattering you. I mean every word."

"If you have nothing to do with her, why then do you keep communicating with her?"

He nodded. "Yeah. I guess I'm just letting her fill the space until someone else comes to fill it."

"That is cowardice. You don't mean your words. So, if no one comes along to replace her, you'd remain stuck with her till you end up in a miserable marriage?"

He laughed. "She does the calling. I don't call her. She's the one dating me. If she has any iota of pride left in her, she should have backed off."

Tolu sighed. "I don't know what to believe. You men can be quite cunning. And I don't even know why you are telling me these; after all, I'm not your girlfriend."

"Come on, Tolu. Don't pretend we do not feel something for each other."

"So? I should let go of my senses and let you play with my feelings?"

"I wouldn't do that."

"That line is familiar."

"It's coming from me, so you have to believe it."

Tolu nodded.

She cleared her throat. "Well, I was…"

"Hi."

It was from Daniel. They had been so engrossed in their talk that they didn't see him through the transparent window when he passed.

"I'm sorry I interrupted. I'll come back," Daniel said.

"No, it's fine. My mission here was informal. I'm sure yours is official," Bisi said, smiling, and got up from his seat. "Please answer my calls and reply to my chats tonight. We have a lot to talk about," he said to Tolu.

Feeling uneasy in her seat, she also got up with the stack of case notes in her hands. "I'll try."

"Hi," Bisi muttered to Daniel on his way out.

"I'm sorry I have to attend to my patients," Tolu said to Daniel before he could say anything.

"Okay. How long would that take?"

She glanced at her wristwatch. "One hour."

"That means you would be through at 5 p.m.," Daniel said, glancing at his wristwatch.

"Yes, but I'd be taking another round at 6 p.m."

"When does your shift end?"

"8 p.m."

"Do you mind if I come then? I can also drive you home. I wouldn't feel comfortable if you have to drive yourself home after work at night when I'm around."

"You can come at five. I would be free for an hour if there's no emergency surgery." She knew she shouldn't be granting him an audience, but she wanted to satisfy her curiosity. "And don't worry about driving me home. I've been driving myself home at night before you came."

Daniel smiled. He missed her greatly. "I'll see you at five." He turned and left.

CHAPTER SIXTEEN

Tolu was attending to the last patient, Emem, a teenage mother, when Daniel walked in. She gestured to him to enter the nurses' station. He sat on one of the chairs while she continued her discussion with Emem.

"Why didn't you inform your *madam* when her husband started abusing you sexually?"

Emem, seventeen years old, was brought to Akure from her village in Calabar to work as a house help for the Okoyes. Jude Okoye was a forty-year-old tutor at the School of Health Technology while his wife, Janet, owned a foodstuffs stall at the main market. The couple had two kids; a boy aged nine and a five-year-old girl. Janet, thirty-two, was hardly home during the day as she resumed at her shop at 8 a.m. and closed at 7 p.m. The kids usually went to their mother's shop after school until their father complained that he found it shameful for his kids to roam the market after school. Since he wasn't ready to look after the kids, they requested a househelp from Madam Ufoma, a child labour agent, who brought Emem to them.

Janet expressed her fears when she set eyes on Emem because she could pass for a twenty-one-year-old. She looked physically mature beyond her age; tall and slender with voluptuous breasts that protruded through the tight T-shirt she wore. Her hips were just appropriate for her size. Despite her poor background, her chocolate skin glowed, and her thick afro hair shone.

Janet called Madam Ufoma who had brought Emem, to the dining section.

"This girl is too big *o*!"

"Big, *ke?* She's just seventeen."

"This one that looks ripe for marriage?"

"Haba!"

"Yes *na!* I don't want a rival or a second wife in this house. You know how these men are."

Madam Ufoma roared with laughter. "What will your husband see in this one?"

"These men's amu no dey look face o. This girl too ripe. Even me wey be woman, my mouth dey water."

"Ah! Me I no see anything wey dey for this one body o. Your husband na professor na. Wetin he wan take this village girl do? You sef you be fine woman na."

"*Na so.* That's how village girls end up becoming the madams of the house."

"See, all you have to do is buy her oversized dresses to hide whatever you think she can tempt your husband with. No trousers or any skimpy clothes. That's how people do it."

Janet wasn't convinced.

"Where is your husband?"

"He's not in."

"Don't you think he should see the girl so that you'd know what he thinks as the head of the family?"

"In fact, I don't want him to see this one. He already permitted me to employ a maid as long as I get the one who can take care of the house and the kids. I would have preferred a boy, but I fear for my daughter. The stories of sexually abused girls we hear these days are scary. I could kill if such happens to my daughter. I don't want to commit murder."

"A boy is not even available now. So, what is your conclusion? Emem is a very pleasant and hardworking girl. She has been with me for three weeks, and I can vouch for her. If not that I already have a girl working for me, I would employ her for myself. *I bring am for you because you be my personal person."*

"Ehn ehn?"

Madam Ufoma was doing a great job at convincing Janet.

"Yes. But since you said you don't like her; I'll return her and bring someone else for you. It's not advisable to employ someone you don't like."

The door opened, and Jude came in before Janet could reply to Ufoma.

"My husband is back," Janet said. "Welcome, honey," she called out from the dining room.

Jude greeted Madam Ufoma as he hugged his wife briefly and later went inside the room. Janet excused herself and went in with him. She returned two minutes later.

"My husband says she looks like a good girl, so she can stay," she said, still looking uncertain.

Madam Ufoma laughed. "I told you. Your husband is a correct man! That's how you know *professors*."

"I just hope he said that with the right intention. I do not doubt that the girl might be a good girl, but these men..."

Madam Ufoma cut in, "Don't you trust your husband?"

"I do." Janet sighed.

"Why then are you getting yourself unnecessarily worried? Please, don't invite fear into your heart. The Bible says whatever you fear shall come upon you. Just do what I told you to do and be vigilant. I'll also talk sense into her head. I'm sure you will give me good reports in a few weeks."

"If you say so," Janet resigned.

Six months later, Emem was confirmed pregnant.

"He said he would kill me and send hired assassins to kill my family in the village if I dared say anything to his wife," Emem replied. Her baby girl was sleeping in her cot. She was the cutest baby Tolu had seen since she started working in the hospital.

"Did you believe he would do that? That was just a threat. He bullied you into silence. That is what abusers do."

"I was scared. He said he loved me and would protect me. He said his wife would not believe me if I told her and my life would end up becoming miserable. I was also concerned about my family because Madam Ufoma usually sent half of my salary to my family after removing her commission. The rest is saved for my schooling. I want to go to school. I don't want to go back to our village and continue that life of poverty." Tears streamed down her face.

Tolu briskly wiped off a teardrop. "But why didn't you use protection? You could have prevented this. You know what I mean?"

She nodded. "He never used condoms. He said he liked it without condoms."

"And you could have gotten some pills to use after the sex, anything to protect yourself." Tolu assumed that she would know about the pills since she knew about condoms.

"I didn't know about that. Even if I did, I didn't have any money to buy anything."

"What about Madam Ufoma? You could have told her or any adult in the neighbourhood if you couldn't tell your *madam*," Tolu questioned further.

"He warned me not to tell anybody. Telling an outsider would have been worse. Don't you think?"

"I don't think so. Silence never solves anything. It only makes things complicated, just like they are now."

When Janet got to know that her husband was responsible for Emem's pregnancy, she called Madam Ufoma to come and take her away, but Jude protested. He said Emem was not going anywhere; she was his responsibility, and he would take care of her. When Janet threatened to move out of the house with the kids, the family elders intervened. After a long stormy meeting, it was concluded that Emem should remain in the house until childbirth, after which she would move to the apartment that Jude would rent for her. However, things never remained the same between Jude and Janet. The former cordiality between Janet and Emem fizzled out as Janet frustrated Emem in every way possible.

Emem sobbed. "I wish I had opened up. I wish I had spoken to someone. Now my life has become worse than it was."

Tolu patted her shoulder. "It's not over for you, Emem. You can still achieve your dreams, only that you would have more sacrifices to make."

Emem shook her head. "I don't think my life can be better again. I ruined my *madam's* family. I have a baby I don't even know how I would take care of. I don't trust Mr. Okoye's promises. He is only after my body, that stupid man!"

Tolu supported Emem's anger. Anger was the right thing to feel, not self-pity. She believed she would be able to make better decisions if she was angry at her situation and the man who put her in it.

"Which man will even marry someone like me?"

"That should be the least of your worries now. You should be thinking of how to deal with the mess you are currently in and how to achieve your dreams."

"I know *aunty nurse,* I know. I'm just thinking." She smiled weakly.

Tolu smiled too. She wasn't surprised. In most of Africa, she had come to know, a woman is expected to aspire for marriage because a woman is perceived to be incomplete without having a husband and children to call her own.

"I don't want you to give up, Emem. I come across many teenage mothers often, but you strike my heart differently. I strongly believe you can still achieve your dreams. This is just an event in your life. It may cause a stir and temporary delay in your life, but it shouldn't bring your life to a halt. You know what? I'll give you my phone number. It's unlikely that I'd meet you here tomorrow. Make sure you call me." She tore a piece of paper from the prescription note where she wrote her phone number and gave it to Emem.

"God bless you, *aunty.* You are giving me so much hope. I'll surely call you. The old fool said he would buy me a phone."

Tolu laughed. Jude was indeed a fool. The baby stirred in the cot and let out a whimper.

"Attend to your baby," Tolu said and got up from the chair. She packed the case notes she had left on Emem's table and headed to the nurses' station with a sense of fulfilment at giving someone hopes for a better life.

She sauntered into the nurses' station. Daniel looked up from his iPad where his head had been buried in.

"I'm sorry for keeping you waiting," she said, relieving her hands of the case notes. The time was 5:30 p.m.

"No *wahala.* I understand. That was why I suggested coming after your shift."

"My discussion with the last patient took longer than I expected." She opened the fridge and took out a can of malt drink. She offered him the drink and sat from across him.

"Thank you. "Daniel smiled and opened the drink.

Tolu exhaled. "This is one of the times I wish I were a millionaire already."

"Let's *collabo,* and your wish will become a reality." He took a swig of his drink.

Tolu eyed him. "Because you are the son of a rich man, *abi?* I hope you know that there is a difference between being a wealthy woman and being the wife of a wealthy man?"

"In marriage, two become one. Whatever each person has belongs to both of them. Whatever I have belongs to my wife as well."

"Isn't that what you all say until you have what you want? The story changes when you become the head of the family. Many wives of wealthy men in this part of the world have nothing to their names. They drive their husbands' big cars and live in mansions. Some of the men ban their wives from working, so they can be dependent on them, and that makes it difficult for them to quit if the marriage becomes abusive. They cover their swollen eyes with sunglasses in their posh cars."

Daniel shook his head. "Tolulope! Where do you get your stories from? I'm not saying that stuff like these aren't happening, but you should feed your mind with positive stories and not ones that would make you prepare in advance for a nonexistent battle. All men aren't the same. There are stay-at-home wives of wealthy men who are equally wealthy. Some men appreciate the sacrifices that women make in raising the kids and keeping the home. Any man who makes light of the sacrifices of his woman is foolish," he enthused.

Tolu seemed to agree.

"Are you saying you are different from the majority of men?"

"Majority? Where did you get your statistics from? Beware of generalizations."

"Stories abound..."

Daniel cut in, "That is their reality. You choose your reality."

"I don't even know why I'm having this discussion with you."

"Because you can discuss anything with me."

She scoffed and changed the topic. "So, what are you doing here? You were supposed to be back in Lagos. After all, you've got what you came here for."

"You think so?"

"I gave you the forgiveness you came begging for."

"Well, my mission is yet to be accomplished, and I'm not leaving this city until that happens."

"And what could that be? Your new job here?"

"You'd know when the time comes."

She rolled her eyeballs. "All the best."

"Is that him?" he asked.

"Who?"

"Your boyfriend."

"Oh." She raised her eyebrows.

"Yeah?"

She hesitated. She and Bisi were not officially dating but judging from their last discussion, that would soon happen. "Yes," she replied, avoiding his eyes.

Daniel nodded slowly.

"What?" she asked.

"Nothing. I just hope he loves you as much as I do."

She snickered. "You?"

"The fact that I was immature and made some mistakes two years ago doesn't change the fact that I love you deeply. I've tried other relationships, but they never measured up to what you and I shared."

Tolu felt a glint of jealousy and pride. So, he dated while she veered off the dating track because of what he did to her. Who were the ladies and what did they look like?

"Why me?" She was curious.

"I ask myself the same question. God must have planted your love in my heart for me to have hung on despite the way you treat me with contempt and derision."

"Yeah, right? I hope it wasn't God that told you to abandon me when I needed you most."

"Tolu, you know that if people died from nagging, I would have died. You would have killed me."

She laughed contentedly.

"What is nagging compared to what I went through?"

"I haven't been able to forgive myself for it. You said you have forgiven me, but you keep mentioning it. We both made mistakes. Let bygones be bygones and let's move on."

"That's so easy for you to say. I have forgiven you. You don't expect me to restart a relationship with you, do you?"

He shrugged.

"Look -"

"Tolu, look into my eyes and tell me you don't love me."

She looked into his eyes. "I don't hate you."

"But you don't love me either?"

She didn't reply.

"I better be on my way so that you can concentrate on work." He rose to his feet. "By the way, I have some gifts for you. I didn't bring them to our previous dates because I feared you might accuse me of wanting to bribe my way into your heart."

Tolu didn't miss the hurt in his voice, and somehow, her heart softened towards him. "You can bring them to the office."

"Can I call you or chat with you on WhatsApp?"

"Fine."

"I'll see you around. Take care."

Tolu watched him leave. She wished she could call him back to stay a little more. She enjoyed his company. She couldn't tell whose company she enjoyed more between him and Bisi's. She loved being with each of them.

Apart from what happened between them, Daniel was her dream man—handsome, intelligent, and responsible. And now that he confessed to being serious with God; that was the icing on the cake. Though she attended church on Sundays when she wasn't at work and also joined her family for the morning devotion, she knew she should do more. She remembered spending a lot of time praying and reading her Bible before she met her ex,

Sylvester, who deflowered her. She sunk into guilt and self-condemnation which eventually pushed her off her faith. Her faith in God was now at a low ebb and she desired to have someone who would encourage her in the faith.

From the little she knew about Bisi, he seemed to be her kind of man too. He was intelligent, he was handsome but not as much as Daniel, and she found his company enjoyable. He had also said he cared about her. What else did she need in a partner?

She scooped the case notes from the table and walked out of the nurses' station.

* * *

The car beeped as Tolu unlocked it.

"Hey!" a familiar voice called behind her.

Startled, she said, "You? What are you still doing here?"

"Waiting for you to close," Daniel replied.

"You are a stalker now?" She was surprised and impressed that he waited for her.

He laughed. "Come on, Tolu. I'm not a stalker. Like I said earlier, I would love to drive you home."

Tolu made to protest, "I -"

"Yes, I know you've been driving yourself home at night, but I'm here now. Let me, please."

She resigned. "Okay." She tossed him the key. She was tired too. Enjoying a ride wasn't a bad idea.

Daniel opened the door for her and closed it behind her. He walked around the car and settled into the driver's seat. Tolu gave him directions as they drove in silence.

"I live two houses away. I think I am fine now. Thank you," she told him when they arrived at her street.

"You know I won't come visiting without being invited."

Tolu nodded. He had read her mind. "Let me see you off back to the junction. I'm on my street, so I'm safe."

Daniel smiled. "Don't worry. I can take care of myself. Goodnight." He opened the door and stepped out of the car.

Tolu got down and watched as his silhouette disappeared into the night's darkness before getting into the car.

CHAPTER SEVENTEEN

Tolu was glad to have finally come to the end of her shift for the week. As she drove home, she recalled the events of the week. The week had been hectic—the c-sections, the emergency cases of two women who had their wombs ruptured due to the improper delivery procedures that they went through at unregistered birth Centers. The health team had put in frantic efforts to save the lives of the women. The blood bank was nearly exhausted as several bags of blood were dispensed for transfusion pre and post-surgery. The CMD finally decided to organize a conference in conjunction with the O & G department on how to curb the high rate of womb rupture in the community.

She and Bisi didn't talk much that week. They bumped into each other on a few occasions at the theatre when she went to check on a patient. All they exchanged most of the time were a smile and a nod. She was usually too tired to chat with him when she got home from work. He must be exhausted too, she guessed.

She hadn't seen Daniel at the hospital nor heard from him since the night he drove her home. She didn't call him either even though her heart went out to him. She was always too tired to do more than freshen up and slip into bed each night. She hardly ate dinner all week.

After having a dinner of rice and spicy catfish pepper soup, she logged on to YouTube to watch a movie—her sleeping pill. Her phone rang. The caller

ID showed up to be Bisi. With her heart pulsing with excitement and a smile playing on her lips, she answered it.

"The week was mad!" Bisi screamed into the phone.

Tolu laughed heartily. "Tell me about it."

"The conference the CMD is planning is very much needed. Recall I have been saying that something needs to be done about women seeking medical care in the wrong hands. I mean, it's crazy—two hysterectomy cases within two days! *Kilode?* These are wombs getting ruptured and removed, not balloons."

"I'm happy that something is about to be done. Pregnancy or childbirth might be a common experience, but that doesn't trivialize the risks and complications associated with it. One cannot be too careful."

"You are right. The week was tough; a boring weekend would be extra torture. I have an idea on how to have an exciting weekend. It occurred to me some minutes ago, and I was like, Eureka! But I'm afraid you would say no. You don't seem to be keen on adventures these days."

"What is it?"

"How about a kind of road trip to Ibadan tomorrow? Believe me, it would be fun. My weekend will be ruined if you say no."

He was greeted with silence on the other side.

"Hello?"

"Yeah?" Tolu replied, her mind jumbled with many thoughts.

"It's a bad idea? I knew you'd say no."

Tolu smiled. "Of course, it's not a bad idea." The thought of spending time alone with him in the car thrilled her and made her shudder at the same time. They were still friends, but the chemistry between them was getting stronger. She avoided talking about their status because she didn't want to appear desperate—that was a total off for most men. Staying together alone—for that long would only get their hormones running wild. Stashing condoms in her bag would pass a message across—she looked forward to them having sex. She did not want that although she fantasized about it.

"So?"

"It's an interesting idea, and I might get to see my alma mater again. But why a road trip to Ibadan?"

"Well, I think it's more exciting than this place. I've been there many times. My aunt lives there. There are places we could go to catch fun—Agodi Gardens, Ventura Mall, the popular *Amala* joint at Bodija, and the trip itself. Spending time with you in the car would be great fun. You're fun to be with."

Tolu grinned. "Are we returning tomorrow?"

"Sure. The trip is less than three hours. That's why I call it a kind of road trip. It's not a long trip."

"Would it not be too stressful?"

"Stressful is the new fun, babe."

"Hmmm. It sounds like it would be fun indeed." She didn't dare to turn him down.

"Yes, that's the spirit!" He threw a fist in the air. "All expenses are on me. I will fuel your car and drive." He had once told Tolu that buying a car was not his priority because he lived close to the hospital, and if it became one, he could get one from his father's garage which housed three cars.

"Alright. See you tomorrow at -?"

"7 a.m.?"

"I am game."

"I'm so excited. This is going to be my best weekend in a long while."

It would be the same for me too. She thought.

When the call ended, she analyzed the decision she just made. Should she tell Gold? She didn't think it was a good idea to inform her. Although Gold respected her decision and wouldn't stop her from going, she would express her fears which would include the risks of kidnapping and road traffic accidents. This would douse Tolu's excitement towards the road trip.

She had given Bisi her word, and there was no way she could cancel. She had considered the physical and emotional risks involved, but what was an adventure without some risks? Since they would return tomorrow, there was no point informing Gold and getting her unnecessarily worried. And to handle the emotional risk involved, she would resist every urge to get physically intimate with him. Since they were going to be in public throughout the day, she was certain she would not do something as crazy as having sex in the car or anywhere in the public.

Once she had her head cleared, her excitement towards the road trip heightened. She jumped out of bed to pack her bag for the trip.

* * *

One hour into the trip, Tolu was convinced that the road trip was a good idea. She had knocked at his door at 6:45 a.m., dressed in jean shorts, polo shirt, and blue sneakers. Her sunglasses perched on her forehead, with its arms tucked in her braided wig. She wore large hoop earrings and light makeup. As if on cue, he too was wearing a pair of jean shorts, a polo shirt, and sneakers. When he saw Tolu's sunglasses, he dashed into the room to fetch his pair. They started on the journey at exactly 7 a.m. as planned. Bisi drove at a moderate speed while they chatted away. Tolu worried a little if he was not distracted by their talks.

"I've been driving since I was seventeen. So, relax, you are in safe hands. I can even jump and drive."

Tolu screamed. "You can do that when you are driving alone. Life is beautiful."

He laughed.

"I told you we lived here," she said when they entered the old city of Ife one hour twenty minutes into the journey.

Bisi nodded. "What was growing up here like? Boring, I guess."

"You bet; especially as a lone child of teachers. Books became my companion. It helped my reading culture though. Even now, there is always a book to read every week."

"I can't imagine being an only child. Life was fun with my siblings until we lost my brother, Tayo. You deserve an award—in the form of a kiss." He leaned towards her and kissed her cheek.

She giggled and pushed him away. "Please concentrate on driving before we end up inside the bush." Her body tingled from the kiss.

Fifteen minutes later, they parked at the roadside to buy bread and freshly fried *Akara*. When they returned into the car, Tolu sandwiched three pieces of the *Akara* in a medium-cut loaf and handed it to Bisi.

"This is bliss," he said after taking a bite.

"I always looked forward to this stop each time I was travelling to school. The softness of the bread and the hotness of the *Akara* gives one *foodgasm*."

Bisi burst into a laugh. "Wow! *Foodgasm.*" He laughed again.

"It's a combination of *food* and *orgasm*," she explained, giggling.

"*Foodgasm*—food and orgasm," he repeated after her slowly. "It's been a while since I had that," he added, grinning.

"What?"

"Orgasm."

Tolu's eyes widened.

"What about you?" he asked. "When last did you have an orgasm?"

Tolu was taken aback. The discussion was getting rather sensual, but she didn't want to appear prudish. "Two years ago," she replied. "The only time my daughter's father and I had sex. I can count the number of times I've had sex in my life. Yet, having a child makes you look as if you have sex every day," she added.

He smiled. "Sex in a relationship is as natural as the air, so you don't have to feel bad about it."

"While I agree that it is natural to feel sexually attracted to someone you love, I also think sex complicates relationships, especially for a woman—I speak for myself. No matter how casual sex has become, I can't give my body to someone with whom I have no emotional connection. And when physical intimacy mingles with an emotional attraction, it beclouds one's judgment and thinking especially when the sex is damn good. You get *dickmatized*."

Bisi roared with laughter.

"Yes. I think I find it easier to walk away from a relationship if sex has not been involved. I know sex is sex for some people, but for me, it is..."

He cut in, "What do you say about *friends with benefits*?"

"Hell no!"

Tolu thought for once if that was what he wanted with her.

"Can you do it? Or have you?" she asked.

"A couple of times." His lips cornered in a smile.

Tolu stared at him.

"Hey, don't look at me like that," he said, his gaze fixed on the road. "You know what? Sex is sex to most men. It's just physical. A man can have sex with a woman without any string attached."

"What about female prostitutes?"

"Well..."

"I think you should speak for only yourself. Sex is just sex to some women too," she argued.

He paused and continued. "I've had two friends with benefits in the past, but we are no longer friends."

Tolu shook her head. "There I was, thinking you were a gentleman."

He laughed. "Come on, Tolu. A gentleman has urges too. When you are in a foreign land with beautiful and curvaceous ladies flocking around you but not ready for commitment, what do you do?"

"Whatever happened to zipping up your pants?"

"Not when half-naked ladies constantly throw their stuff in your face."

"I don't think anyone has ever died from not having sex. Abstinence doesn't kill."

"Yeah, right?" He nodded.

Tolu shot him a look.

He looked away.

Cars sped past them as they continued the rest of the journey in silence. Bisi increased his driving speed since they were not talking and in thirty minutes, they entered the ancient city of Ibadan. Tolu smiled as memories of the five years she spent in the city replayed in her mind.

"Here we are. Where should we go first?" he asked, looking at her.

Tolu shrugged. "You choose." Her grim face was fixed on the road.

Bisi pulled over to the curb and covered her hand with his. "I'm sorry for upsetting you. It wasn't intentional. I felt we were adults and friends and we could discuss our sexual lives without being judgmental of each other."

"You are right. I have no right to judge you of what I was guilty of."

"Come on, Tolu. That's not it."

"I understand sarcasm when I hear it."

He sighed. "Alright, I'm sorry. I regret my words. Forgive me."

Looking into his pleading eyes melted her heart and her lips straightened into a smile. "It's okay. I'm sorry for being judgmental too."

"You are forgiven." He ruffled her hand and pinched her cheek softly. "So where do we go?"

"Let's go see a movie at Ventura Mall."

"Check for the movie that would be showing at 11 a.m." The car clock read 10:30 a.m.

Tolu browsed through her phone while Bisi started the car engine and joined the flow of traffic.

"You are in Ibadan, consider everyone else behind the wheel as not normal, especially the taxi drivers."

Bisi laughed. "No kidding. I've seen that in my ten minutes' drive here."

* * *

Daniel parked the car beside Tomiwa's car in the large compound, exhausted from the four-hour drive from Lagos to Akure. He had travelled to Lagos on Tuesday to meet with his father and some of his father's friends concerning his hospital project. His mother, Chizurum, and his sister, Susan, were all over him, overly ecstatic to see him. His mother had thrown tantrums on several occasions to get him to come home, but Daniel did not budge. He missed his family, but he had his own life to live.

He met five of his father's friends including his father, Chief Justus Okojie, and presented the list of the needed equipment to them. There's no way private individuals could supply all the equipment that a state-owned hospital needed, but they promised to be of help in their own way. Daniel knew that their donations would go a long way in getting some of the necessary equipment and hoped that the government would be inspired to embark on this project when they see what individuals could do.

Chief Justus Okojie commended his son's passion for contributing to society. He owned one of the three largest pharmacy stores in Lagos, and the largest pharmacy stores in Abia and Imo states. Daniel admired his father's business acumen, but he did not admire his insatiable love for women.

"Why should I marry one woman when I can take care of a hundred?" he would say and also claimed that he was helping the society because there were many nubile women but just a few marriageable men.

Daniel knew that apart from marrying three wives, his father also kept several side chicks. That was one of the complaints that his mother lodged to him when he was home.

"Just make sure you protect yourself whenever he comes knocking at your door," was his reply to her.

"Which is like twice in a month," she said sadly. "And is that what you will say? Can't you advise your father? Aren't you a man?"

Daniel laughed. "Mum, you bargained for this. When you, a graduate, decided to marry a man who already had two wives, what did you expect? That your beauty and charm would cure him of his love for many women? It probably did until you became older. You are almost fifty; he would need younger ladies to keep him warm. You know what I'm saying? I'm sorry if I sound harsh but it's the truth."

Daniel knew that his mother married his dad for his money, which was an accomplished mission because she was enjoying his wealth. Chief Justus opened a large fabric and jewelry store for her in Lekki, which was populated by corporate moguls and celebrities. He provided all that the children needed and gave his three wives monthly allowance, so Chizurum only spent her money on designer fashion items. If money could buy affection and attention, she could afford it.

Chizurum slapped Daniel's head. "If I hadn't married him, would you have been born?"

Daniel laughed, rubbing his head. "Another couple would have birthed me."

"And you wouldn't have had access to all the luxury you've been enjoying all your life because a poor couple in the village would have been your parents."

Daniel rolled on the floor laughing.

His mum and his sister were sad when he was leaving. He loved and missed them, but he had to fight for the love of his life. He didn't say anything about Tolu to his family yet. He needed to clear his mess first. He spent two nights at Wale's place and updated him on his plans.

He walked to Tomiwa's flat, wheeling his luggage behind him. Tomiwa flung the door open, his face broke into a big smile when he saw Daniel. He hugged him and helped him with his luggage. Tomiwa missed him greatly and wondered how he would cope when he eventually left.

A lady was in the sitting room with a bottle of wine and a half-filled glass before her. "You have a guest?" Daniel whispered to Tomiwa who replied with a wink. After a brief introduction, Daniel headed to his room, sizing up the lady cursorily.

Thirty minutes later, Tomiwa entered the kitchen where Daniel was scooping some *jollof* rice into a plate.

"I guess someone is hungry."

"That is an understatement. Someone can eat an elephant right now," Daniel replied, placing a drumstick chicken piece beside the rice. He put the food in the microwave and set the timer. "Would you like some rice too?"

"No, I ate already. Nice car, by the way."

"Oh, thanks. It's my mum's. My kid sister now drives my car. That girl can be a pain in the neck sometimes."

Tomiwa laughed. "Be thankful you have a sister. I don't have one. There are three of us, all boys."

"I pity your mum."

"Yeah, right?"

The timer beeped. Daniel retrieved the food from the microwave and placed it on a tray. He reached for a bottle of water from the fridge and settled at the table to eat the meal. He gulped some water.

"That's her, Adenike. The Masters student I told you about."

Daniel nodded. "She's adorable. I hope she feels the same way you feel for her?"

"Well, I haven't made my intention known to her, but if the look I see in her eyes is anything to go by, then she feels the same way. I am positive about it."

Daniel grinned.

"How was your trip?"

"Positive, I mean very positive. My father and his friends promised to help."

"That's good news. Good job, man." He gave him a high five.

"Thank you."

"And Tolu?"

"Remember I told you I met her boyfriend at the hospital, and that Tolu told me that nothing could happen between us again? I've not called her since Monday that I drove her home because I was trying to recover from that day's events. I also don't want to appear desperate or be a distraction to her relationship. Honestly, it hurts. Anyway, I arrived this early to see if I can hang out with her today."

"Nice move; don't be too far from her. You have to be consistent to show that you're serious about having her back. She might need constant assurance from you to be able to consider you. Don't worry about being a distraction. They are not married yet, so he cannot lay a claim on her. You need to step up your game before you receive her wedding invitation."

Daniel's heart sank. He couldn't imagine Tolu getting married to another man. His appetite disappeared suddenly, and he dropped his spoon.

"Desperate times require desperate measures. You have to act fast if you want to get this girl. Stop being a gentleman," Tomiwa added.

Daniel picked his phone from the table and dialed Tolu's number. He tried three times without any response. His frustration peaked.

* * *

Tolu switched off her phone after ignoring Daniel's call the third time. They were at the cinema, seeing the much-talked-about Nollywood movie, *The Wedding Party.* The cinema room was sparsely filled because it was morning. A scene showed the couple kissing in the car; Bisi slid his right arm behind Tolu. She got the message. He wanted to kiss her. She wanted to kiss him too. She looked around the dim room. The few people in the room had their eyes fixed on the screen. Slowly, she brought her head closer to his and their lips locked.

After the movie ended, they drove to Palms Mall at Ring Road for window shopping and left there at 1 p.m. From there, they went to Bodija market to eat at the popular local restaurant, after which they headed to Agodi gardens to have more fun. They rode on horseback and took pictures. Tolu laughed heartily while the horse took her around the barricaded arena. Bisi felt proud to see her happy. The road trip was a good idea after all. They went boat-paddling afterward, and when they stepped out of their boats at 4 p.m., Tolu suggested they set out on their journey back to Akure to avoid a late-night trip.

"It's just 4 p.m., and you want us to leave already? Let's have some more fun *jare*."

"I think we've had enough fun. I don't want to get Gold worried."

"Gold?"

"Yes, my mum. That's what I call her."

He smiled. "Cute. I wish I could call my mum that but what I feel for her is anger and sadness."

Tolu rubbed his back.

"How can a mother lose herself because she lost a child when she has two other children? It only shows she values the dead one more than the rest of us."

"It's not easy to lose a child, Bisi."

"I know, but a woman must learn to be strong. I have accepted the fact that I've lost her. I only feel for my dad who is stuck with her for life. I would be glad if he had another woman somewhere that makes him happy - my mum is just a bag of sadness."

"Come on!" Tolu cautioned.

"But it's true. If only you know what it feels like to see your mother once full of life, then turn to become a complete shadow of herself." He shook his head sadly.

Tolu pitied him.

"Everything will be fine."

"I don't believe that. It hasn't been fine all these years, what miracle can happen again? It doesn't get to me anymore because I've decided to live my life to the fullest. My mother has chosen the way she wants her life to be."

"That's a good attitude." Tolu nodded. "Do you think your dad has another woman somewhere?"

"I would be the happiest person on earth if he does, but he is a pastor, and that is what irks me," he screamed.

"Why?"

Bisi stopped walking when they passed by the swimming pool. "Do you mind if I swim for some minutes? I want to swim away from these awful memories."

"Okay." If he weren't getting moody, she would have refused.

"Care to swim?"

"You go ahead and entertain me."

He gave a cheery smile and headed to the bathroom to change. Tolu found an empty lounge chair under a shade beside the swimming pool and sat in it. Bisi came out two minutes later clad only in a pair of boxers. Tolu's heart skipped at the sight of his half-naked form. He wasn't entirely muscular, but his body made her long for his touch. Her eyes travelled to the bulge in his underpants. Good Lord! Was he trying to seduce her or something? He flashed a smile at her before diving into the pool. Tolu decided to return Daniel's call to distract her from the temptation before her. The phone barely rang when he answered it. She stood up and paced the surrounding.

"What happened? Where have you been? Is everything okay with you?" Daniel asked, his voice a mix of anger and concern.

"I am fine. I missed your call, that's why I'm calling."

"You got me worried," he said, raising his voice. He was angry she was trivializing his concern.

"Are you alright? You are not my boyfriend, remember? You don't have any right to be angry that I didn't pick up your calls."

He sighed. "You are right. I'm not your boyfriend, but courtesy demands that you…" he stopped, not wanting to say anything to upset her. "I was just checking up on you."

"Aww. How nice of you, since Monday."

Daniel smiled. "Really? So, you cared that I didn't call you?"

"No. Why should I? You are not my boyfriend."

"You said that earlier. Judging from your insistence, I incline that you'd like me to be."

She laughed. "Dating two men at a time is not my thing."

"You are not married, so you don't belong to anyone yet. This is your husband speaking with you."

Tolu laughed a bit loudly and cast a glance at Bisi who was also looking in her direction questioningly. She moved further away from the poolside.

"What makes you think you are my husband?"

"I love you deeply in a way that I can't explain. I want to make you happy. I see my future with you in it. We enjoy each other's company, and I know we can be happy together. I'll try all in my power to be the best husband to you and the best father to our children; God help me. Believe me, Tolu. I'll never disappoint you, not again. Please, give me a second chance."

Tolu's heart softened towards him, and she was tempted to believe him. Despite what had happened between them, she had a strange conviction that she could be happy with him. But there was Bisi, who was also a good catch for her. "My boyfriend can offer all of what you mentioned, so you don't have a point."

"What gives you the assurance that he can?"

"And what is the proof that you can, especially after what you did to me?"

"I am wiser now. I wouldn't make such a mistake again. If I didn't care about you, I would have been long gone. I would have left after you said you forgave me. But here I am still begging for your love."

"It doesn't matter. Men can pretend for as long as they want."

"You know what? Just pray about me. If after praying, you remain unconvinced that I am for real, I'll back off like you want me to. This time, to be back no more."

Tolu laughed, even though she shuddered at the thought of Daniel leaving her life for good as if he had been a part of her life in the last two years. "Prayer? So funny."

"What's funny? Aren't you a Christian?"

"I am, by religion. I've not been living like one for years. I don't even remember the last time I prayed."

"It doesn't matter. Start from where you are now. God's arms are ever wide open to receive us whenever we come to Him, no matter how long we've been away from Him."

She sighed. Daniel was right. "God doesn't choose a partner for anyone," she said.

"Yes, but He guides His children towards making the right choice. It's left for you to ask for and follow his guidance. He doesn't force His guidance on us; He respects our power to choose."

Tolu was impressed. "Daniel, really?"

"Where are you?"

"Road trip to Ibadan."

"With who?" His heart thumped.

"Who else? Sorry, I have to go now," she said and ended the call when she saw Bisi climbing out of the pool.

"Feel better?" she asked when he came close to her. The sight of his wet body which made the bulge in his underpants more visible sent shivers down her spine.

"Yes. Swimming is therapeutic for me."

Tolu's eyes went with him as he walked to the bathroom to change. If they could get home safely without getting physically intimate, she would never expose herself to such temptation again except they were married. Married? She had never imagined Bisi and her as husband and wife. The picture of it was somewhat blurry to her. She believed it would become clearer with time.

They headed back to Palms Mall from there. When they stepped out one hour later, it was cloudy.

"This mall could be so deceiving!" Tolu cried. "The weather has changed, and we didn't even know it. We shouldn't have come here. We should have left after you swam."

Bisi held her hand. "Come on, Tolu. You worry too much. You are with me. Feel safe. Please don't ruin the fun we've been having since morning. Think about it; if we had gone when you asked us to, we would have been trapped in the rain on our way."

"What do we do now?" She checked her wristwatch for time. "It's five-forty. There is no way we can avoid a late journey and the rain..."

"How about sleeping over?"

Her face creased in a frown. "How? Where? What will I tell Gold?"

Bisi touched her shoulders and looked into her eyes. "I need you to calm down, Tolu. Will you?"

As if he used magic on her, she calmed down. His gentle rub on her shoulders was so soothing.

"Call Gold and inform her that you will be sleeping over at your friend's place tonight."

"Who and why?"

"Don't you have friends in Akure?"

She looked away. "I don't. My friends are in Lagos and Abuja."

"What about that snob in your ward?"

She smiled. "Lucia? I told you she's not a snob."

"Whatever. Isn't she a friend?"

"She's just a colleague." Tolu liked her though and wouldn't mind being friends with her, but she was wary of workplace friendship.

"Then use her name. She's your friend for tonight. You are with her and sleeping over at her house."

"I've never slept out before."

"There is always a first time. What are you? Ten-year-old?"

She laughed. A heavy thunder sent some people who were standing outside back inside the mall, and then a heavy downpour followed. Bisi held Tolu's hand, and they went back inside the mall to have dinner in one of the restaurants.

* * *

Tolu froze when the lady receptionist informed them that there was only a double room available.

"It's the weekend; hotel rooms are usually fast occupied. People make bookings for the weekend during the week. You are very lucky because a customer just checked out about three minutes ago, which is very unusual," she explained.

Bisi and Tolu looked at each other. It was 9 p.m., and the darkness outside was thick. When they went back into the mall, Tolu called Gold to tell her she was sleeping at Lucia's place. She remembered mentioning Lucia to her mum whenever she was sharing happenings in her ward with her. She also spoke with Lola, asking her what she ate throughout the day. She promised to be back early enough to take them to church, even though the church was a walking distance from home.

"What do we do?" Bisi asked.

"Check other hotels, maybe."

If Bisi's face showed reluctance, he tried his best to mask it.

The receptionist chipped in, "I can bet you won't find any hotel with vacant rooms in this area at this time. It's the weekend. The vacant room we have here is by sheer luck. I'm sure the room would be taken in a matter of minutes. I work here, so I know how things run."

Tolu glowered at her. She found her quite intrusive. Did she care about them or was she after her gains?

Before Bisi could respond, a young couple dressed in native attire entered the reception, looking spent. Tolu guessed they were party guests who had been stranded at the party venue because of the rain.

"Can we get a room?" the man asked, ignoring the receptionist's greeting.

"Yes, there is only..."

"We will take it," Bisi interrupted her.

The receptionist gave Bisi and Tolu an I-told-you-so look.

"I am sorry sir, there is no vacant room," she said to the couple.

The man sized Bisi up, hissed, and went out with his wife.

"Nuisance," Bisi muttered under his breath.

Tolu looked on tiredly. If she had found her voice earlier, she would have persuaded Bisi to give up the room for the couple because the tired look on the wife's face unsettled her.

"I'll sleep on the couch," Bisi whispered in Tolu's ear.

She smiled. She wasn't sure she would let him do that. The cold weather reminded her of her desire to feel his arms wrapped around her. She was trapped between two emotions – excitement at the opportunity to be relieved of the sexual tension that had been building up since morning and the burden of having unprotected sex with him when their relationship was yet to be defined.

* * *

Daniel turned restlessly in bed with his phone in his hand. He had been agitated since he spoke with Tolu. Apart from the feeling of jealousy that consumed him knowing that the woman he loved was with another man, he also wanted to know if she was fine and back in town. He had called her number three times but hit the red button before the phone could ring. He didn't want to appear intrusive, but there was no way he would sleep without knowing if she was safe where she was, so he damned the consequences and called her again.

* * *

Tolu swiped the call to the silent option, contemplating whether to pick Daniel's call. When she heard Bisi turn on the shower in the bathroom, she answered it.

"Where are you," he asked.

"Ibadan."

"Why?"

"Why what?" She was getting miffed.

"Did you plan to sleep over?"

She hesitated. "It rained."

"Where are you staying or who are you staying with?"

Tolu lost it. "What rights have you to question me? Are you aware that you are intruding on my privacy?"

"Calm down, Tolu. I'm sorry if I'm intruding. I was just looking out for you. I wanted to be sure you are safe."

"Your concern would have been more appreciated two years ago."

"Anyway, don't do anything silly."

Tolu couldn't believe her ears." What the -?" She hit the red button. What a nerve!

"Are you okay? I heard your voice." Bisi stepped out of the bathroom with a big white towel wrapped around his waist. Tolu imagined pulling off the towel and fondling him down there. How big could he be? She shook her head to shake off the thoughts, but her body had responded to her imagination. The sexual tension that dwindled after she had a warm bath started rebuilding.

"It's one important," she replied and dropped her phone on the bedside stool.

"You sounded upset, and now you are frowning."

Tolu drew the duvet to her chin and turned her face towards the wall.

"Goodnight then if you don't want to talk about it. Do you sleep with the light on or off?"

"Off," she lied. She preferred sleeping with the light on.

He switched off the light and stretched on the tiled floor. His clothes were spread on the floor while he covered himself with the towel.

Two minutes later, Tolu asked, "Aren't you coming to bed?"

"No. I want you to be comfortable."

"What? Please come to bed. It is meant for two people. I wouldn't be comfortable knowing that you are sleeping on a cold hard surface after a stressful day."

"Thank you." He got up.

That was fast, Tolu thought. It was hard being a gentleman after all. When he settled in bed, she resisted the urge to place her head on his chest.

"Who was making you laugh that hard on the phone back at the gardens?" he asked.

Tolu's heart skipped. She had thought he didn't care about it. "My daughter's father."

"You guys must be friends."

"Why did you say that?"

"You were laughing so easily. Do I make you laugh like that?"

She smiled. "Are you jealous or something?"

"I just want to know."

"You do."

"Are you sure or you just want me to feel good about myself?"

"Like you don't know."

She sensed his smile.

"You haven't told me about your daughter's father, you know? Don't you think it's high time you did?"

"Well," she cleared her throat, "as you said, we were very good friends, and we liked each other, so we started dating." She told him all that he needed to know except that Daniel was the new guy at the hospital.

"Now he wants you back. How do you feel about that?"

"I don't feel any way. Moreover, he is only trying his luck."

"Do you still love him?"

"After everything that happened?"

"Never say never. Women could be unpredictable sometimes."

"Not me. Even if I love him, the thought of the past won't let me take him back."

"Isn't that what you all say?"

"Now I'm getting pissed. Do you want me to regret sharing the most sensitive part of my life with you?"

"I'm sorry if I upset you. I was just thinking you might consider taking him back since he's serious about wanting you back."

"And so?"

"I am sorry anyway," he replied.

Tolu wasn't satisfied. Why was he not making his intention known? She understood the danger of being in an undefined relationship, and she didn't want to fall victim, yet she didn't want to appear pushy or desperate. She hoped he wasn't trying to be her friend for just the benefits. If he had done it twice, what made her different from the other ladies? He liked her, she knew, but he hasn't said he loved her. Maybe he was taking his time before he declared his love.

She shut her eyes but opened them when she felt his lips brush hers. The fragrance of soap wafted into her nostrils.

"Can I?" he asked whisperingly.

She nodded.

He covered her lips with his. She also kissed him back. Even though she appreciated that he always sought her consent before going sensual with her, she couldn't help but think of him as a sly fox. They shared chemistry, and she wouldn't mind a relationship with him, even more, to keep Daniel away. If they didn't end up dating, there was no way she could accuse him of using her to satisfy his sexual desires because it was consensual. If she didn't want it, she would have declined. But how could she resist him after all that she had been exposed to during the day and even at the moment?

His warm hand travelled over her body stopping to explore her sensitive parts.

"Just a moment, please," he said and got out of bed. Tolu shut her eyes, reveling in the lingering effect of his touch. He rummaged his bag and was back in bed in ten seconds after Tolu heard the rustling of nylon.

She was not sure if she should be happy that he delivered them both from the consequences of unprotected sex or be bothered that he probably had everything planned out.

CHAPTER EIGHTEEN

Tolu tried to make sense of Bisi's unusual excitement since they started on the journey an hour earlier. It was probably because of last night. He was gentle with her, yet firm. He made her feel like a woman with the manner he adored her body with his touch. He knew the right places to touch and when to do so. He was mostly in charge, bringing her to the realization that she needed to up her game. They made love three times before they eventually slept at 3 a.m. Bisi had complained of hunger after the first round, so they ordered French fries, roasted croaker fish, and a bottle of wine. They ate in bed while they saw *The Handmaiden* on Tolu's iPad but started making out before the movie ended.

The pleasure of the night didn't shove the question that screamed for an answer in her mind. Bisi had a pack of condoms in his bag; he was sheathed the three times they made love. Was he taking care of his sexual health or he had it all planned out? The road trip was his idea after all. But the heavy rainfall was not his idea, she argued. Were it not for the rain, they would have been back to Akure.

"Are you okay?" Bisi asked, observing that her words had been laconic, and he had driven past the bread and *Akara* stop without her showing interest in buying. When they woke up at 9 a.m., she felt bad because she had promised her mother that she would be back early enough to attend church with them. He urged her to call Gold, and she did.

"Aren't you feeling guilty?" she asked.

"About what?"

"Last night."

"Why? I don't remember us committing murder last night."

She eyed him. "You know what I mean."

He laughed. "Why? Didn't you have a nice time?"

She smiled.

His lips curled into a self-satisfying smile. "So why should I feel guilty?"

"Don't you think having sex outside marriage isn't right?"

"No, I don't believe that crap. Where is it written? Who made the law? Sex is one of the most natural things in the world."

"I know sex is a physiological need, but it should be gratified in marriage."

"Says who?"

Mouth agape, she asked, "Aren't you a Christian?"

"And I thought you said you were irreligious."

"Yes, but that is different from not being a Christian."

"Oh." He raised his brows. "Well, I don't do any religion. It's all trash. If not, why should we feel guilty for such a beautiful thing as what we had last night?"

Tolu couldn't believe her ears. "Didn't you say your father was a pastor?"

He hit the steering wheel, making her jerk. "Yes!"

"And you don't do any religion?"

"Yes," he fumed.

"Are you an ath-" she drawled.

"Yes, I'm an atheist."

Heat descended on her despite the cold interior of the car. Bisi increased his speed and overtook some vehicles. She fanned her face with her palms.

"What happened?" she asked.

"I don't believe in a God who rewards his worshippers with evil or who cannot protect those who serve him. What kind of a god is that? We've been scammed. There is no God anywhere and if he exists—which I greatly doubt—then He's either weak or wicked. Only a sadist would derive pleasure in humans' suffering. Only a wicked person would have the power to prevent a disaster but prefers to fold his arms and watch like it's not his business. After all, he lives in heaven, so we can all rot on earth."

Greatly stunned, Tolu asked, "Would you like me to take over driving?"

"No, I'm fine," he snapped and reduced his speed.

She sighed. "Why are you angry with God?"

He scoffed. "Angry? That's being euphemistic. I'm mad at him. In fact, I hate him! What am I even saying? I don't believe a god exists."

Tolu managed to contain her shock so that he could let off his steam. She also wondered at the ridiculousness of him hating someone he believed did not exist.

"Is it that bad?"

"What could be worse than realizing that you've been fed with religious crap all your life? That a *so-called* God is loving and kind and would protect His own, yet he couldn't save my brother from dying? He could have done something, but He didn't. He watched as my family languished in agony. He could have stopped the accident or done something to ensure that my brother did not board that ill-fated vehicle. Even if the accident was bound to happen because of bad roads or reckless driving, He could have kept Tayo alive either with a fracture or even a spinal cord injury that would confine him to a wheelchair all his life. At least, he would be alive. But no, God wanted to prove that He could do and undo." Tears streamed down his face.

"They say God is still a loving Father regardless of our sorrows. Fine, I believed that until my mother was losing herself. I forgave God for my brother's death, but what about my mum? I prayed so hard that God should touch my mother so that she could snap out of her depressive state and to restore our family to the way we were. He refused. He wanted to make a show of our family. He was having fun with our woes." He sobbed and further reduced his speed.

Tolu wiped her misty eyes with a palm. She understood that losing a loved one was a great blow when she lost her father. Even though she now doubted if she would have mourned him the way she did had she known about his ugly secrets. Not only did Bisi lose his brother, but he also lost his mother even while she was alive, and that deepened his pain.

He continued, "I grew up knowing my dad as a pastor and my mum, a Bible teacher. Growing up, we were all committed to the church. My sister sang in the choir while my brother and I played the drums and the piano. My late brother was an executive in the Christian Corpers' Fellowship. So, why would God do this to our family? Would it not be foolish of me to believe in a God that watched a family that served him become an object of ridicule?" He sobbed and pulled the car to a stop, a few meters from the Obafemi Awolowo University. His sobs grew into wailing, not caring that his face was messed up with tears and snot.

Tolu kept patting his back as tears coursed down her face. Her heart melted seeing him in such a pitiable state. He had an avalanche of hurts bottled up inside of him, and crying could help him let off some steam. Since she didn't have answers to his questions, she kept on patting his back and mopping her wet face with the other palm.

After five minutes of intense weeping and sobbing, Tolu reached for the box of Kleenex in the car, and they both cleaned their faces.

"Thank you," he said.

Fresh hot tears stung Tolu's face when she saw his red and swollen eyes.

"Please take over the driving." He alighted from the car.

They continued the journey in silence with Tolu behind the wheel. One and a half hours later, she dropped him off at his house before driving home. Comforted by hugs from Gold and Lola, a warm bath, and a plate of spicy plantain and fish pepper soup, she crashed into her bed.

* * *

"Cheer up, man. It might not be what you think," Tomiwa said to Daniel on their drive home from church.

"I can't think otherwise. I mean, what do you expect? A fine young man and a beautiful lady staying together in the same room on a rainy night."

Tomiwa couldn't help laughing. "I think your imagination is going wild. From what you told me; she didn't say they were together in the room."

"She wouldn't have reacted angrily if that was not the case," Daniel replied.

Tomiwa sighed. "You think they kept each other warm throughout the night?"

Daniel managed a smile. "Why put it so mildly?"

"What do you intend to do?"

"Sincerely, I don't know. I feel like I'm losing control. What could be worse than knowing that another man is exploring every nook and cranny of the woman you love?"

Tomiwa laughed as he turned the car into the street that led to his house. "I'm sorry for laughing. Listen, if you want this girl, don't give up. And you have to stop imagining what she and the guy might be doing together. Your imaginations may be wrong after all."

"I hope so."

CHAPTER NINETEEN

On Wednesday, Tolu attended the departmental meeting with the CMD although she wasn't on duty. Suggestions were raised on how to curb the increasing maternal emergencies in the hospital, which were eventually streamlined into three focus actions—following up on every pregnant woman that registered in the hospital till delivery, the use of various social media platforms to enlighten the public on the dangers of not seeking appropriate health care, and monthly community health education.

After the meeting, Lucia, who was on duty, persuaded Tolu to keep her company till the nurse on the afternoon shift took over because her shift partner had gone to the crèche to attend to her baby.

Lucia brought out a sachet of dark chocolate from the fridge when they got to the ward and extended it to Tolu. "You are my guest," she said.

"Thank you." She ran her eyes over Lucia. She was a pretty ebony-skinned lady with curves in the right places. Her face glowed under the light makeup she wore. Tolu liked her and wished at that moment that they were friends. She wondered if it was her looks that attracted her to Lucia or the feeling that she would be a nice lady.

"Congratulations on the opening of your salon and makeup studio," Tolu said as she tore the chocolate open.

Lucia's face beamed. "Thank you!" She settled in the chair from across her guest.

"You didn't invite us from here."

She sneered. "Here? So that they can have something new to gossip about? No, thanks."

Whew! Tolu was amazed she knew that she was an object of hot gossip in the hospital. "Really?"

"I know they say stuff behind me here, but I don't care as long as it does not add a penny to my bank account."

"How do you know they say stuff behind you?"

"I see it in their stares and glares and the way they look at me with envy and helpless admiration."

Tolu laughed. "I am happy you are not bothered; even people talk about the dead."

"Yeah."

There was a pause. Tolu loved the taste of the dark chocolate with chili spice.

"Away from me, when are you guys bringing your wedding invitation to the ward?"

Tolu was lost. "Pardon me?"

Lucia made a face. "Yes, you and your fiancé."

"Fiancé?"

"Stop pretending *jare.* You and Doctor Ayoade."

She almost choked on her chocolate. "Where did you get that from?"

She laughed. "The walls have ears."

Tolu was dumbfounded. Hospital romance stories were not uncommon, but she didn't want to add to the statistics, especially if it was just a fling. She thought she and Bisi had been discreet enough. Who could have seen them together enough to conclude they were dating? Now she understood what it felt like to be the object of gossip.

"Don't believe everything you hear," she said when she found her voice.

"Anyway, congratulations if it's true. I know people keep their relationship away from public glare these days until we start seeing pre-wedding photos." She laughed. "You're lucky, girl. Your guy is cool. I've seen him a couple of times. I envy you."

"Envy me? I hope you know that you're the envy of many ladies."

"I wish."

That was a pregnant response, Tolu thought. She made up her mind to become friends with Lucia.

Aminat Aminu, the nurse on the afternoon shift entered the ward, dressed in a blue scrub and black hijab. She was a thirty-year-old Hausa woman who usually attended to Hausa patients who didn't understand English in the hospital. She once joked about having her own office since she was always called upon to attend to Hausa patients in every department of the hospital. She loved her job, so it wasn't a burden to her.

Lucia excused herself to hand over to Aminat while Tolu scrolled through her phone absentmindedly. Was it so obvious that she and Bisi had something going on between them? Did anyone see her in Bisi's house? She hoped that no one saw them together on their trip to Ibadan or even at the hotel. Her heart raced. Could it be Daniel? She doubted it. Even though she was always rude to him, she believed Daniel wouldn't start a gossip just to get back at her. Somehow, she knew he cared about her. He hadn't called since that night. He was mad at her certainly.

Breaking into Tolu's thoughts, Daniel walked into the ward and their eyes met. He ignored her and proceeded into the ward to meet the nurses who were now at the last bed. He shook hands with Lucia, who laughed at something he said. Both of them sauntered towards the nurses' station, talking and laughing. Tolu felt like sending a wave between them to pull them apart.

What? Was that jealousy ringing? No. She didn't love or want Daniel, not after what he did to her. He could date any lady for all she cared! She fumed.

She imagined Lucia and Daniel together as a couple. Truthfully, they looked cute together. Her heart missed a beat at the thought of Daniel getting married to another lady.

The duo stopped right at the entrance of the nurses' station. Tolu fixed her gaze on Daniel who acted oblivious to her presence.

"So, when are we getting the equipment?" Lucia asked.

"Next week, by God's grace. I am making orders this week."

"We can't wait."

He smiled. "Will you be on duty tomorrow?"

She nodded.

"Alright, I'll see you." He shook hands with her again before leaving the ward without throwing as much as a glance in Tolu's direction.

Tolu felt slighted. Daniel was really mad at her. This was a man who would do anything to be in her good books again. Was he so mad at her enough to start dating Lucia? She got teary.

"You know him?" Lucia's voice interrupted her thoughts.

"The Biomed engineer?"

"Yeah. He's cool. He was here yesterday and was so helpful."

Tolu craved the magic of Merlin to smack Lucia's lips with her eyes and to disrupt the smile that was playing on her lips. She felt betrayed by both of them. How could they? She knew her thoughts were irrational because Lucia didn't know who Daniel was to her and Daniel hadn't done anything wrong exactly. After all, she insisted to him that she didn't want him despite his persuasion. Why then was she losing control because he was getting close to another lady, especially a Diva like Lucia? Tolu had always been confident in her looks, but Lucia would command a second stare from any guy. She was curvier than Tolu, with unmistakable feminine charm.

Tolu felt she should not be bothered. After all, she had Bisi. They hadn't talked since she dropped him off at home from the trip. She longed to hear from him and wanted to be sure that all was well with him, but she was also happy that he didn't reach out. Bisi seemed kind of complicated, and he being an atheist disturbed her. She wasn't judging him, after all, she hadn't been a serious-minded Christian over the years, but she would prefer a spouse who would encourage her to take her faith seriously. More so, she didn't want to raise confused kids who wouldn't know whom to believe about the existence of a 'god'.

"You are free from my hold now. Thanks for the company. I need to change."

"I'll take you home," Tolu offered.

"Are you sure?"

"I've never been so sure of anything in the last one minute." She was willing to do anything to snap out of the moodiness that she crawled into the moment

Daniel walked in.

Lucia laughed and hurried out of the ward.

* * *

"FUTA," Lucia replied when Tolu asked where she lived after settling in the car. She had changed into a fitted black jumpsuit that accentuated her features

"Why? Isn't it too far from the hospital?" She pulled out of the parking lot.

"It's because of my business. Who cares about hairdo and makeup if not young ladies? If it were Lagos, it would be a different ball game."

"I know, right?"

"I would have preferred to work in Lagos if not for the fact that I got this job immediately after serving here. This town is too boring for me. That's another reason I decided to live in the students' area. It's livelier than other parts of the town."

Tolu nodded. The change of location didn't make any difference to her. Her life had always been unadventurous, but there seemed to be a promising change with Bisi in her life.

"My consolation is my thriving business. I even attend one of the students' fellowships close to my house. Where do you live?"

Tolu found it amusing that Lucia attended church. "Alagbaka."

"We live far apart in the opposite direction. Are you sure you want to do this?"

Tolu smiled. "We are on our way already."

"Thank you." Lucia smiled back. "Your place is far from work too, but you have a ride."

"Why not get one?"

She rolled her eyeballs. "And risk losing my mum?"

"How?"

"She said I would chase men away."

Tolu laughed. She understood her plight and was grateful that Gold was not an African mother who believed that a single lady should not flaunt her achievements in order not to scare men away.

"In fact, I didn't tell her I had started my salon and makeup studio because when I mentioned it to her, she said I should wait till I get married."

Tolu laughed again.

"She's hypertensive. Her blood pressure will rise if she discovers that I have started the business. If I add a car to it, she will simply slip into a coma."

Tolu shook her head. "An African mother's obsession with marriage is bothersome. To her, a woman is incomplete without a man to call her own."

"And children to call her own," Lucia added.

"So, a woman shouldn't have a life or acquire properties until she gets married."

"Or risk being eternally single."

Their laughter filled the car. Tolu felt convinced that becoming friends with Lucia was a good decision.

"The men who are intimidated by me are the ones I'm not interested in."

"Exactly!"

Thirty minutes later, Lucia directed her into the street that led to her house. Students thronged both sides of the street. Tolu reminisced about her days as a student; how she was usually flanked by Chisom and Maryam, chattering excitedly on their way to class.

A gold BMW SUV appeared behind them and later overtook them.

"And here we are. The second house to the left."

The jeep was parked opposite the house Lucia pointed at. Tolu pulled up in front of the house. It was a bungalow, swallowed by a gigantic black gate.

"Thanks so much for the ride. I appreciate it." She freed herself from the seat belt.

"It's a pleasure."

"Would you like to come in for a drink?" She threw her head back. "Why do you make me feel like I need some company today?"

Tolu laughed, happy that the feeling was mutual.

"My friends are all in Lagos, and they are yet to wrap their heads around what I'm doing here."

"It's fine. I don't have any urgent business at home so I could use some company too."

She heaved a sigh. "Thanks for being kind enough to spend today with me."

Tolu laughed, and they both alighted from the car. Another car had pulled up across the road.

"Really? What are you doing here?" Lucia screamed ecstatically at the driver of the jeep who had just climbed down from the car.

Tolu looked up to see Daniel with a smile plastered on his face. She nearly jumped out of her skin as Lucia crossed the road to meet him.

"I live here," he said. He had his sleeves rolled up and a bottle of water in his hand.

"Are you serious?"

"Yes, serious. I live with a friend here. Upstairs."

"The lecturer?"

He nodded.

"How come our paths never crossed?"

Daniel glanced at Tolu, who looked away immediately when their eyes met. He shrugged. "I guess we are very busy people. I've not been here for too long anyway, almost a month maybe."

"We are neighbors! Interesting!"

"You can say that again."

"Your car?"

"Well, yeah."

"Do you mind if I hitch a ride with you to and fro work?"

"Not at all. We will need to exchange phone numbers so that we can make that happen."

"Sure." She rummaged her bag for her phone and gave it to Daniel.

Tolu's heart was beating faster. Though she pretended to be disinterested in their conversation, she was listening in. Was Lucia crushing on him already? Or, were they crushing on each other already? And where did he get the posh car from?

"I have your number now," he said and returned the phone.

"That's my colleague, Tolu. She brought me home. I don't know if you guys have met."

"Hi," Daniel called out.

Tolu replied with a brisk wave and reached for her phone in her jeans pocket. She faked a call when Lucia walked back, and Daniel was opening the gate.

"I'm sorry I have to go now. I received an urgent call from my mum." She retreated to her car.

"You live with your mum?"

"My mum lives with me." She opened the car door. "I'm also on morning shift tomorrow. I'll see you." She jumped into the car.

"Alright, drive carefully," Lucia said.

Daniel and Lucia watched as she reversed the car and zoomed past them. Tolu struggled not to make eye contact with either of them. She grabbed the Kleenex box as she drove out of the street and made a mental note to replace it because she was sure going to exhaust the box soon.

CHAPTER TWENTY

The morning shift commenced on a very busy note as three pregnant women had been booked for surgery since the previous day. The shift, although busy, would have been calm save for the emergency case earlier that morning. A woman who was seven months pregnant was rushed to the emergency after being beaten severely by her husband who left her writhing in pain and bleeding profusely. She was brought to the hospital in a semi-conscious state by their neighbours. After arresting the hemorrhage and ensuring that the baby was safe, she was transferred to the intensive care unit for close monitoring.

"What kind of a man hits a pregnant woman if not a devil?" Lucia said. She was thoroughly shaken by the incident and kept on raining vituperations on the man as they walked back to their ward.

"I am sure today wasn't his first. She has been enduring domestic violence for a long time. Didn't you see some old scars all over her body? I don't know why women put up with this kind of torture," Tolu replied.

Lucia replied with a sigh.

"Today has been crazy!" she said as she slumped into a chair when they got into the nurses' station.

"Tell me about it." Tolu also lowered herself into a chair.

They hadn't sat for thirty seconds when they heard what sounded like a slap from the left-wing of the ward, where women who had vaginal deliveries were admitted. They hurried out of the office into the ward. Voices of reprimand sprang from different angles.

"What is happening here?" Lucia demanded.

"This man slapped his wife," Jumoke, one of the patients replied. She was a thirty-year-old woman who had a stillbirth earlier in the morning.

Tolu and Lucia sized the man up. His wife had had a forceps delivery of a male baby in the morning.

"You were nowhere to be found after your wife gave birth and needed some food to eat. When you eventually arrived, from God knows where, the best thing you could do is hit her? What is wrong with you men? What is it with you and hitting your vulnerable wives today? Are you all crazy?" Lucia burst out. There was a deafening silence.

The man growled at Lucia. "How dare you talk to me like that? An ordinary woman like you!"

The sight of the unkempt man who was probably in his early forties so disgusted Tolu that she wondered how his wife made love with him.

"This one is a..."

"Certified unrepentant wife-beating bastard," Lucia interrupted Tolu as tears coursed down her cheeks.

The man lunged at Lucia, but the patients' loud rebuke stopped him. Two hospital security men walked in and took him away.

"Please detain him until the police arrive," Lucia called after them as she headed back to the nurses' station.

The man's wife flinched at the mention of the police. Even though Tolu felt like skinning the man alive, she was taken aback by Lucia's reaction. She restored order to the ward and comforted the man's wife before returning to the office.

"The police are on their way," Lucia informed her in a shaky voice before hurrying out of the office into the bathroom.

Tolu was disturbed when she heard her crying afterward but she didn't want to intrude on her privacy. When the crying grew intense, she hastened to the bathroom and tapped the door. Lucia kept on crying without answering till Tolu opened the door gently. Her heart melted at the sight of her new friend.

Her makeup was smeared with tears.

"Oh dear," Tolu entered the bathroom and shut the door. She reached out to her and embraced her. Lucia, who was a few inches taller, buried her face in Tolu's shoulder. Tolu didn't bother that her white scrub would get stained with Lucia's messy face. That was the least she could do for a hurting sister.

"Do you want to talk about it?"

She sobbed the more before lifting her head from Tolu's shoulders. She turned her back to Tolu and pulled up her scrub. "He used to hit me with a belt."

Tolu was gripped with panic at the sight of Lucia's back, marked with linear and wide contusions. "Jesus!" She ran her hand over her back.

"The events of today brought back the awful memories I've been trying to bury."

"I'm so sorry, Lucia. I…" The intercom buzzed.

"Go and get it. It's probably from the theatre. We'll talk later."

"Alright." Tolu stepped out of the bathroom and shut the door after her, still shocked at what she had just seen.

* * *

At five minutes before the hour of two, after they had fulfilled their shift duties, they settled in the nurses' station and awaited the nurse on the afternoon shift.

Lucia started, "He was so insecure and possessive. He had the password to all my social media accounts and my devices. If he saw anything fishy, he would descend on me before I could explain jack."

"What a bastard!" Tolu cursed under her breath. "Why didn't you break up with him the first time he beat you?"

She smiled. "It was complicated. Tokunbo and I dated for seven years, I finally found the guts to quit after my NYSC. I was a fresher, and he was a final year student of Petroleum and Gas Engineering at the University of Lagos. His father was a senator. You know what that means?"

Tolu nodded.

"My family isn't a comfortable one, you see. Don't be deceived by my good looks." She let out a rueful laugh. "We are just blessed with good looks and brains. You think I'm pretty? You need to see my two sisters and my brother. When I gained admission, my parents were only able to pay the acceptance fee while they struggled to raise my school fees without success. I had gone to school that day to print out my acceptance form when I met Tokunbo. He was driving in his car with his friends while I strolled to my department with my new friend, Kofo, just to see what my department looked like. He drove us there in his car, and we exchanged phone numbers afterward. That was how it started. He asked me out later. I didn't want a relationship. In fact, I had just broken up with Kwame, my first boyfriend. He was a family friend, and we grew up in the same neighborhood. All I wanted to do was focus on my academics, graduate with an impressive result, and get a good job that would enable me to help my family enjoy some comfort. When..." she stopped when she saw Aminat, the nurse on the afternoon shift, enter the ward. "Can we do this later?" she asked.

"Sure," Tolu replied and scooped the pile of case files from the table. Both of them went into the ward to hand over the patients to Aminat.

* * *

Daniel poked his head into the ward and entered when he sighted Lucia. After exchanging pleasantries with Aminat, he asked Lucia if she was ready to go.

"Yes, please," she replied. They had just finished handing over.

Tolu broke out in a cold sweat as Daniel's eyes were fixed on Lucia. Why was he acting this way? Didn't he say he loved her and would do anything to be back into her life? And just because she put up a little resistance, he was frolicking with another lady. She was right after all; men weren't worth it. She was tempted to call him when she arrived home the previous day, but she didn't want him to think she was feeling threatened by his budding closeness with Lucia.

"I can drop you off at home," she said. Aside from her eagerness to know the end of Lucia's story, the thought of Daniel and Lucia alone in his car unsettled her.

"Oh thanks, but that would be too much to do after such a hectic day."

"It's not a bother."

"That would be selfish of me. You've been so kind to me since yesterday. I even stained your white scrub. We will continue our talk tomorrow. Let me go with Daniel since we are neighbours anyway."

"Okay." She smiled wryly, trying to mask her disappointment.

"You remember where I'm parked. I'll be in the car," Daniel said to Lucia.

"Hey!" Bisi appeared at the door. He shook hands with Daniel and greeted Lucia before turning to Tolu. "Do you have an hour?" he asked.

Tolu smiled as Daniel looked at her. Did she say Bisi was complicated? Yes, he was sweetly complicated. "I have two," she replied.

Lucia winked at her.

* * *

She closed her eyes, relishing Bisi's succulent hands on her feet. She was lying on the couch in Bisi's house. She had missed him and was happy to spend some time with him, but she couldn't help thinking what Daniel and Lucia could be doing.

"I learned the hospital was chaotic today and I knew you would be on the morning shift, so I thought I could offer some comfort. How do lunch and a foot massage at my place sound? I'll drive you to my place and also drive you home when we are done," he had said when they got to her car.

She made a face.

"It's just that. I promise. You know I won't do anything you don't want."

That was not the problem, Tolu thought. The problem was that she would want it. "Okay." She tossed the car key to him, feeling physically and emotionally exhausted. She could use some pampering too.

After a lunch of oatmeal fufu and spinach vegetable soup garnished with beef, fish, and smoked turkey, she stretched on the couch for the foot massage Bisi promised. Waves of pleasure shot through her body as he worked his hands through her toes.

"You must have been wondering why I didn't reach out to you since last weekend."

She shrugged.

"I was thinking about me. About us." He bit his lower lip.

Tolu opened her eyes and stared at him, her heart beating faster and her feet turning cold.

"I apologize for my outburst in the car the other day. I guess I bottled up a lot of things and I just had to let off some steam."

"I understand."

"Ever since my mother became a shadow of herself and I watched my dad become an unhappy man, marriage became unappealing to me. Don't get me wrong. I know marriage is not a bed of roses, but a couple should be able to weather the storm together. Married people need to be strong, if not for themselves but their partners because if they lose it, their partners will suffer for it. I thought my mother was a strong woman because she could pray down hell, but when adversity came, she crashed like a house of cards. You know, if you faint in the day of adversity, your strength is small."

Tolu sat up. "You just quoted the Bible."

He frowned.

"Yes, the book of Proverbs." She smiled.

"I was a Christian for most of my life, and I have a good memory."

She laughed. "But you believe that verse of the Bible and support your point with it."

"It doesn't mean anything. Even a madman makes sense sometimes."

"Okay." She laid back on the couch.

"So, I told myself if I ever get married, I must marry a strong woman. I like and respect you a lot. You are not just beautiful and intelligent; you are also resilient. I feel so much at home with you and spending that night together in Ibadan further convinced me that we can be happy together. I mean, that was the sweetest lovemaking I had ever had. I'm yet to get it out of my mind. I love you, Tolu. So much."

She removed her legs from his thighs and sat up; surprised and confused, but happy.

"What about your girlfriend?"

"Ex-girlfriend."

She stared at him.

"I blocked her on social media and blocked her number."

She sighed.

"I don't know if my being an atheist is a problem for you, but I know a happy marriage is independent of religion. There are a lot of happily married people on earth and all of them are not Christians. Humanity is the first religion. I know I'm a good person and I promise to make you happy."

"What does your dad say about this?"

"I'm an adult. He can't decide for me what to believe."

She rose to her full length. "I have to go now."

He stood up too. "Did I say anything wrong?"

"No. I just need some time to think about what you said."

"Take all the time you want. I'll be waiting."

She looked at him and struggled with the temptation to kiss him like she did the other night.

"Yeah."

"It took me some days to think this through. I want you to know that I'm serious about this."

"I know."

"I'll drive you home."

"No, I'm fine. I'll drive myself home."

CHAPTER TWENTY-ONE

Tolu's heart was laden with many thoughts as she drove home. Why was it so complicated? She liked Bisi but picturing both of them as a couple was difficult. Even if she could deal with their religious differences, what about their children? Would they be able to deal with parental conflicting convictions about the existence of a supreme being? She longed to talk to someone. Gold would not stop her from marrying any man of her choice, but she wouldn't encourage her to marry a man who didn't believe God exists. She didn't want to involve Lucia in very intimate issues of her life yet because they were just getting to know each other. And Daniel? She always felt that she could tell him anything. He was intelligent, and she respected his opinions, but he was also implicated in the matter, he would be biased. More so, they were not on good terms. She swallowed her pride and called him anyway. He answered on the third ring.

She cleared her throat. "Hi."

"Yes?"

"Good evening to you too."

"Cut to the chase, please."

"Why are you being unkind?"

"And why are you so proud and disrespectful?"

"What?"

"Yes, Tolu, you are so full of yourself and very disrespectful. You talk me down like I'm the worst criminal on earth. Yes, I love you, I want to be a part of your life again, but it's your decision, and I can't force you to love me back. You don't have to make me feel less of myself. I left everything I was doing, my plans, privileges, and family for a town I'd never stepped foot in just to make things right with you and you are driving me nuts!"

"Okay, can we see?"

"No! Not after you've given your boyfriend the two hours that you've got."

She laughed silently, happy that he was jealous. "So, what now?"

"Let me be and let me find my love since you do not need me."

Her hands trembled on the steering wheel. "Lucia?"

"What about her? Isn't she cute and adorable? She's also intelligent and fun to be with."

Hot tears welled up in her eyes. "Really? You claim to love me, and you are busy fucking another lady!"

"Mind your language, young lady!"

"What if I don't? Fuck! Fuck! Fuck!" Grateful that she was off the busy road, she veered into her street.

"Really? Scream it louder baby, because that's all you do with your boyfriend."

She steadied her grip on the steering wheel as tears cascaded down her face. "Yes, that's all I do with him."

"Good. I hope you had a nice time on Saturday night?"

She sniffed. "Yes, I did. I'm yet to recover from his touch."

"Good for you," he replied in a low voice.

She broke out in a flood of uncontrollable tears as she pulled up in front of her house.

"Why are you crying, Tolu? I'm the one who is hurting here. I'm the one enduring another man touching the woman I love. I'm the one who is being rejected and treated like a leech by the woman I love. So, quit playing the victim here." He started crying too.

"You are only reaping the consequences of your selfishness and wickedness. I was the one who endured the shame of carrying a pregnancy without being married. I was the one who asked to be opened up when I couldn't bear the bone-breaking labour pains, and I am the one who has been seeing to the financial welfare of your daughter for two years! Tell me who the victim is here!" she burst out.

Tolu was greeted by silence on the other end, followed by an intense weeping and gut-wrenching sobs.

"You are the victim, continue to play the victim," she added.

"I- I- am so sorry, Tolu. I didn't know you kept the pregnancy. Oh my God! I feel so terrible. I have a daughter?"

"No, you don't. You have no right to call her your daughter because you wanted her killed."

"That is not true. I was young, stupid, and afraid. I wouldn't do such a thing now. I didn't know any better back then."

"But you did want an abortion."

"And I regret it. I find it hard to forgive myself for being so selfish and stupid. That's why I'm here to fix things. Think about it. If I didn't love you or care about you, I wouldn't be here. Two years is enough time to forget about you. We need to see it. We need to talk."

"Go and see Lucia."

He laughed despite himself. "Are you jealous? After all, you have a boyfriend."

"Fuck off, Daniel."

"When did you become so vulgar? You need Jesus."

"And you need to get off my phone right now."

"How about dinner tonight? Please don't say no. I'll pick you up at eight."

"Bye." She tidied up her face before stepping out of the car.

* * *

"What? Why are you staring at me as if you've never seen me before?" she said after settling in Daniel's car three hours later. She wore a short red dress and a pair of black heels with light makeup on. Her braided wig fell loosely on her shoulders. Daniel had driven into her street and parked where she had asked him to stop the day he drove her home.

Sniffing in her perfume that diffused in the car, he replied, "You look and smell nice."

"Thank you. Will you drive now?"

"Sure." He was dressed in black pants and a lilac T.M. Lewin shirt.

"This is not your car."

"It's my mum's. My sister drives mine now. Her excitement that she would drive my car when I traveled was more than her thought of missing me."

She laughed. The thought of meeting his family, especially his younger sister, gave her a momentary thrill. Maybe she could be the sister she never had.

"How did you get it?"

"I traveled to Lagos last week and returned on Saturday; the day you went on a trip with him."

"Oh." She raised a brow. "Where are we going?"

"Somewhere nice."

"And nameless?"

"I can't kidnap you. Don't you trust me?"

"I did."

"Why can't you just let go of the past?"

She shrugged. Daniel slowed down and pulled up in front of a hotel gate located just along the road.

Tolu sighed. "Great. Not far from home. How did you get this place?"

"Imagine the present world without Google."

They got down from the car and made their way into the hotel restaurant. The beautiful chandeliers, the smile on the face of the waitress that led them to their table, and the soft music that played created a romantic atmosphere that Tolu found so relaxing. The sight of the buffet and the aroma of the food caused her stomach to churn. There were three other couples in the restaurant. Daniel pulled out a chair for her to sit before he sat. They scanned through the drinks menu and ordered fresh mango juice and water.

"This smells delicious," she said.

"We can do this again on any day and time of your choice."

She rolled her eyes. "Let's get to it already; it's late." She led the way while he followed. She filled her plate with some peppered snails and shrimps. Daniel did the same. The waiter had brought their drinks to the table before they returned to their seats.

"Where do I start from?" he said.

"Your choice," she replied, picking a piece of snail meat to her mouth.

"I couldn't stop imagining what my daughter looks like. Thank you for not getting rid of the pregnancy."

"You don't have to thank me for not killing my child."

"What can I do to make you forgive me? I mean, let go of the past and start afresh with me?"

"I don't know."

"You need God's help."

She gawked at him. "This," she pointed at her plate, "is too spicy and delicious to make me get angry with you."

He smiled and picked a snail. "Can I see her?"

"Omolola? No."

"That's her name? Omolola. Child is wealth."

She smiled at him.

"I was born and bred in Lagos. Don't forget I understand the Yoruba language as much as I do Igbo."

"I remember, but you will not see her."

"On your phone, I meant."

"Yes, that too."

"Please."

She looked into his eyes and fetched her phone from her black purse, scrolled through her gallery for Lola's most recent picture, and gave him the phone.

He fixed his gaze on the picture as tears formed in his eyes. "I can't believe this is my daughter. She's so cute." He ran his fingers across the phone screen. "She looks so much like me."

"Indeed."

"You know it's true."

"That is the innocent girl you wanted dead. Don't call her your daughter because you never wanted her."

He continued as if she hadn't spoken. "The resemblance is so striking. She's a chip off me." He dabbed his misty eyes with a handkerchief.

Tolu sneered. "Can I have my phone, please?"

He gave her the phone.

"Again, what do you want me to do? Tell me. I'll do anything to be a part of your lives."

"It's not that easy."

"Why?"

"You can't disappear and reappear and want to continue where you stopped with me."

"So, what should I do? Disappear till eternity?"

She took a sip of her juice before picking the last piece of snail on her plate. She stretched her hand and picked the three snails on Daniel's plate.

"Why can't you just let go seeing that I'm penitent and willing to do anything to have you and ..."

Tolu stared at him. "Don't you ever think you can take my daughter away from me. From Gold. From us."

"I'll never do that."

"I don't know what you can do."

"Trust me, please."

"I'd rather trust these peppered snails. I'm going to get some more." She picked her plate and sauntered to the buffet table. Daniel followed suit hesitantly. Tolu filled her plate with some snails, peppered fish, a drumstick, and a meatball while Daniel repeated his first pick.

"Can you marry someone who doesn't believe that God exists?" she asked him when they were back at their table.

"An atheist?"

"Is there any other name for it?"

He smiled. "Are you one?"

"What if I am, will you still love me? Will you still want to marry me?"

He grinned. "I hope this is not a trap."

"It's not."

"Okay. It all depends on my values, that is, the things I hold dear. My faith in God is one of them, and I won't compromise it for anything. So yes, I love you, and I'll still love you, but no, I will not marry you."

Tolu almost choked on the fish in her mouth.

He poured water into a cup and gave it to her. "Here."

She collected it and took a gulp.

He continued, "To be in love is one thing; to be compatible is another. It takes more than love to have a successful marriage. There should be compatibility of values because your values will guide your actions and inactions. Someone whose core values do not include faith in God will have no problem marrying an atheist. I want to be able to pray with my wife, share the insights I get from reading the Bible, and listening to sermons with her. I want to be able to attend church services with my wife and children. You know, as a family. I just want to be on the same page with my wife spiritually."

"Have you always been this wise or you just became wiser?"

He laughed. "I miss you, Tolu. I miss us—the laughter, the talks, the outings, the kisses." He winked at her. "Everything. I thought about you every day while I was away. At a point, I was so mad at you for blocking me on social media and even changing your phone number. You are too stubborn, but I love you the way you are. I came back to the country because of you."

"You came back because you were done with your Masters."

"Do you need proof?"

"I don't care."

"Of course, you do. I know you still love me. I can see it in your eyes, but you are concerned about what people would say. You don't want to be called weak for letting me back into your life after saying I didn't want a baby. Even though you were the one who broke up with me."

"What did you expect me to do when you insisted I get rid of the pregnancy? Beg you or summon the whole universe to beg you to let me keep your pregnancy, our pregnancy?"

"No, but you didn't give me a chance to have a rethink."

"Not like you were ready to change your mind."

"It was complicated. I didn't know what else to do. But I'm back, and I'm ready to pay for my foolishness."

"Oh sweetheart, it's complicated. There is someone in my life now." She glanced at her wristwatch. "It's almost 10 p.m. Please take me home. Today was terrific, and I need some sleep. Morning shift continues tomorrow."

Daniel wasn't happy that the date ended too quickly. He wanted them to talk more. He wanted them to talk about the possibility of them getting back together again and the possibility of him meeting his daughter. But he didn't want to upset her, so he replied, "Okay."

"Thanks for the meal," she said.

Daniel nodded and walked to the counter to pay for the buffet. After fifteen minutes of a quiet drive, Tolu climbed down from his car at the spot where he had picked her and walked home.

CHAPTER TWENTY-TWO

At noon the following day, Tolu and Lucia summoned Comfort, the woman who was hit by her husband the previous day. She had her hair weaved in three large loose cornrows and had a wrapper tied over her breasts.

"He has been beating me since I got married to him six years ago. It became worse when I gave birth to two girls. He promised to stop beating me if I gave birth to a boy. When I got pregnant after the second girl, and the scan showed it was a girl, he beat me till I lost the pregnancy."

The nurses were irked.

"Why didn't you run away from him? You could have died, you know?" Tolu said.

"I have nowhere to go with two children. I'm an orphan, and I have two stepsisters who have their own families too. We are not even close. My only brother died three years ago. He was the only one that my husband feared." Tears streamed down her face.

"Why don't you rent an apartment far away from him and leave with your kids?" Tolu further asked.

She smiled sadly. "I don't have a penny to my name. I don't work. He didn't allow me to work."

"Why?" Lucia asked.

"I was doing well in my hairdressing business and had about six apprentices. He accused me of being disrespectful to him because I was making more money than him. He got home before me one evening and was angry I didn't return early enough to prepare him dinner. He hit me and told me that was my last time at the shop. All my pleadings fell on deaf ears. People said I should obey my husband and be a submissive wife, especially because of my children. I have been dependent on him for four years now."

The two nurses sighed simultaneously.

"Even when I became pregnant with a boy, he didn't stop beating me as he promised." She sobbed. "I never dreamt that I would end like this. I had dreams. I wanted to be a nurse like you, but my dreams went down the grave with my mother. I had no one to sponsor my education. That was why I learned how to make hair. I'm tired of living. I'm tired of this life. If not for my children, I would have killed myself. My children are the only reason why I'm living."

Lucia and Tolu's eyes became misty.

"Are you ready to break free from him? Are you ready for a new life?" Lucia asked, placing a hand on Comfort's shoulder.

"I want to, but I can't. I don't have any help."

"You did not answer my question."

She nodded. "I am ready." She sniffed.

"Good. I will make sure he signs an agreement at the police station never to lay his filthy hands on you again and also to let you resume your hairdressing business. I'll meet with the CMD to see if he can contact the Commissioner for Women Affairs. I'm sure there should be a provision for domestic violence victims." She tore a sheet from the prescription booklet, scribbled her phone number on it, and gave it to her. "This is my phone number. Call me if there is any problem." She reached for her purse inside her bag and counted five one thousand naira notes. "Have this too. I'm sure you'll need some money."

Challenged by Lucia's act of kindness, Tolu also reached for her purse and gave Comfort the three thousand naira that was left in her purse.

Comfort broke out in fresh tears. "Thank you," she said amidst sobs.

Lucia wiped the tears that welled up in her eyes while Tolu's throat stung as she fought back tears.

"Thank you," she said again, her voice quavering as she went on her knees.

The nurses helped her up and later dismissed her.

Tolu smiled at Lucia. "That was kind of you," she said.

Lucia smiled back. "Experience teaches you empathy. You see, one of the ways a man exerts control over a woman is through financial dependency. You don't have a voice if you don't have money of your own. What can you do without money? What decision can you make? Whoever controls your finance controls your life. I gave in to Tokunbo when my parents couldn't pay my school fees. It would have killed me to miss the admission to study nursing at UNILAG. You know how competitive the course and the school are and how difficult it is to secure admission in this country. So, I saw him as a godsend. He got a mini-flat apartment close to school for me, which became his second home. I had all the comfort I needed. T.K, as he was fondly called, was a good spender. He even drove me to class sometimes. I became the envy of my mates, but they didn't know what I was going through. T.K was also a sex freak. He loved sex more than food." She smiled wistfully.

Tolu felt sympathy for her.

"We had sex every day, I mean, whenever we saw, we had sex, even if *Aunt Flo* was around. Do you blame him? I had to give something in return. I feel like I have had enough sex to last me a lifetime." She let out a pathetic laugh. "He became so possessive of me. I must not have anything to do with another guy, no matter how harmless. I'm a pretty lady; I've always had lots of guys on my neck, including married ones. Whenever he suspected anything fishy, he would use his belt on me, beg me later, and take me shopping. That was the cycle."

Tolu sighed. "I'm so sorry for your experience, Lucia. How were you able to cope with that and your academics?"

"I was brilliant. I guess I still am." She chuckled. "I just needed to work harder. Even with all my hard work, I couldn't graduate with a first-class as I had desired. I am human. The physical and psychological abuse affected me."

" I can imagine. I'm so sorry. Forgive me if I sound silly, I want to ask..." she hesitated.

"Go on. Ask," Lucia prodded.

"Did you enjoy frequent sex? You know, as a teenager, having sex in a comfortable apartment is some sort of freedom. Did he rape you at any time?"

"I didn't have the guts to turn him down in the first place, so there was no reason for rape. At first, I enjoyed it, but along the line, I felt used and dirty. It's a different thing if I had sex because I was in love but giving my body to a guy because he felt he owned me murdered my self-esteem."

"So, you never loved him?"

She smiled. "I don't know. Maybe I did at the beginning. Maybe I got used to him."

"I'm so sorry for your experience," Tolu said again and reached out to embrace her. Her eyes fell on Daniel through the windowpane. With a surprised look on his face, he slowed down his steps.

When they broke the embrace, Lucia said, "That is why I'm working hard to be financially independent. I don't want to find myself or any of my children in such an unpleasant situation ever again. Before, I wanted to be a nurse because they said it was lucrative. But now, I want to be more. I want to be wealthy. I want to have businesses and investments, and when they become big, I'll quit this job to manage them. I can't be a wealthy woman with only this job."

Daniel was standing at the door before Tolu could reply.

"Hi," Lucia said, her face breaking out into a smile.

"Hello, ladies." He stepped into the office. "I hope I didn't interrupt anything?" He had his sleeves rolled up as usual.

"You did, but it is fine," Lucia replied with a wave of the hand.

Tolu shared her gaze between Daniel and Lucia. Lucia seemed to like him already, and that needed to stop! She fumed within.

"Set to go?" she asked.

"No. I wouldn't go without you," he replied, taking a glance at Tolu.

Tolu's heart thumped. Was that an attempt to make her jealous? She felt like punching him in the face.

"I'm here to inform you that by Monday, this ward would have five full electric hospital beds, a vital signs monitor, and a suction machine."

"Wow! That's good news. Thank you."

"I'll see you in two hours," he said to Lucia and stole another glance at Tolu before leaving the ward.

"You don't like him?" Lucia asked.

"Why?"

"I've never seen you talk to him or reply to his greetings. You even go silent whenever he's around."

She shrugged.

"Oh! You like him!" Lucia said, her face lighting up as though she just had an epiphany.

"No, you like him."

"At least I am honest about my feelings. He's not only good-looking but also fun to be with. I love conversing with him."

Tolu felt a glint of jealousy. "What about him? Do you think he likes you? Do you mind dating him?"

"I don't mind. After my ordeal with Tokunbo, I've been skeptical about opening my heart to another man, even though I have many of them on my neck - single and married. I need me some good man. Daniel looks like one to me. I need someone to treat me with the tender loving care that I deserve." She crossed her arms over her chest. "I want to love for real this time. About him liking me..." A seductive smile played on her lips. "What kind of man wouldn't like me?"

Tolu forced saliva down her dry throat.

"Excuse me, please."

Tolu watched as Lucia sashayed out of the office to the toilet. Maybe it was high time she was honest about her feelings too.

* * *

Tolu had a cold shower when she arrived home and later settled for lunch—beans porridge and *dodo*.

"I know you can't eat beans without *Garri,*" Gold said, placing a bowl of the processed cassava flakes before her daughter.

Tolu smiled and thanked her as she poured some iced water into the *Garri.*

The aroma of the food wafted up to her nostrils and caused her mouth to water. It was 2:50 p.m.; Lola was still at school. The beans porridge was spicy, just the way she liked it.

Gold pulled out a dining chair and lowered herself on it. After some seconds of staring at her daughter, she asked, "What is on your mind?"

She feigned surprise. "What?"

"I'm your mother. You don't need to pretend. I know you've had a lot on your mind lately, but I thought you'd let me know if you wanted me to. Since you're not coming forth, I can't fold my arms and watch as you shoulder your burdens alone. I'm your mother, and I care about you."

Tolu couldn't resist her mother's pleading eyes and the genuine concern that laced her voice. She gulped some *Garri* water. The tanginess of the cold *Garri* water sent ripples of pleasure to her oral cavity.

"Daniel wants us to start dating again. He now knows about Omolola," she said, willing her voice to dangle between seriousness and nonchalance.

"And?"

"How possible is that? He can't treat me like crap and expect a grand welcome."

"So, you hate him?"

"I don't. Maybe I am still angry with him."

"Or angry with yourself that you still love him?"

Tolu glowered at her mum.

"You don't like him?" Gold probed.

"I don't know." She continued eating.

"You need to know what you want, Tolulope, and be honest with yourself. Tell him if you don't want him and let him go."

"I have told him many times; he wouldn't listen."

"Maybe he loves you."

"Indeed." She rolled her eyes.

"I thought you said you broke your SIM card and blocked him on social media? You also moved from Ibadan without letting him know of your whereabouts. Do you know the kind of psychological torture that would have caused him? I think you were the one who disappeared and not him."

Gold's words hit her like a tsunami. She was soft but stern.

"Sorry if I'm hard on you, but I need to tell you the truth. Look, I'm not excusing Daniel's faults. I do not support the fact that he wanted an abortion. I'm saying you should take responsibility for your actions too. Own up to your part in this issue. You don't have to take him back if you don't love him. You don't have to accept him because of Lola. But if you think you still love him, let go of every bitterness and open your heart to love again."

Tolu wanted to reply that her heart had been opened to love since she met Bisi, but she found herself nodding absentmindedly. Gold's advice was too easy. If only it could be as easy as she had said it. In fact, it shouldn't be that easy. She believed women of Gold's generation were too easy and forgiving. That was why her father could spend his salary to raise his other family in his village while Gold took care of the family with her income. Gold said it was love; Tolu regarded it as stupidity. She was certain that a twenty-first-century woman wouldn't agree to such gullibility.

CHAPTER TWENTY-THREE

Bisi grinned as Tolu entered the cafeteria. He was halfway through a meal of rice, *Moin Moin,* meat, and Coca-Cola. Tolu returned his smile and sat from across him. The cafeteria was filled with hospital workers in scrubs of different colours and relatives of patients who had come to eat or buy food. Bisi spread a palm on the table. Tolu took a cursory look around the room before placing her hand in his. Everyone seemed to be too hungry to notice them. She, however, knew that no matter how busy hospital workers appeared to be, they were always alert enough to catch any gossip.

"What? We are adults," he said, squeezing her hand softly and making her skin tingle.

"I don't want to be the next topic of hospital gossip."

"We would make a good topic for gossip, don't you think?"

She gave a wry smile and removed her hand from his.

"You know what? I like you a lot, and I'll be happy if you become mine, but I'm not desperate. Take your time to think about it."

She sighed.

"And if being an atheist is a problem for you, I'll understand, because I don't see myself changing my mind about that."

Tolu's fears about him skyrocketed. She had comforted herself with the possibility that he might have a change of mind about God with time, but Bisi's words had just punctured her hope.

"I know I'm a good man and I'll do all I can to make you happy in every way. As in, in every way." He winked at her.

She smiled longingly, the memory of their lovemaking playing in her mind.

"Eat up before your food becomes irredeemably cold."

"I'm sure you are here to eat and not to talk with me. What would you like to eat?" He beckoned on one of the servers. Before the server arrived, Tolu noticed Bisi smiling at someone or something in the opposite direction. When she looked in the direction of his smile, she froze at the tall image that greeted her.

What the heck? Was Daniel stalking her now?

"Hi," Daniel said, extending his hand towards Bisi for a handshake while he muttered a 'hello' to Tolu. "May I?" He pointed at the empty seat at their table.

"Sure," Bisi replied, obviously pleased to have him join them.

Tolu felt like pulling Daniel with her outside and giving him a piece of her mind. Why on earth did he choose their table when there were other vacant seats he could have sat on?

Bisi tapped her. "Make your order."

She had been lost in thought and was oblivious of the server's presence.

"I think I just lost my appetite." She rose to her feet. There was no way she would not choke on her food if she ate under the watchful eyes of the two men that wanted her.

Concern was etched on Bisi's face. "Why? What happened?"

"I'll see you later," she said to Bisi and headed for the exit.

Bisi stared at her retreating figure in amazement. "Can one ever understand women? One minute they are bubbling with excitement, the next minute they are as cold as ice."

"Yeah, right? Mood swing. Blame it on their hormones," Daniel said.

They laughed.

Bisi resumed his meal while Daniel gave his order to the young lady who was patiently waiting on them.

"What are you doing this weekend?" Daniel asked.

He shrugged. "Nothing important. I will be home because I am not on call this weekend."

"How about a picnic?"

Bisi thought about it. He desired to have Tolu visit him during the weekend for a repeat of what they had at the hotel in Ibadan. He had not been able to get that night out of his mind.

"Tell me about it."

The server returned with Daniel's order—*jollof* rice, *MoinMoin,* and chicken. He thanked her and asked for a bottle of Coca-Cola drink.

"It's just my idea of having a relaxing weekend with friends after a hectic week. We will be having my host and his girlfriend, Lucia and I, and then you and your woman - if you honour my invitation. My host, Tomiwa, lectures at FUTA, he'll take us to a field or garden we could use."

"Sounds interesting. I'll tell her about it."

"Cool."

They exchanged phone numbers before they left the cafeteria.

* * *

Lucia entered the office and saw Tolu pacing the room. "Are you alright? Have you eaten?"

"No."

"Why? You said you were famished and could even eat three plates of food."

"Yes, I was famished, but now, my appetite is nowhere to be found."

Lucia laughed and dropped the case notes she was holding on the table. "But why?"

She let out a puff of air, trying to come up with a plausible reason because she couldn't let the cat out of the bag yet. Bisi appeared at the door before she could speak. Lucia stepped aside to allow him access into the small office.

"Why did you lose your appetite?" he asked.

"I don't know," she replied.

"Are you sure you are okay?"

"I am fine. It happens sometimes."

"If you say so. Guess what? This weekend would be fun!"

"Why?" She hoped it wasn't another road trip, even though she secretly longed for it.

"There is a picnic at FUTA tomorrow."

"With who? By who?"

"Daniel. You know him. He joined us at the table in the cafeteria."

Tolu could feel her heart pounding against her chest. What was Daniel really up to? It was high time she stopped him.

"Oh yeah. He told me about it this morning. It's going to be fun," Lucia chipped in excitedly.

"What do you say?" Bisi asked.

"Okay," she said, not having a genuine reason to turn down the invitation.

"Yes!" Lucia punched a fist in the air.

Bisi planted a kiss on her cheek. "Take care of yourself." He walked out of the office.

"Awwn, that's so cute. I want to love and be loved again." Lucia said as she wrapped her arms around her chest.

"We are still on duty," Tolu said, not too comfortable with Bisi's public display of affection in the hospital since they were not officially dating. She didn't want any scandal attached to her name. With her phone in her pocket, she went into the bathroom and dialed Daniel's number.

"What do you want?" she asked when he picked up.

"You."

"Is that why you are stalking me?"

"I'm not stalking you. Lines are only falling in pleasant places for me."

"Planning a picnic and inviting Bisi isn't part of the lines falling for you. That was a deliberate act."

"I don't remember when planning a picnic and inviting a friend becomes a crime."

"Bisi is not your friend."

"That is not yours to decide."

"Just leave me alone. Stay away from me. Is that too much to ask?"

"Yes, it's too much to ask. I agree that planning the picnic was a deliberate act to get close to you. Once again, I'm sorry for all the pain that I've caused you. My work here will end next week, and I'll leave this town by next weekend if you want me to stay away from you."

"Is that a threat?" she asked.

"No, it's me respecting your wish. Isn't that what you want?"

Fear and confusion overwhelmed her.

"Whatever," she replied and ended the call.

* * *

At 2:30 p.m. when the shift was over, Tolu received Bisi's message via WhatsApp.

How about spending the rest of today at my place? It's the weekend, let's spend some time together. I've missed you.

He added a winking smiley.

She fumbled with her keypad as she thought of a reply. A surge of adrenaline shot through her body at the thought of what the visit held. She typed, *fine.*

"I'll see you tomorrow," Lucia called behind Tolu who was standing with her head buried in her phone. Lucia had changed into a knee-length flared Ankara gown and a pair of black heels and had her bag perched on her arm.

Tolu turned to look at her.

"Daniel is waiting for me in the car," she added.

Tolu's chest tightened. "See you tomorrow," she managed to say. Her eyes followed Lucia as the latter walked majestically out of the ward. What if Daniel falls for Lucia? It was Friday, and the atmosphere was quite idle and flirty. Strangely, she found herself trusting Daniel, but Lucia getting close to Daniel was just like dangling a banana before a monkey. What kind of man wouldn't jump at the opportunity of laying hands on a lady like Lucia especially when she was offering herself as a sacrifice on the altar?

A vibration on her phone intruded her thoughts. It was a message from Bisi asking if she was ready. She replied to him and left for the changing room.

* * *

Bisi had barely opened the door when they started kissing voraciously.

"I've missed you," he said huskily as he kissed her neck.

Tolu had missed him too, but Bisi's hands on her body left her tongue-tied. He took her bag from her and tossed it on the couch. His hands traveled to her back and unzipped her knee-length Ankara gown. He explored her body passionately before their bodies united in harmonious rhythms.

"Let me get us something to eat," he said after they crashed on the couch and got their breath.

"Okay," she watched him leave in his boxers and shirt. His phone vibrated on the couch almost immediately after he left. The caller ID revealed Ada.

Tolu's heart raced. She couldn't believe her eyes. Bisi lied to her. He was still in contact with his girlfriend or so-called ex-girlfriend. She felt used and stupid. She picked up her bra from the ground and wore it and later struggled with her zip.

Bisi appeared from the kitchen with a tray containing a bottle of wine, two wine glasses, and a bowl of potato chips. "Are you alright?" he asked.

"Maybe you should ask your girlfriend who just called."

"You called me?" He dropped the tray on the table.

Tolu was mad that he had the guts to trifle with her.

When he saw that she wasn't sharing in his humor, he picked his phone on the couch.

"It's not what you think, Tolu. I can explain it."

She shook her head in disbelief. "Isn't that what people say when they are caught red-handed?"

"Just listen to me. I've not done anything wrong."

The fact that he was calm and not looking guilty angered her the more. It made her seem like the one overreacting.

"Ada called with this number some days ago, and I warned her never to call me again after I realized she was the one. I had to save the number with her name so that I could ignore her calls."

Tolu searched his eyes. "And you want me to believe that?"

"What do I have to gain from lying to you?"

He was probably right.

"You know I took my time to ask you to date me. Why would I ruin my chances by giving my ex attention?"

Tolu felt stupid for overreacting. She lowered herself on the couch with her dress unzipped.

"Jesus." He sat beside her.

"Don't call him. After all, he doesn't exist."

He laughed. "Are you now fighting for him? Of course, he's powerless. He can't fight for himself. That's why his followers fight for him."

"You need to stop being bitter against God."

"How can I be bitter against a god who doesn't exist?"

"You told me you hated him. You are just confused."

"Now you need to shut up." He brought his face close to hers and sealed her lips with his.

* * *

While she drove home from Bisi's house, Tolu wondered if she had not been fooled by Bisi. If indeed he didn't want to have anything to do with Ada, he would have barred the number instead of saving it for future recognition. Even if he was being honest, for how long would he ignore her? Wasn't he setting himself up for temptation? Talk about old flames. He could ignore her calls, but he wouldn't be able to ignore her messages. He would read them before deleting them. So, what was the sense in his decision?

She rubbed her temples, trying to massage a budding headache. As sweet as Bisi was, he was also complicated. One minute she could boast that she knew him, the next minute he would throw her into an abyss of confusion. Her body still tingled from his touch. If passionate lovemaking were all she desired in a relationship, she would not think twice before agreeing to date him, but she believed that there was more to relationship and marriage than good sex.

She needed to let out her burden to someone—Lucia. She deserved her full disclosure.

CHAPTER TWENTY-FOUR

Tolu saw Daniel and Lucia standing outside the large school gate as she approached the school. Bisi was sitting beside her in the car. She had gone to pick him up at home. He had appeared at the door clad in a pair of boxers making Tolu flustered for a second. She knew he was trying to seduce her. As much as she longed for his touch, she made up her mind not to fall for his seduction, not after what happened yesterday. What if he was only using her to satisfy his sexual needs until Adaora returned to Nigeria? She wouldn't forgive herself for being played again.

"Why are you not dressed? It's ten-thirty already. We are thirty minutes late," she said, feigning anger and walking past him into the house.

"We are the guests. Normally, they arrive there first to receive us."

"And who says they wouldn't have been there before ten?"

"We will be on our way in five minutes. I'm a man; I don't wear makeup."

"Whatever. Some men do." She lowered herself on a couch while he headed into the room.

Tolu swallowed hard as she watched him leave. He must have been disappointed at his failed attempt at getting her to open her legs for him again. Even though her body longed for him, she acted contrary to its desires. That was self-control. She felt in charge and was proud of herself. She was not some booty call.

Bisi appeared in the sitting room in three minutes dressed in a pair of jean shorts, a black Polo shirt, and white sneakers. His perfume wafted into her nostrils. She got up and led the way out of the house. She was dressed in a loose sleeveless jumpsuit. They didn't talk much as she drove to the school. Turning him down must have hurt his ego.

Daniel and Lucia approached Tolu's car when they sighted it and hopped in. The four chorused their greetings. Lucia was dressed in a sky-blue playsuit which Tolu swore could give a eunuch a hard-on. Tolu was thrown into a jumble of emotions—admiration, jealousy, indignation. Why did she wear something that sexy? To seduce Daniel? Was Daniel impressed? Was he falling in love with her already? Was Lucia not concerned that her exposed skin would be a feast for mosquitoes?

Daniel gave Tolu directions, and they were in the garden in ten minutes.

"I need to get something from the boot," Tolu announced.

Daniel followed her to get it. "How are you?" he asked.

"I am fine," she replied without looking at him.

"You look good."

"Thank you." She got the package from the car and handed it to him. She was angry with him for the picnic, for Lucia, in fact, for everything.

They walked to where Tomiwa and his girlfriend, Adenike were seated. There were two large picnic mats spread on the neatly manicured lawn.

Daniel introduced the guests, "Tomiwa, Nike, meet my friends from work, Bisi, and Tolu. Tomiwa has been the one hosting and feeding me since I came to this city."

"Come on," Tomiwa said and the others laughed as they all exchanged pleasantries.

"There is a lot to eat and drink, so feel free to eat anything as much as you want," Daniel said. He and Tomiwa had bought some pastries, roasted chicken, soft drinks, and two bottles of wine at the eatery. Tolu brought some peppered meat and plantain chips. She had implored Gold to help her prepare them when she arrived home the previous night.

"Shall we pray over the edibles?" Daniel asked.

Bisi giggled while Tolu pinched him gently on the arm. Everyone closed their eyes, except Bisi as Daniel said a brief prayer.

"You religious people never cease to amaze me. Why pray over picnic food? Do you fear that some demons could have possessed the food? Religion is the mother of paranoia," Bisi said.

Tolu wished there was a hole she could hide her face. Did Bisi have to say that?

"Do you have a problem with praying before eating?" Daniel asked.

"No, I don't. I just have a problem with praying to a god that doesn't exist."

The others exchanged glances, unable to hide their shock. Tolu sought refuge in her phone as she surfed the internet.

With a smile playing on his lips and a knowing glance at Tolu, Daniel encouraged them to serve themselves. Everyone took what they wanted. Tolu picked a meat pie and put some peppered meat in her disposable plate and grabbed a can of Coca-Cola. She secretly prayed that no one would further Bisi's controversial stance or else the picnic would be ruined. Religious discussions had always been murky water to wade into.

When everyone had settled with their food, Daniel asked, "Bisi, do you mind sharing why you think God doesn't exist?"

Tolu wished she could punch Daniel in the face. Her angry stare met with Daniel's smiling one.

With a mouthful of doughnut, Bisi replied, "Because I know he doesn't. From experience, he has proven himself to be nonexistent."

Tomiwa laughed. "I find that contradictory. How can someone who doesn't exist prove himself to be something or not?"

All eyes were on Bisi while Tolu fixed her gaze on her phone as she nibbled on her pie.

"Okay, how do you explain the case of a family that served the *so-called* God for years and ended up being messed up by the same God? The father was a pastor, the mother taught the Bible, and all the three children were active in the choir. About ten years ago, the first child died in a fatal vehicle accident on his way home after finishing his NYSC. Not only that, the mother did not recover from the grief and later slipped into depression. Why would a good God watch such a family that was faithful to Him become a home of ruin?"

Tolu could swear she heard everyone heave a sigh. A silence ensued in which Bisi basked in his momentary victory.

Daniel broke the silence by clearing his throat and saying, "That's a very sad one. Losing a loved one is one of the most painful things that can happen to anyone. It's an experience I dread, even though death is an inevitable end for us all. I can't claim to understand the agony of the aggrieved family, but I do not think blaming God for the outcome of the family is entirely the solution. Did it ever cross your mind that, maybe, just maybe, God could have given the guy a signal not to travel that day or even board the vehicle? Sometimes God speaks to us, but we are too distracted to hear. Don't you think it's possible?"

Tolu raised her head to look at Daniel before resting her gaze on Bisi, whose face was creasing into a frown.

"I agree with Daniel. It's a possibility, but there is no way to confirm that, sadly," Tomiwa said.

"Even if that was not the case," a feminine voice started, commanding the attention of others. It was Adenike, Tomiwa's girlfriend. "I believe the primary gain of being a believer is eternal life through Christ Jesus. No matter how many years we spend on earth, we'll still die. The gospel according to John chapter three verses sixteen says, "For God so loved the world that He gave His only begotten Son, that whoever believes in Him should not perish but have everlasting life." The everlasting life is the eternal life I'm talking about. Death is a transition unto eternal life. Believers in Jesus do not die, they sleep, and they will rise when Jesus comes the second time. In fact, they will rise first, before those who are alive. I have forgotten the scriptural reference. This is our comfort as Christians. Plus, God doesn't want us to be Christians who only think He is good when things are good."

Tomiwa smiled at her and pulled her close to him.

"Easier said than experienced," Bisi chipped in.

Lucia sighed, not knowing what to say.

"I agree with you, Bisi. Like I said earlier, losing a loved one is a deadly blow and it takes a great level of faith to accept what Adenike explained. But I maintain that being a Christian does not shield one from the harsh life circumstances that everyone, regardless of their religion, is exposed to."

"So, what's the point of serving a God who cannot protect you? What explanation will you give to the many tragedies that plague the world—injustice, sicknesses, terrorism, natural disasters, poverty, wars, and even innocent children dying of hunger and sicknesses? Where is God in all these? Why would a good God open his eyes and let people suffer if he indeed cares? Why would he create a world like this?" Bisi asked.

"Generally, life is unfair, but God is fair. We live in a fallen world. I'm not saying God does not protect His own. He is a good Father, and He protects us even without us knowing sometimes. If God were to open our eyes to the dangers He daily keeps us from, we would be more grateful. But the truth remains that life is full of good and evil. Sometimes we enjoy the good, other times, we endure the bad. That is life. Why do we focus on the things that aren't going fine in our lives and the world entirely? Is it all bad? Isn't there anything to be grateful to God for? Think about it," Daniel said.

Tolu found herself agreeing with Daniel while Bisi gulped his drink.

"I think I agree with you, Daniel," Lucia chipped in, finding her voice since the discussion started.

Like you had a choice, Tolu thought. She didn't understand why she was envious of Lucia's admiration for Daniel.

"I agree that it's not right to blame God for all the things that are going wrong in the world. After all, we are rational beings, meaning every action has a consequence. Take, for instance, a man who gets drunk and drives a truck, runs into a car consisting of a family of five, killing them in the process. The silly driver killed innocent people with his carelessness. Why is the consequence of the drunk driver's action not limited to him? Is God to be blamed for that? If we are to be spared of all the consequences of our actions, what kind of world would we have? We humans usually believe that God should be able to stop every bad thing from happening just to prove his goodness and power. I believe God does this sometimes out of his mercy and omnipotence but it's not the norm."

"Why?" Lucia asked, still in awe of Daniel.

"Okay, imagine a world where God stops each of our thoughts and actions before we carry them out. We would become robots. And… who wants to be controlled? Also, God said He has given the earth to us to dominate. So, we are in charge of what happens here. God has given us the power of choice and He respects that. God needs our permission to do things in our lives and on the earth. That's where prayer comes in."

Sighs flew in from different directions.

Tolu was certain that Daniel had been doing a lot of reading.

Adenike spoke again, "I also believe that every country is what the people make of it. While some countries are named as the happiest countries in the world, some are filled with hunger, poverty, pain, and wars. Is that God's fault? The welfare of a country is determined by the policies the leaders make and their passion to make things work. Our country is blessed with amazing natural and human resources that many countries of the world cannot boast of, yet there is great poverty and unemployment. Why? Greed. Corruption. A handful of people steal the billions meant for the welfare of millions of people. So, the majority of the problems in our world today are caused by humans and will be solved by humans. After all, life is all about solving problems to make life better. Even with that, we may never understand why innocents suffer in the face of a loving God. There are some things we will never understand, no matter how much we try. I think we need to accept that some things are beyond our knowledge as humans and that we will not always find an explanation for everything that happens."

Bisi was yet to find his voice.

"That is so true, Adenike. I'm not trying to be insensitive here, Bisi. I understand that it's normal to question our faith in God when we are faced with unpleasant life events. But what measure did the family take in ensuring the effective management of their grief, especially the mother's?" Daniel asked.

Bisi shrugged. "Just a bunch of pastors and church members trooping in and out for two weeks."

"I'm sorry, but that's the mistake we often make as Christians. We think that time will heal our grief or that Jesus will automatically take our grief away. Yes, the Holy Spirit is our Comforter, but that doesn't mean we can't use the services of trained personnel like clinical psychologists or therapists, to help us through our grief. If grief is poorly managed, it can lead to depression."

Bisi let out a sob to the shock of everyone. Tolu dropped her phone and wrapped her hands around him.

"I'm so sorry if my words hurt you, I didn't mean to cause you any more pain," Daniel said, standing up from his position and lowering himself beside Bisi. He draped an arm over him and patted him gently while Bisi broke into bouts of painful tears. The others stood up and gathered around him.

"I went through a season of God-hating and God-bashing when I lost both of my parents in an auto crash the same day," Adenike said. Everyone raised their heads to look at her.

"I questioned His love, faithfulness, and existence. I had the love and support of family and friends. I got better with time. I've come to understand that sometimes we may not understand why some things happen, we may never have answers to some of our questions but trusting in God's love never goes wrong. Even though there is so much evil in the world, God is not evil and will never do evil. He is good all the time."

The crying reduced to sobs and ten minutes later, comforting silence reigned amongst them.

"Thank you, guys," Bisi said in a low voice and sniffed.

The others returned to their former sitting positions, uncertain of what to say. There was an unspoken unanimous agreement that the picnic should be brought to a close. It felt like any other discussion would trivialize Bisi's pains. Daniel packed the foods and drinks for each of them, and twenty minutes later, they dispersed with warm hugs.

Bisi was quiet throughout the drive to his house. Tolu cast occasional glances at him, wondering what was on his mind, but she didn't say anything to him. He alighted from the car when they got to his house and said a brisk 'thank you' to Tolu. She watched him enter through the gate before driving off.

When she arrived home, she was emotionally exhausted. She dried herself after a cold bath, then read a text message from Daniel.

I keep asking myself where I would be this time next week – on my way to Lagos or with you? You decide.

Not sure of the reply to give, she tossed the phone on the bed.

CHAPTER TWENTY-FIVE

The following day, Tolu went to church with Gold and Omolola. For the first time, she chose to attend the youth church while Lola went with Gold to the adult church. Praise and worship session was in progress when she entered the hall. The usher directed her to a vacant seat in the fourth row. She scanned the hall before lowering herself on her seat. Most of the people consisted of teenagers and people in her age group. Some of them were even married. They must have preferred the youth church because it was livelier there.

She said a brief prayer and joined the excited congregation. The praise session ended twenty minutes later, much to Tolu's displeasure. There were sessions of testimonies and prayers before the sermon, which was delivered by the youth pastor. He was married and couldn't be older than thirty-five. He preached on 'Loving God in an Unloving Generation'.

When he finished, Tolu was convinced that the sermon was meant for her and resolved to get serious with God. She craved the peace and joy that only having a relationship with God could give.

She wished to share her experience with a friend after the service ended at 11 a.m. Bisi seemed to be her only option as Daniel was probably in church, plus, she was still angry with him. Lucia was out of it. While she waited for her family in the car, she dialed Bisi's number. She also wanted to know how he was faring after the picnic ended abruptly yesterday.

"Hey," he said when he answered the call.

"How are you today?" she asked.

"I'm good. Still in bed. Thinking about my life."

"Really?"

"Yeah."

She exhaled, thinking of what next to say.

"You?" he asked.

"I am fine. Just finished at church, waiting for my people in the car."

"You went to church. Cool."

She laughed. "I go to church whenever I'm available. Only on Sundays though. Not good enough, I know, but it's better than nothing."

"I'm not judging you. After all, you are better than me."

"I'm not judging you too. Your situation is understandable. And with God, no one is better than the other. We are all loved by God, no matter who we are and what we have done. Jesus died for everyone, remember?"

"Hmm. Well, I need to see Daniel today, he would have left the hospital before I resume tomorrow."

Tolu's heart skipped. Why would Bisi want to see Daniel? "Why?" she asked.

"Just some personal stuff."

Not wanting to intrude, she said, "Okay." She saw Gold and Lola approaching the car via the front mirror. "I have to go now."

* * *

After lunch, Tolu felt a pressing desire to talk with a friend—a girlfriend who would understand her plight. Maryam and Chisom didn't know the latest about her life, so Lucia was her only choice. More so, Lucia deserved it; she had told her intimate things about her life. She also needed some company to take her mind off worrying about what Bisi could want to discuss with Daniel. If Bisi needed male company, she needed female company too. What's sauce for the goose is sauce for the gander. She picked her phone and called Lucia to inform her that she was visiting. Lucia was so excited to hear that and said she couldn't wait to have her around.

One hour later, she was lying on the only couch in Lucia's small but decent sitting room while Lucia, clad in bum shorts and a T-shirt sat on the rug from across Tolu. Lucia served her with potato chips and orange juice. A music video was showing on the TV.

"Life could be complicated for some of us, you know. Some ladies are just fortunate. They meet someone they love and who loves them, get married, and raise a family. It's not that simple for some of us," Tolu said.

Lucia laughed. "Tell me about it. As pretty as I am, one would think I have an enviable love life. Yes, I have men on my neck, but I know sex is all they want, and I am not ready for that. But you? You have a man to call your own *na.*"

Tolu sighed. "It's not that simple. Bisi and I aren't dating yet. He asked me out already, but I'm yet to give him my response."

"Really? Why? What are you waiting for?"

"It's complicated."

"How?"

"Let me ask you, can you marry an atheist?"

Lucia thought for a while." No, I don't think so. Not that I have problems with someone being an atheist; everyone has a right to their beliefs. I just feel that I've spent many years not acknowledging God in my life; I don't want that to continue in my marriage. I know there are terrible church guys just as there are good church guys. But I'd rather wait on God for a good church guy."

Tolu stared unbelievably at Lucia and understood the foolishness of judging people based on physical appearance. Who could have thought a lady considered to be a side chick by some women was once an abused woman who also cared about her faith and the consequences of marrying someone who didn't share her faith?

"Is this about what Bisi shared yesterday at the picnic?"

"Partly. I care about my faith too. Bisi is a cool guy, though he acts complicated sometimes. I understand his struggles with religion because of his experience, but I'm quite skeptical. I have my fears. I don't feel completely at peace about having a relationship with him or marrying him."

"What if he changes his mind about being an atheist? Will you still consider him? He seemed touched by the discussion at the picnic yesterday."

"Hmmm. Honestly, I don't know. I enjoy his company and all that, but I don't see us as a couple."

"Oh well, then you should give him your answer and not get his hopes up."

"Yeah, and more importantly, my ex, my daughter's father is begging for a second chance."

Lucia's eyes bulged. She didn't know Tolu's story, only speculations from ward gossip. Tolu rarely shared her issues at work, so no one knew her story exactly. Lucia felt privileged to be hearing it from Tolu herself.

"We broke up, rather, I broke up with him when we discovered I was pregnant."

"Why?"

"Fear of ruining his dreams of having his master's degree in Canada sponsored by his father. He said if his father got to know I was carrying his baby; he would insist on us getting married and starting a family."

"Wow."

"How selfish of him to suggest abortion to me. I'm an only child for God's sake. I couldn't imagine risking my life and my mum losing me after losing my dad, but he insisted. I was angry with him, and I broke up with him. I cut communication with him. I even destroyed my SIM card. Now he wants my daughter and me in his life after two years. He must be mad." Tolu felt a new surge of rage.

"This is serious. I don't know what to say. What do you want to do now?"

She sighed. "I'm confused. Do you think it makes sense if I take him back?"

"This isn't a matter of if it makes sense. The question is, do you still love him?"

"Now you sound like my mother."

Lucia laughed. "It's true. Does he love you? Is he genuinely sorry for his wrongs? Is he ready to make amends and take responsibility for his child? Is he ready to play by your rules? These are the questions you should be asking yourself and not if it makes sense. If it makes sense to you, why not? It doesn't have to make sense to others. It's your life. You owe nobody any explanation for your decision. Remember you were the one who cut communication with him. What if he changed his mind without you knowing?"

Tolu wondered if Lucia would give her the same advice if she knew that Daniel, her crush, was the man in question.

"The answers are positive so far. He's genuinely sorry, he's ready to make amends, he loves me, and I'm afraid I still love him. How silly! I'm not supposed to love him after everything."

"Our heart betrays us sometimes."

"What if I tell you Daniel is my daughter's father?" she dropped the bombshell.

"Which Daniel?"

"Same Daniel you know. Your friend or your crush, the Biomed engineer, your neighbour." Just then, it occurred to her that Bisi and Daniel were probably together. She wondered what they could be discussing.

"No way! Are you kidding me?"

Tolu shook her head. "I kid you not."

"And you didn't tell me?" Shock and disappointment showed on her face. "How did you two manage to carry on like you didn't know each other? Oh! You are the one!"

"What?"

"Daniel told me he came to Akure because of his ex, but she has been proving stubborn. He told me how much he loved her and would do anything to have her back. That was all. He didn't tell me about the child or where you work."

"I'm so sorry. I was looking for a perfect time to tell you everything, and that's why I'm here. It's been so tough for me." She rubbed her forehead.

"You could have just spared me from crushing on him." She laughed. "Anyway, seriously, what is your decision? The dude is leaving town this weekend."

She ran her hand through her braids. "He told me. I don't just know..."

"You know. Maybe you don't just want to take the step. Whatever you have to do, you have to do fast because time is what you don't have here. From the little I know about him; Daniel seems to be a good guy. Good men are hard to find at this age. Don't lose this one. If he came from Lagos to Akure just to right his wrongs, I think he's for real. If I were you, I'd turn Bisi down and let him go sort himself out. He has a lot of baggage, and I wouldn't want to add that to my life. Then I'd give Daniel a chance and see how things would go between us. You should count yourself lucky. Do you know how many jilted single mothers wish their child's father would come begging?"

Tolu rolled her eyes.

"Seriously."

"Well, I'll give it a thought."

"Please do. Look at you. Aren't you so lucky? You have two eligible men begging for your love."

Tolu laughed. "Thank you, Lucia. I feel better talking with you."

She smiled. "What are friends for?"

"I pray you find a man who is worthy of you because you are a beautiful soul."

"Awwn. Amen."

"Now I'm hungry."

"Me too. Let's go make some spicy noodles." Lucia got up from the rug and led Tolu by hand into the kitchen.

CHAPTER TWENTY-SIX

It had been a busy week at work for Tolu and Lucia such that they had no time to spare for their talks. At the end of their morning shift on Wednesday, Lucia asked if Tolu had spoken with Bisi and Daniel.

"No, I haven't. You know it's been a crazy week. I just manage to drive home, have a shower, eat lunch, and crash in bed. Before I know it, it's almost midnight. I am sure Daniel has even been busier since he's been dispensing equipment in the wards."

"Tell me about it. I haven't been to my studio this week. My days have been running pretty much like yours. And you are right about Daniel being busy. We've not been coming to work or going home together because he comes earlier and leaves late."

"He hasn't called me."

"We won't be coming to work in the next two days. I guess you'll have enough time to fix things."

"I hope so. Let's change so I can drop you off at home."

"Thank you, but I'll be fine. You go home. It's been a hectic day."

"It's not a bother. I can also spend some time with you."

"Really? Let's go then."

* * *

The following morning while still in bed, Tolu called Bisi to ask if they could see. She knew he had the day off too.

"I'll be out on my way to Ado-Ekiti in ten minutes."

"Is everything fine?" she asked.

"Yes. I just want to see my family. It's been a while."

"Oh, good."

"Why do you want us to see?"

"Well, it can wait till you return."

"I'll be back tomorrow afternoon. I'm on weekend call."

"I'll resume the night shift on Saturday. We'll see then. I pray we have a calm shift."

"I say 'Amen' to that because this week was hellish."

"Really? Amen?"

He laughed. "I gotta go. Enjoy your days off."

"Have a safe trip."

She hit the red button with her lips parting in a smile. She swallowed her pride and put a call through to Daniel, which he answered almost immediately.

"So, you've been too busy to call me, right?" she queried.

"Good morning to you too."

"Tsk tsk."

"Yes, I have, and I'm even on my way to the hospital now. Will heavens fall if you call me?"

She took the phone from her ear to check the time. "It's six thirty-five."

"Yes. I have a lot to do, and I have just today and tomorrow. All roads lead to Lagos on Saturday morning."

Tolu's heart fluttered. "I guess you have accomplished your mission here."

"If you say so."

"Really? Working at the hospital was your mission?"

"Tolu, has anyone ever told you that you are proud and stubborn?"

"No, just you. It shows the problem is with you."

"The day is just starting, please don't ruin it for me."

"I didn't call you to be insulted."

"How did I insult you?"

"Have yourself a good day. I better go so that I won't ruin your day."

"Thank you."

The line went dead. Tolu stared unbelievably at her phone screen. Had Daniel given up on her? Hadn't he come from Lagos for her? She had expected him to intensify his pursuit when he learned of his daughter. Had he developed cold feet because of her resistance? She held onto her phone with the hope that he would call back. Was it not Daniel who had been trying to be in her good books?

When her phone did not ring after ten minutes, she threw it on the bed and went into the bathroom to brush her teeth. If he'd be traveling back to Lagos on Saturday, he'd surely reach out to her. This time, she wouldn't resist.

* * *

Tomiwa leaned against the table and watched as Daniel folded his clothes into his suitcase. It was 10 p.m. on Friday and they had just returned from a bar where they had goat meat barbecue and malt drink. Tomiwa had told him he wanted him to have a feel of the city one last time.

"I'm going to miss you here. I guess I need to get married as soon as possible. I can't imagine living here alone now."

Daniel laughed. "It's not good for a man to be alone. Loneliness isn't fun."

"Now I know. I've always loved my space, but now I want someone in it."

"You have your girl already. Just shoot."

Tomiwa laughed.

"And I'm grateful for all that you've done for me. I cannot thank you enough."

"The pleasure is all mine. It was great having you around."

There was a momentary silence.

"She hasn't called yet?" Tomiwa asked.

Daniel shook his head.

"Why not call her? She might be expecting you to, you know?"

"I'm tempted to, but I won't. I've been chasing her all this while without any result, so what difference would it make now? Because I'm leaving tomorrow?

More so, I want to see if she wants me. I don't want to pressure her into accepting me. She's an adult. She should make her choice. If indeed she wants me back in her life, she'll call me. She knows I'm leaving tomorrow."

"And your daughter? What do you intend to do about her?"

"I've been thinking about her ever since I saw her picture on Tolu's phone. I'm afraid I'd be attached to her if I set my eyes on her, and with her mother not cooperating, I might be tempted to take legal steps against her, just to be a part of my daughter's life. That would mean going against Tolu, and I don't want to wreck more havoc than I already did."

Tomiwa nodded in understanding. "I hope she calls before you leave tomorrow morning."

"I hope so too, and if she doesn't, I'll move on with my life. Life must continue."

"Yeah."

* * *

Tolu woke up drenched in her sweat with her phone in her hand and her heart pounding out of her chest. She pressed her phone's power button to check the time. 6:15 a.m. She had slept off with her phone in her hand, expecting Daniel's call. She switched on the bedside lamp and said a brief prayer absentmindedly.

If Daniel was leaving town this morning, he'd call her to discuss them and Lola, and the way forward. Wasn't that what he wanted? Maybe he couldn't call yesterday because he was exhausted since it was his last day at the hospital. She went into the bathroom, holding her phone tightly. She was not only anxious but scared. Now she realized how much she still loved him and wouldn't want to lose him. She regretted not giving in to him when he was desperately after her. Talk about leaving the stage when the ovation is loudest.

At 7 a.m., she became restless and went into the kitchen where Gold was making sandwiches for breakfast. She passed by Lola who was eating biscuits with her eyes fixed on the TV.

"Daniel is leaving this morning," Tolu announced. She stood by the door and rested her head against the wall.

Surprised, Gold turned to look at her. "Why? Have you guys settled?"

"No, not really. I think he's waiting for me to call him and fix things."

"Then do that. After all, he has been the one begging you all these days."

"Then he should finish what he started."

"You are too stubborn. I hope you don't regret it." She put some water into the electric jug and plugged it into the power source.

"That's mean, Gold," she whined.

"Truth can be bitter."

Her phone vibrated in her hand. She jerked and checked who the caller was—Lucia. A wave of sadness and disappointment swept over her as she swiped to the green button.

"Hey, Tolu. I'm sorry I should have called yesterday, but I got in from the studio late. I fell asleep almost immediately."

Before Tolu could reply, she continued, "How far with you and Daniel? Have you called him? Is he still leaving today?"

"He hasn't called. I called him yesterday morning, but we ended the call in a minor quarrel. He hasn't called since then."

"Then call him! What are you doing, Tolu?"

"I don't know." Her heart beat faster. "Let me call him. I'll call you back."

She ended Lucia's call and dialed Daniel's number. Gold cast intermittent glances at her. Daniel's number was switched off. Not believing her ears, she redialed it and got the same response.

"His number is switched off, Gold."

"Maybe it's the network. Try it again," Gold said, afraid for her daughter.

Tolu tried it again but got the same response. She called Lucia to inform her.

"What could be wrong? Hold on; let me check if his car is in the compound. I'll call you back," Lucia replied.

Lucia called back three minutes later. "His car is not in the compound. He's probably gone."

Weak from shock, Tolu turned on the waterworks.

"Hold on, Tolu. Don't give up hopes yet. Let me go upstairs to Tomiwa's flat to find out about Daniel's whereabouts. It might not be what we think after all."

"Okay," Tolu replied, crying.

Gold shook her head and carried the tray containing their breakfast to the dining table while Tolu walked behind her.

Tomiwa was still in his pajamas when he opened the door for Lucia.

"Good morning. I'm sorry to bother you. Please, where is Daniel?" she said.

"He left for Lagos a few minutes ago."

Lucia heard Tolu scream into the phone.

"Relax, Tolu. We've got this," Lucia said.

She faced Tomiwa. "Tolu has been trying his number, but it's switched off."

Tomiwa shook his head. "Too late. He had been expecting her call for days. Why didn't she call him since? He must have destroyed his SIM card as he said."

"Jeez. What do you think we can do? We have to do something." Lucia heard Tolu sobbing.

Tomiwa ran his hand through his hairless head. "I don't know what we can do. I..."

"How far do you think he'd have gone?"

"I don't think he should be out of this city yet."

"Lucia?" Tolu called.

Lucia put her phone to her ear. "Yes?"

"I'm going after him. I might catch up with him if I drive fast."

"Ah. You think so?"

"There is no harm in trying."

"Please drive carefully then," Lucia warned but Tolu was already off the line. "Do you mind if I stay here till she calls back?" she asked Tomiwa.

"That's no problem."

Lucia lowered herself on a couch, feeling tired.

"Coffee and toast?" Tomiwa asked.

"I think I'm too nervous to eat, but I'm hungry. So, yes, please."

They laughed, and Tomiwa disappeared into the kitchen.

Tolu ran into her room to fetch her car key and later dashed out of the house.

"Drive carefully *o!*" Gold screamed after her.

"God, please help me. Jesus, help me," she prayed as she sped through her street. She tightened her grip on the steering wheel as her hands trembled and her heart slammed against her chest. "God, do this for me. Help me to catch up with him, and I promise...I promise...to...I don't even know...just help me," she sputtered as tears rolled down her cheeks. "I don't want to lose Daniel. I still love him." She sniffed.

* * *

Daniel wiped a bead of sweat from his forehead with his palm, casting frustrated looks at the two soldiers at the checkpoint who had ordered him to park. He had shown them what they requested; his driver's license and car documents. Then they asked for his fire extinguisher; when he couldn't produce it, they ordered him to park and continued with their duty.

"What's all these for God's sake?" he muttered under his breath.

After fifteen minutes of waiting without being attended to, he approached one of the soldiers. "Officer, what do you want me to do now? I have a long journey ahead of me."

"Gentleman, be patient!" the officer barked at him.

As Daniel turned to walk back to his car, he was stunned by the sight of an approaching car. *This looks exactly like Tolu's car, but it can't be her. What would she be doing here?* He thought.

The driver of the car slowed down and parked behind his car. Daniel couldn't believe his eyes as Tolu alighted from the car and walked briskly towards him. She threw her hands over him and hugged him tightly, with tears trickling down her face and wetting his shirt.

"What are you doing here?" he asked when he finally found his voice.

"Stopping you, idiot. How dare you?"

He hugged her tightly in return. "How did you find me? How did you know I'd be here? I can't believe this is happening."

"I decided to try my luck, but I have Tomiwa and Lucia to thank for this."

"How?"

"I'll tell you later."

"I go love o!" The soldiers teased them.

They disengaged and looked into each other's eyes. Tolu's eyelids were puffy.

"You have been crying," he said, his eyes welling with tears.

"And you look stressed."

He shrugged. "Tolu, I'm so sorry for everything. I am."

"I know. Let's go home. "

They both thanked the soldiers. Tolu led the way as they drove back into the city to her house.

* * *

Daniel prostrated when Tolu introduced him to Gold and refused to stand up even when Gold asked him to.

"Please forgive me, ma. I know I have hurt your family so deeply. Forgive me," he said.

Gold blinked, fighting back tears.

"Stand up, Daniel. You were forgiven a long time ago," Gold said.

He stood up and sank his weight into a seat. He was exhausted and glad that his journey was interrupted. How could he have driven to Lagos in such a state?

Tolu brought Lola, who had been watching them, to him. He carried his daughter on his lap and hugged her warmly, feeling guilty that he had wanted her aborted. Lola reached for Daniel's face and wiped his tears gently. A small smile took over his lips as more tears flowed down his face.

CHAPTER TWENTY-SEVEN

Tolu hosted Daniel for one week. During his stay, he told her he had a job waiting for him in Canada. He decided to come to Nigeria because of Tolu after a successful interview for the job which was to start three months later. He asked Tolu if it was possible to have their wedding done within a month so that he could return to Canada to resume work and await her coming. Tolu promised to get back to him before the end of his stay with them.

Bisi came to Tolu's ward on the second day of the night shift and Tolu told him all he needed to know.

"Are you serious? Daniel is your daughter's father?"

She nodded.

"Why didn't you tell me before now? You women can be...."

"No, don't you start."

He smiled and shook his head. "I can't believe it."

"I am so sorry. I should have told you earlier. I was angry and confused."

"Is he aware that we have...you know?"

"Yeah."

"And he doesn't mind?"

"No. You and I have been getting along before he came back into the picture."

"So, you still love him?"

She hesitated. "Yes. Look, I am sorry..."

"It's okay. My prediction back at the hotel was right after all."

Tolu remembered it.

"It hurts, but it's okay."

"I'm so sorry, Bisi. I really like you, I'm sure you know that."

"But you love him more. More than an atheist like me."

"Come on, you know it has nothing to do with that. My feelings for you didn't change despite that. That wasn't an issue." She knew she wasn't sounding convincing even to herself.

"It's not even an issue anymore."

"How?"

"I spoke with Daniel and Tomiwa last Sunday."

Tolu's eyes lit up. Now she knew why Bisi wanted to see Daniel. "So?"

"I'm good."

"Talk to me."

"This is not the best time. I have to go now." He rose to his feet and walked out of the office.

Tolu was troubled that he was hurt and hoped that he would get over it with time.

* * *

Daniel couldn't have enough of his daughter. He would drive her to school with Gold and also picked her up after school. He helped her with her homework and played with her afterward. He took them all shopping, bought clothes and toys for Lola despite Tolu's protest.

"She has enough already," she told him.

"These are from me, her father."

On Saturday evening, Daniel and Tolu invited Tomiwa, his girlfriend; Adenike, Lucia, and Bisi to a hangout at Nevado Gardens. This time around, it was all fun and laughter. They all ordered fish barbecue and their preferred drinks. There, Tomiwa told Daniel how Tolu was able to find him at the military checkpoint.

"While Lucia and I were having breakfast, she asked me if there was a way, we could stop you at a checkpoint. That was when I remembered that I had the phone number of a soldier that I'd become friends with. He usually stays at Ondo road military checkpoint where Tolu met you. He told me he wasn't on duty, but he'd call those who were. I gave him your description and that of your car."

"Really? No wonder..."

The others laughed.

"Thank you, Tomiwa, and you too, Lucia," Daniel said.

When they arrived home from the hangout at 8 p.m., Tolu told Daniel her decision in the presence of Gold while Lola was fast asleep.

"I'll only marry you and relocate to Canada only on one condition," she said.

"What?" Daniel asked, his heart racing.

"Lola stays with Gold."

Daniel was shocked. Lola was his daughter, and he wanted to be part of her life. He wanted his family complete.

"It's tough enough that I'd leave her. Taking Lola away from her would break her, and that'd be unfair. She has been the one responsible for Lola since I gave birth to her. In fact, Lola calls her 'mummy'. Of course, you can play your role in her life as her father. We can spend time with her during vacations and visitations. I'm not sure if Gold would want to relocate anytime soon but for now, this is my decision, and I'm not reneging on it."

Gold had her eyes fixed on her neatly done pedicure. She knew nothing of her daughter's decision. Gold had dreaded that Lola would be taken away from her, but she didn't voice her concern to her daughter so as not to appear selfish.

Daniel exhaled deeply. This was a tough choice. Maybe he deserved it. After all, he was the one who didn't want the pregnancy.

"I accept your condition," he said, even though he wasn't happy about it. If that was Tolu's condition, then he had no choice. He hoped Gold would consider the option of relocating to Canada someday.

Gold's face lit up with tears in her eyes. "Thank you!"

After church service the following day, Daniel and Tolu set out for Lagos.

They spent the trip reminiscing about old times and discussing what the future held for them. Tolu constantly pushed back the memories of her road trip to Ibadan with Bisi. She was having fun with Daniel on the trip as much as she had fun with Bisi. She was happy she would be relocating to Canada soon, so, won't have to see Bisi at work. She liked him and hoped he would find love soon.

Tolu heaved a sigh as Daniel pulled the car into a free space in the garage in his father's house in Lagos five hours later. He placed a hand on her thigh and stroked it.

"Relax, they'll like you. They have no choice. Even if they don't, I don't need their opinion. I only brought you to be introduced to them and not for you to be assessed by them. My family is pleasant anyway. Don't concern yourself with the other wives and children. My mother and sister are your business."

She managed a smile and nodded.

They stepped down from the car. Daniel held her hand, bracing himself up for the many explanations he owed his family as they walked into the house.

THE END

About the Author

Olubunmi Mabel is an RN and a graduate of psychology from Nigeria's Premier University, University of Ibadan. She blogs at www.olubunmimabel.com where she shares practical relationship and personal development tips for women.

A romantic wife and a lover of God, her fiction centers upon complex romantic relationships and not-so-unusual marital challenges.

Aside from watching her kids laugh and joking around with her husband, Olubunmi enjoys reading and collecting books, interacting with her virtual friends, and eating carrot cake with coffee and Greek yogurt.

She currently lives in Copenhagen, Denmark, with her husband and two children.

You can connect with me on:

- https://olubunmimabel.com
- https://twitter.com/olubunmi_mabel
- https://www.facebook.com/olubunmi.mabel
- https://www.pinterest.dk/olubunmimabel90

GLOSSARY

Abi- right?
Akara- bean cake
Amala- yam flour meal
Amu- penis
Booli- roasted plantain
Dodo- fried plantain
Efo riro- vegetable soup
Garri- cassava flakes
Inugo- have you heard/you hear?
Kilode- what happened?
Mo n bo- I am coming
Na- now
Na so- indeed
No dey- do not
Oga mi- my boss
Okwaya- isn't it?
O se- thank you
Wahala- problem
Wan- want to
Wetin- what?
Yeye- silly

Printed in Great Britain
by Amazon

55213059R00135